"Would you like to go for a ride?"

Marco knew Gretchen meant the car, but he couldn't help but think of the far different, exceedingly intimate kind of ride he would like to take with her. "I don't know how to drive a stick shift," he said.

She maneuvered her long legs into the driver's seat. Looking at him expectantly, she replied, "That's okay. I do."

When he hesitated, she patted the leather of the passenger seat with bright red fi_____ils "Don't worry, Dr. Garibaldi. I prom____ bite."

She might not, but he was afraid i____ cooped up in close quarters with____ long, *he* might.

"Marco," he said. "The name's____

"Call me Gretchen."

"Very well, Gretchen." Swing____ ____er door open, he sank with a sigh onto the____ leather seat. Inhaling a heady breath of new-car aroma, he said, "Take me away from all my troubles."

"My pleasure."

Dear Reader,

Once again, Silhouette Intimate Moments brings you six exciting romances, a perfect excuse to take a break and read to your heart's content. Start off with *Heart of a Hero,* the latest in award-winning Marie Ferrarella's CHILDFINDERS, INC. miniseries. You'll be on the edge of your seat as you root for the heroine to find her missing son—and discover true love along the way. Then check out the newest of our FIRSTBORN SONS, *Born Brave,* by Ruth Wind, another of the award winners who make Intimate Moments so great every month. In Officer Hawk Stone you'll discover a hero any woman—and that includes our heroine!— would fall in love with.

Cassidy and the Princess, the latest from Patricia Potter, is a gripping story of a true princess of the ice and the hero who lures her in from the cold. With *Hard To Handle,* mistress of sensuality Kylie Brant begins CHARMED AND DANGEROUS, a trilogy about three irresistible heroes and the heroines lucky enough to land them. Be sure to look for her again next month, when she takes a different tack and contributes our FIRSTBORN SONS title. Round out the month with new titles from up-and-comers Shelley Cooper, whose *Promises, Promises* offers a new twist on the pregnant-heroine plot, and Wendy Rosnau, who tells a terrific amnesia story in *The Right Side of the Law.*

And, of course, come back again next month, when the romantic roller-coaster ride continues with six more of the most exciting romances around.

Enjoy!

Leslie J. Wainger
Executive Senior Editor

Please address questions and book requests to:
Silhouette Reader Service
U.S.: 3010 Walden Ave., P.O. Box 1325, Buffalo, NY 14269
Canadian: P.O. Box 609, Fort Erie, Ont. L2A 5X3

Promises, Promises

SHELLEY COOPER

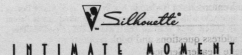

Published by Silhouette Books

America's Publisher of Contemporary Romance

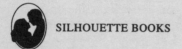

SILHOUETTE BOOKS

ISBN 0-373-27179-4

PROMISES, PROMISES

Books by Shelley Cooper

Silhouette Intimate Moments

Major Dad #876
Guardian Groom #942
Dad in Blue #1044
Promises, Promises #1109

SHELLEY COOPER

first experienced the power of words when she was in the eighth grade and wrote a paragraph about the circus for a class assignment. Her teacher returned it with an "A" and seven pluses scrawled across the top of the paper, along with a note thanking her for rekindling so vividly some cherished childhood memories. Since Shelley had never been to the circus, and had relied solely on her imagination to compose the paragraph, the teacher's remarks were a revelation. Since then, Shelley has relied on her imagination to help her sell dozens of short stories and to write her first novel, *Major Dad,* a 1997 Romance Writers of America Golden Heart finalist in Best Long Contemporary, and all those that have come after. She hopes her books will be as moving to her readers as her circus paragraph was to that long-ago English teacher.

To Charles and Joan Cooper
for raising an incredible son, and for treating me,
a daughter by law, like one of their original eight.

Prologue

Eyes stinging and heart pounding, Gretchen Montgomery sat motionless at her desk, staring at the items scattered across the blotter. An empty padded manila envelope. A letter from an attorney named Martin Sanders. A portable tape player. A cassette.

The cassette was what had her thoughts in turmoil. It was labeled "Jill Barnes—Tape for Gretchen Montgomery" and dated eight days prior to Jill's death three months earlier. The letter, stating that the tape was an addendum to her best friend's bequest to her, was from the executor of Jill's estate.

Gretchen reached for the tape with trembling fingers. A minute, then two, passed before she found the resolve to insert it into the tape recorder. After drawing a deep breath and letting it out slowly, she pushed the play button.

"Surprise!" Jill's voice trilled, weak but full of the humor and vivacity that had been Jill all over. "I bet you weren't expecting to hear from me again."

Though Gretchen had steeled herself for it, the sound of her best friend's voice had emotion swelling her throat.

"I was going to videotape this," Jill's voice echoed in the silent room, "but let's face it, I look like death."

Gretchen choked out a laugh. Even at the end, when Jill's pain had been great, she hadn't lost her sense of humor.

"Are you smiling, Gretch?" the tape continued. "You'd better be, 'cause if you're sitting there boo-hooing over me, I'm going to be highly pissed."

"I'm smiling," Gretchen said softly, her lips turning up as she brushed away a tear.

"Good. Now, where was I? Oh, yeah, videotaping. Since that was out, and since I've never been much of a letter writer, I chose this method of communicating with you. I hope you don't mind."

"I don't mind."

Gretchen knew she was talking to the air, that Jill couldn't actually hear her, and that anyone chancing upon her would think she'd lost it. She didn't care. She'd been so lonely these past months with Jill gone. It was wonderful to hear her friend's voice again, even if it was just a recording and not the real thing.

"We've been through a lot together," Jill said. "Wouldn't you agree?"

An understatement, if ever there was one. Best friends since kindergarten, and the only family each had had after the deaths of their parents, it had taken the marauding power of cancer to part them.

"More than the average bear," Gretchen murmured.

"Matter of fact," Jill stated, "I can't think of a single area of our lives we haven't shared. Training bras and braces. Pimples and periods. The hard times your family went through. Unrequited crushes and failed romances. The struggle to build a successful career. Regrets and unfulfilled dreams."

There was a pause. "It's the regrets and unfulfilled

dreams I want to talk about today. I can't tell you how many regrets I have for some of the things I've done during my life. But they pale in comparison with the regrets I have for the things I didn't do. The things I won't get to do now.

"I have a question for you, Gretch. What is the best thing a person can say about you? And I don't mean your appearance. I mean you—Gretchen Montgomery the person."

The tape whirred silently while Gretchen pondered the question. What was the best thing a person could say about her? That she was neat, clean and dependable. That she was loyal to those who had gained her trust. That she showed up at work on time every day and did a thorough job. That she had the respect and admiration of her colleagues.

She felt her lips twist. Just how boring could you get?

The sudden sound of Jill's voice made her start. "Do you have the answer yet? Well, here it is. Other than that you are the most wonderful friend a woman could ever hope to have, for which I thank you from the bottom of my heart, the best thing a person can say about you is that you never break a promise. Ever. You've made quite a few promises over the past twenty-nine years, haven't you?"

Yes, Gretchen acknowledged, she supposed she had. Her family, particularly her mother, had been great on the making and keeping of promises. But for the life of her, she couldn't figure out what any promise she'd made had to do with Jill's unfulfilled dreams, with Jill's regrets.

As if reading her mind, Jill said, "I suppose you're wondering why I'm bringing up those promises of yours. Because there's something I want you to do, and I want you to do it for both of us. In the name of our friendship, Gretch, I'm going to ask you to make a few of those promises you're so good at keeping.

"First, I want you to celebrate every day by living in the moment. That means you have to let go of the past and stop waiting for the future. Now is the only time that counts. Now is the time to tell the people who are important to you how much they mean to you. Now is the time to not put off, hold back or save anything that will add laughter to your life. Now is the time to tell yourself that the day is special, that each minute, each second, each breath is a gift that must not be squandered. Can you promise me that?''

''I think so.''

''Good. Now for the hard part. I want you to take the money I left you out of the nice, safe money-market account I'm sure you've invested it in. You have enough put away for the future, you don't need any more. This is your mad money, Gretch, and you are to spend every penny of it. You are not to give it to charity. You are not to spend it on anyone else. Every cent must be spent on you, and you are to buy things that you never in your wildest dreams imagined you would find yourself buying. Some necessities, yes, but mostly wild, crazy, impractical things. Fun things. Promise?''

''But why?'' Gretchen asked, appalled at the thought of throwing away good money on items she neither wanted or needed. It went against everything she'd been taught, against the philosophy of her chosen career. She was a CPA, for heaven's sake. Frugality was her middle name, alongside practicality.

Again, as if anticipating her question, she heard Jill say, ''It's important, Gretch. Because, if you keep going on the way you are, your nose to the grindstone, always doing the safe thing, when your time comes you're going to have as many regrets as I do. You still have a choice. God willing, you have many years ahead of you, a lot of life to live. That's why I had my lawyer wait three months before sending this tape to you. Surely by now you've started questioning the meaning of your life.''

She had. Mostly at night, in the stillness between wakefulness and sleep, when she could no longer escape the discomfiting thoughts with activity.

"Promise me, Gretch," Jill insisted. "If you promise, I know you'll follow through."

"I promise," Gretchen whispered.

"Good. Remember how, when we were kids, you used to dream of being a concert pianist? Well, I want you to promise to enter a piano competition. ASAP. I want you to find out, once and for all, whether you have true ability. After that you can choose what you do with the knowledge."

Gretchen's head whirled. "You have my word. Anything else?"

"One last thing, and I'll let you go. I gotta warn you, though, it's a biggie, so prepare yourself. Ready?"

"As I'll ever be." Gretchen wondered what, after everything she'd already heard, could be left to surprise her.

"Okay, here goes. I want you to promise to have a wild, crazy affair. No more Ms. Practical for you, when it comes to men. No siree, Bob. You are now going to be Wild Woman."

For a second or two, Gretchen stared at the tape recorder, her mouth slack with shock. Then, giving a small shake of her head, she smiled ruefully. She should have known better than to wonder what Jill could have had left to surprise her.

"I told you it was a biggie." Jill's voice sounded amused, but determined. "There are also a few stipulations with this one. The man can't be anything like the men you've dated in the past. He can't be steady and unimaginative when it comes to both work and play. Especially play. He can't be more focused on his career than he is on your figure. And he can't be more comfortable in a suit than he is in a pair of jeans. In a word—and no offense, Gretch, 'cause I'm also describing every man I've ever dated—he can't be dull. Dull, dull, dull."

"No offense taken," Gretchen murmured.

''You'll know you've met the right guy, when just a mere look is enough to curl your toes, when your heart all but stops when he smiles at you and when you think you're going to incinerate on the spot when his fingers chance to brush against yours. And if he sports a tattoo, wears a leather jacket and rides a Harley, all the better. That's a guy you can let your hair down with. That's a guy you can have a wild, crazy affair with.''

Of all the promises Gretchen had been asked to make, this one gave her the most pause. In the simplest terms, she was not the wild, crazy affair type. Even if she had been, she didn't know any men like the one Jill had just described.

Or did she? Her thoughts flew to her tenant, the man who rented the other half of the duplex she'd grown up in, and which had been left to her when her parents died. Dr. Marco Garibaldi. She rarely saw him, but whenever she did she experienced all the reactions Jill had just described, and then some.

''Yeah, right,'' Gretchen muttered wryly. She had about as much chance of having a wild, crazy affair with Marco Garibaldi as she did with a movie star. Still, the thought filled her with a restless yearning she couldn't deny.

''Promise me, Gretchen.'' Jill's voice filled the room with a determined strength. ''For the first time in your life, I want you to be totally selfish, to for once do things for you and only you, and to hell with what anyone else thinks or says. I want you to live the life we always talked about living but were too scared or busy with our careers to actually get out and live. I want, when you lie on your deathbed, for you to have no regrets.

''Remember that line from *Auntie Mame?* 'Life is a banquet, and most poor suckers are starving to death.' I want you to feast, Gretch. Feast like no one has feasted before. Promise me you'll do everything I asked.''

Despite her conviction that Jill's request was beyond crazy, Gretchen felt a growing excitement in the pit of her stomach. Sitting in her office, listening to the voice of a dead woman and making outrageously impractical promises, she felt more alive than she had in months, maybe even years.

"I promise." The words slipped out before she was consciously aware she intended to utter them.

Could she really do it? Could she do all the things Jill had asked? Could she actually have an affair with Marco Garibaldi, or any other man like him?

One thing was certain: she had to try. After all, she had made a promise, and promises were to keep.

Chapter 1

Something was up with his landlady.

Marco Garibaldi didn't know precisely what that something was, only that she was behaving totally out of character. Even worse, her out-of-character behavior was making it impossible for him to sleep.

Gritting his teeth against the swell of music echoing off his bedroom walls, Marco rolled onto his back and stared wide-eyed at the shadows flickering across the ceiling. A wave of frustration consumed him. The sheets were a tangled mess around his waist from all his tossing and turning. Air-conditioning, set on high, did little to cool a body that refused to stay in one position long enough to benefit from the chilled air pumping into the room.

The music ended and silence fell. A blessed silence, during which Marco closed his eyes and prayed for sleep to finally claim him. Just when he thought his prayers might be answered, once again the lilting notes of a piano sonatina filtered through the wall separating his half of the duplex from his landlady's.

Marco groaned. Would it never cease?

It wasn't that the music wasn't nice. On the contrary, it was beautiful. Chopin, if he wasn't mistaken. Or maybe Beethoven. He was too tired to try and figure out which.

Which was the entire point. Having just come off a six-teen-hour shift in the E.R., he was exhausted. Not only that, he was expected back there, bright and early tomorrow morning at six. And tonight, of all nights, his landlady had decided that midnight was the perfect time to play a CD at top volume, an unprecedented action on her part.

But what really had him stewing in aggravation was that she had programmed her CD player to play the same blasted sonatina over and over again. Thirty minutes listening to the same piece, no matter how beautiful, was about twenty-five minutes too long by his reckoning.

For two years he'd lived next door to her. Two years, during which they'd waved hello and goodbye to each other whenever their paths happened to cross, which wasn't often since she seemed to work as many hours as he did. Two years, during which he'd dutifully placed his rent check in her mailbox on the first of each month. Two years, during which she hadn't thrown so much as a tea party, let alone a wild, anything-goes free-for-all. Two years, during which she'd kept her stereo and television volume muted, and during which he'd never heard a peep from her after eleven o'clock at night.

Until tonight.

The sonatina swelled to its now-familiar finale, making Marco's head throb. He winced. Oh, yes, something was definitely up with his landlady. And he didn't like it one bit.

The music wasn't the entire problem, he acknowledged with a sigh as he wrapped the pillow around his ears and turned on his side. Yes, he couldn't sleep, but the music coming from his landlady's apartment was only part of the reason why.

During his years as an intern, and then later as a resident

when he'd worked practically around the clock for days on end, Marco had perfected the art of sleeping on his feet. Normally he could sleep anywhere, at any time and through anything. But tonight his brain wouldn't shut off, no matter how hard he willed it.

He'd had a hell of a day. A record breaker, just like the heat wave that was smashing records that had stood unchallenged for decades. Heat always tended to bring out the worst in human nature. Add alcohol, drugs and handguns to the mix, and you got a violent combination that would inevitably, at some point, find its way into the E.R.

Today had been no exception. Since it was only July sixth, and the mercury had already soared past one hundred for three days running, Marco hated to think what the rest of the summer held in store.

His shift had started at 6:00 a.m. By noon, he'd already seen three shootings, a husband and wife who had knifed each other in a domestic altercation, a child that had been shaken mercilessly by his mother's boyfriend and who might have permanent brain damage, and two drug overdoses.

Things had gone rapidly downhill from there. A bus accident had flooded the E.R. with victims at one-thirty. At three, a heat-provoked quarrel over whose turn it was to walk the dog had sent five members of the same family through the E.R.'s pneumatic doors. Then, at four, just as he was preparing to leave, three of his fellow physicians, who had all eaten a late lunch at the same fast-food restaurant, had come down with a virulent case of food poisoning, and Marco had known he'd be working a second shift.

The icing on the cake, though, had been the appearance of his current steady at six o'clock, demanding a commitment she'd assured him she didn't want at the start of their relationship. When he'd asked if she could wait until he had time to speak in private, she'd refused, insisting he answer her questions there and then. She didn't care who was listening. She'd left him no choice but to tell her that he had no intention of ever entering into a commitment with her, at which time she'd told him they were history. He hadn't wanted things to end that way; he had in fact hoped to enjoy her company for a long time yet to come, but she had given him no choice.

Afterward, the patients who had witnessed the scene regarded him as if he'd suddenly sprouted a tail and horns. At least the nurses, who were even more overworked than the doctors, had gotten some entertainment out of the episode. He knew he'd be the object of a fair amount of ribbing for days to come.

Still, the breakup with Pamela, unpleasant and unexpected as it had been, wasn't what was keeping him awake. The memory of the shaken baby was what tormented him. Despite his best efforts, he hadn't been able to keep the eight-month-old from slipping into a coma. Given the probable prognosis, he didn't know whether to pray that the child would succumb or survive.

Most of his fellow physicians did their best to distance themselves from their patients. Distancing helped to numb the pain and grief they encountered on a daily basis. Despite being advised to do the same himself, when he'd graduated from medical school Marco had vowed never to lose touch with the human side of his job. He never wanted to forget that the families, as well as the patient, were in pain. He didn't want to become immune to that pain, no matter what the personal cost to himself.

Sometimes, though, it all seemed so hopeless. He patched up drug users and battered women who refused to press charges against their abusers and sent them on their way, only to treat them all over again days, weeks or months later. He'd lost count of the number of homeless people who relied on the E.R. to give them some basic human dignity and to help them with medical conditions that were solely a result of their homelessness, and thus totally preventable.

Then there were days like today, when an innocent child was entrusted to his care and he could do little to help. A day like today made Marco question whether what he did made any difference at all. A day like today left him wide-eyed and staring at the ceiling while he prayed for silence and the forgetfulness of sleep.

Five minutes, he thought in desperation. Like the woman married to a chronic snorer, five minutes of uninterrupted silence was all he would need to drift off into lullaby land. After that, his landlady could play that blasted sonatina a thousand times, and he wouldn't hear.

When the song repeated yet again, Marco knew the only way he was going to get those five minutes was to demand them.

Wearily he climbed out of bed. For the sake of propriety, he shrugged a seldom-worn bathrobe over his naked body, then trudged in his bare feet to the front door.

The night air felt like a hot breath on his skin. Raising his right hand, he loudly rapped his knuckles against the aluminum screen door marking his landlady's side of the duplex.

He had to repeat the motion three more times before the music stopped. A few seconds later he heard the soft patter of feet across hardwood. The pattering was followed by a pause while his landlady peered out at him through the peephole.

Then she was opening the door and regarding him through wire-rimmed glasses. It had been months since they'd actually spoken face-to-face, and he'd forgotten how tall she was, just an inch shy of his own six feet.

"Dr. Garibaldi," she said, clearly surprised to see him. "Is there a problem?"

Something was different about her tonight, he realized. He was used to seeing her in suits, so the sleeveless, calf-length sundress was a surprise. But her attire wasn't what had caught his attention. Maybe it was just a trick of the light that silhouetted her figure in the doorway, but he could swear her face was flushed with excitement and that her eyes actually sparkled behind the thick lenses of her glasses.

Was she entertaining? Had his unscheduled visit interrupted a languid seduction scene? Was that what was up with his landlady?

He'd never seen her like this before, so animated, so alive. Prior to that moment, if anyone had asked him to describe her, he would have said she was a woman who took life seriously and who dressed the part. She wasn't plain, nor was she pretty. *Sensible looking* would be an apt enough description. He'd always thought of her as quiet and self-contained, a woman content to fade into the background with her books and ledgers, while other, more vibrant personalities hogged the limelight.

Since when had he turned so poetic?

Since he'd realized that his landlady had gorgeous, thick, waist-length hair. Normally, or at least whenever he'd seen her, she wore it in a French braid or in a bun fastened at the nape of her neck.

Suddenly, Marco was looking at her in a whole new light.

"Dr. Garibaldi?" she repeated, seemingly puzzled at his nonresponse.

He gave himself a mental shake. Given the acrimony with which his most recent relationship had ended, he was in no hurry to jump into another one. Even if he had been, Gretchen Montgomery would be the last woman he'd choose. For one thing, Marco was fairly certain she was a marriage-minded woman, and he was definitely not a marriage-minded man. What was more important, she was his landlady. Never mix business with pleasure, that was his motto.

"I'm sorry to disturb you so late, Ms. Montgomery, but I was wondering if you could turn your CD player down."

She looked more puzzled than ever. "My CD player?"

He felt a surge of impatience. "The piano music. It's keeping me awake."

"You think—" She broke off. A quick glance at her wristwatch, and her eyes filled with contrition. "I'm so sorry. I didn't realize it was this late. Of course I'll turn the music down. I apologize for disturbing you, Dr. Garibaldi. I won't be so thoughtless again."

"Thank you."

"Can I do anything else for you?"

You can let me run my fingers through your hair.

The unexpected thought shot a tingle of awareness through him. Before he could control the impulse, he actually felt his arm reach out as if to do just that. He definitely needed to get some sleep.

"No," he said, quickly backing away. Snatching back his outstretched arm, he thrust his fingers through his own hair. "Nothing else."

"Have a good night, Dr. Garibaldi."

"You too, Ms. Montgomery."

"Dr. Garibaldi?"

Hand on the door to his own apartment, Marco slowly turned. "Yes?"

"Before I forget, I should probably warn you that I'm having some cosmetic work done on the outside of the house over the next few weeks. Most of it should be carried out between nine and five, but if it causes a problem, please let me know. I realize your hours can be erratic, and I don't want to disturb your sleep again."

"Thank you. I'll notify you if there's a problem."

She seemed to hesitate. "Well, good night."

"Good night."

He'd just settled back into bed and closed his eyes, the blessed silence cocooning him like a soft, cotton blanket, when the phone rang. Marco swore. He wasn't on call. Unless there was a huge disaster in the making, or a member of his family needed him, his phone had no business ringing at this hour.

"What?" he barked into the receiver.

"It's me," Brian, his best friend, said.

"Do you know what time it is?"

"Sorry, buddy. It's just... Well, it's Val." A long sigh traveled the phone lines. "We had another fight. A big one. She's threatening to file for divorce. Can I come over? I really need someone to talk to."

Marco swung his legs over the side of the bed. "Sure," he said, running his hand over the stubble on his cheeks. "I'll put the coffee on." What had ever made him think he was going to get some sleep?

As he stumbled into the bathroom to toss cold water on his face, Marco's thoughts turned to Brian and Val. Married just four years, they had already separated and reunited twice.

The problem was that, like him, Brian was a physician. A pediatrician who'd just started a practice of his own, he often worked more than eighty hours a week. And that didn't take into consideration the hours in the middle of the night that he was on call. With a new baby to care for, it was no wonder Val often felt overwhelmed and neglected as far as attention from her husband was concerned. For his part, Brian justifiably felt torn between the pressures of the practice he'd built to assure his family's financial security and the emotional demands of that family.

Marco was thankful for one thing. The day he'd promised to never forget the human side of medicine, he'd also promised that he would never marry. The marriages of too many physicians ended as a result of the very issues with which Val and Brian were now struggling. Issues they would continue to struggle with in the future. If, that is, they stayed married.

During those rare times when the thought of a wife and family to come home to became too tempting, all Marco had to do was think of Brian and Val, and his weakness would vanish. The one thing he never questioned were the promises he had made. His determination to keep them remained steadfast.

So why, even though he knew it was inappropriate, couldn't he stop thinking about the light in his landlady's unexpectedly bewitching eyes? And why couldn't he stop hoping that she wasn't entertaining a gentleman caller, that some other man wasn't this very minute running his fingers through her beautiful, long hair?

Gretchen stood with her back pressed to her closed front door. Her heart thudded and her cheeks felt hot.

"'Well, good night,'" she muttered in disgust. "Is that all you could think to say to him? What about, 'You make my toes curl and my heart pound, and I was wondering if there was any chance I could do the same to you?' Or, 'I made a promise to my best friend that I'd have a wild, crazy affair. You game?'"

Groaning, she buried her head in her hands. She really was hopeless. Having a wild, crazy affair with any man, let alone one as virile as Marco Garibaldi, wasn't going to be easy. In truth, she had to face the fact that it might prove downright impossible.

Gretchen felt herself grow as hot as the air outside as she remembered the way her tenant had looked, his thick, nearly black hair tousled, his well-muscled legs and broad chest on view in a way she had never glimpsed before beneath his loosely belted bathrobe, his smoky, heavy-lidded eyes half-closed from exhaustion. Heaven help her, if he had smiled that slow, crooked grin of his, she would have melted into a puddle at his feet. And the heat would have had nothing to do with it.

There was no denying that he possessed all the qualities Jill had stipulated. Just as there was no denying that, since Jill had put the notion into her head, having a wild, crazy affair with Marco Garibaldi was just about all Gretchen could think about.

She had always pictured herself as the PTA-baking-cookies-and-sewing-Halloween-costumes type of woman. And, if no man ever gave her a chance to exercise those skills, she gave a bang-up presentation before a board of directors and could summarize a company's financial situation in thirty words or less.

When asked for a résumé, *seductress and temptress* had never made the list. For heaven's sake, she wore high-necked cotton nightgowns in the summer and flannel pajamas in the winter. She never slept in the nude, something—if that loosely belted bathrobe was any indication—she suspected Marco Garibaldi was quite comfortable doing. Face it, she knew as much about having a wild, crazy affair as she did about flying a rocket to the moon.

Her recent encounter with the doctor in question more than bore out that conclusion. She hadn't exactly gotten off to a rousing start, so far as seduction was concerned. Although she could have sworn that, for the briefest of seconds, she'd actually seen a flare of interest in his eyes. She'd even imagined that he'd reached out to her. Of course, the minute he'd all but tripped over his feet in his haste to get away from her, she'd realized how mistaken she'd been.

Good thing Jill hadn't given her a time limit to accomplish everything she'd promised she would do, because something told Gretchen her powers of seduction needed a complete overhaul.

She was making headway on the rest of her promises, though. Over the three weeks that had passed since she'd listened to Jill's tape, she'd done a lot of thinking on how she would spend the money Jill had left her. To date, she'd solicited bids to have the years of grit and grime covering the outside of her duplex sandblasted away and to have the bricks themselves repointed. Next week, central air-conditioning would be installed, and she and her tenant could throw away the window units that were working overtime in this heat. While the expenses could hardly be called impractical, it was money she normally wouldn't have spent.

She'd also filled out an application to compete in a piano competition in Morgantown, West Virginia, next November. The age cutoff was thirty, which meant she would just squeak in under the wire. This truly was her last chance to find out whether she had any talent, and, if she was accepted, she had only a little more than four months to prepare. She was nervous, but she was also excited.

Filling out the application and writing the check for the entry fee had been the easy part. Much harder had been sitting down at the piano itself.

Though she'd kept the upright in tune, she'd rarely played it these past years. She didn't know why, other than that when she'd given up her dream she'd also given up playing. She'd even, after her parents died, had the piano moved from the living room into the spare bedroom on the second floor. Out of sight, out of mind, she supposed.

Tonight, however, the minute she'd rolled back the lid from the keyboard, she'd lost herself in the wonder of the music. It had been obvious from the first note that she had a long way to go before she was ready to compete. But, oh, the joy of playing again. She'd forgotten how wonderful it felt to run her fingers over the keys and the sense that always filled her when she sat down to play—that the world was a wonderful place and that all things were possible.

She'd played the same piece over and over again, a Beethoven sonatina that was perfect for stretching lazy fingers. Marco Garibaldi had thought she was playing a CD. Surely that was a good sign. Surely that meant she hadn't grown irredeemably rusty and that she had a chance.

Yes, she decided as she pushed off the door and turned to see that it was properly bolted, she was making progress. She was doing everything she could to keep the promises she had made.

Everything, that is, except try to find a way to seduce

her tenant. She'd been putting off the hardest task for last, which was totally unlike her. When it came to work, she had always done the thing she least wanted to do first, getting it out of the way so she could enjoy the tasks that made her job such a pleasure.

She supposed she was dragging her feet because she had little confidence that she would succeed. Also, she'd never been lucky where affairs of the heart were concerned. An engagement had ended when she'd decided to care for her dying father. Subsequent relationships had all been unsatisfying. When Jill got sick two years ago, Gretchen had abandoned dating altogether, in order to spend as much time as possible with her friend.

She thought of the men she'd dated: sedate, sensible, dependable. Or, as Jill had so succinctly put it, dull, dull, dull. Then she thought of the women she'd seen on Marco Garibaldi's arm. Beautiful. Vibrant. Vivacious. Anything but dull. She'd have to do something drastic, if she was ever going to compete with them.

Just how did a person go about having a wild, crazy affair? How could she make Marco Garibaldi look at her like she was one of the beautiful women he frequently squired, instead of his landlady? Gretchen didn't have the first idea, but she knew someone who might.

"Do you have a minute?"

Gretchen peered around the office door of the senior partner of Curtis, Walker, Davis and Associates. Gary Curtis had been her mentor and friend from the day she was hired to work for the firm. Aside from Marco Garibaldi, he was the most virile-looking and devastatingly handsome man she had ever met. Good thing she loved him like a brother because he was also gay. She'd seen more than one smitten woman delude herself into believing she could change the way nature had made him, only to wind up heartbroken in the end.

Gary closed the file he was reviewing and smiled at her. "For you, I've always got time. Come in."

After carefully closing the door, Gretchen took a seat.

"What's the problem?" Gary asked. "Is this about the Harrison account?"

"No." She made a show of crossing her legs at the ankles and smoothing her skirt while she gathered her thoughts. "It's…personal."

"Sounds serious."

She drew a deep breath. "It is. I need your advice, Gary. About men."

A light of interest gleamed in his eyes. "What about them?"

"This is going to sound stupid, but I was wondering if you could tell me how I should go about attracting one."

Gary spread his arms. "Gay men I know. Straight men…" He shrugged. "That's a whole 'nother story."

"Your brother's straight, isn't he?"

"As a ruler."

"Does he look like you?"

"People have been known to remark on the resemblance. Why?"

"That means he's a handsome devil, which means women must like him."

Gary's lips curved. "Let me put it this way. They often come to blows over the favor of his company."

"That's what I was hoping for," she said. "I want you to pretend you're him for a few minutes. Can you do that?"

"I think I can manage it."

Like an actor preparing for a role, he leaned back in his chair, closed his eyes and drew in a deep, cleansing breath. When he opened them again he said, "Okay. I'm a macho, heterosexual male who is irresistible to women. What do you want to know?"

She knew he expected her to smile, but she regarded

him intently instead. "What would I have to do to get you to want me?"

"Are we talking purely physical here, or something deeper?"

"Purely physical."

He nodded. "You want it flat out on the table, or sugar-coated?"

She squared her shoulders. "Flat out on the table."

Tilting his head, he ran his gaze over her. "Okay. For starters, stop slouching. You're tall. Accept it. And lose the suits. They're way too businesslike, and I assume you have a figure under there, somewhere. Your legs, what little I can see of them, seem nice. You need to accentuate them. Buy lots of dresses. Short dresses. By short, I mean nothing longer than the top of your knees. And a push-up bra. It'll give you cleavage.

"You also need to have a total makeover. Hair, nails, makeup, the works. Take notes. You need to get fitted for some contacts. And you need to go to the bookstore."

Her eyebrows raised. "The bookstore?"

"The bookstore. I want you to buy every book you can find on attracting a man. Study them the way a theology student does the Bible. Once you've done all that, come see me, and we'll talk some more."

Gretchen couldn't help laughing. "You sure you're not secretly straight, and just waiting for the right moment to burst into the closet?"

He grinned back at her. "Not a chance. So, I assume this all has a purpose. Whom are we trying to attract?"

She told him about Jill, the tape and Marco Garibaldi.

"It must have been hard for you to listen to Jill's voice like that."

"In the beginning it was. After a while, though, it was just comforting. I miss her a lot, Gary."

Sympathy filled his eyes. "I know you do. What do you plan on doing with the money?"

"I'm not entirely sure. I've scheduled some maintenance work on the house. I've also made an appointment for lasik surgery, so you don't have to worry about me wearing glasses anymore.'' She spread her arms. ''Other than the makeover and a new wardrobe, I'm still thinking.''

''May I make a suggestion?''

''Of course.''

''Buy a sports car.''

''Why a sports car?''

''Because the car you're driving now is ten years old, and there's nothing sporty about it.''

''It's a Volvo, Gary. It'll still be going strong ten years from now.''

''And what does Volvo say, when the man you're trying to seduce sees you in it? Especially a ten-year-old Volvo.''

Her smile was wry. ''Point taken.''

''Good. Buy a sports car. Park it in your driveway. I guarantee it won't be long before the illustrious Dr. Garibaldi will be begging to take you for a test drive.''

She raised her eyebrows at the vision Gary's words formed in her brain. ''The double entendre was deliberate, wasn't it?''

''Of course.''

''You really think I have a chance?''

''Why would you doubt it?''

''Look at me, Gary. I'm not exactly the temptress type.''

''So what if you're not a raving beauty. Neither are most supermodels before the makeup department gets their hands on them. All you need is a little confidence in yourself. A makeover and the appropriate wardrobe should give you that.''

''If you say so.''

''Smile for me, Gretchen.''

She curved her lips in a perfunctory motion.

''No.'' He shook his head. ''Really smile.''

This time the smile she gave him let him know how precious he was to her.

"Honey," he said gently, "when you smile like that, you make me wish I hadn't been born to an alternative lifestyle."

"Have I ever told you how good you are for my ego?"

"A time or two." Gary regarded her for a long minute. "Can I ask a personal question?"

"Sure."

"Are you a virgin?"

Gretchen felt her cheeks heat. "I was engaged at one point, remember?"

"So?"

"No, Gary, I'm not a virgin."

"Thank God." He looked relieved. "There are some things I just can't teach."

Gretchen laughed. "I love you, Gary."

"Where did that come from?" he asked, looking startled.

"From Jill. She told me to tell the people who are most important to me how much I care for them."

He seemed to think it over, then his expression softened. "I love you, too. Now get a move on. You've got a lot of work to do. And I don't mean in the office."

"Thanks for the advice." She headed for the door.

"Anytime. Know something? I like this. I'm starting to feel like Professor Higgins in *My Fair Lady*. Between you and me, I always thought the man was gay."

Gretchen laughed. "Well, Professor Higgins," she said, "I'll let you dress me up and make me over. But I'm telling you right now, this Eliza Doolittle draws the line at filling her mouth with marbles and singing about the rain in Spain."

"We'll see about that." Gary waggled an eyebrow at her.

Chuckling, Gretchen returned to her office. As she opened one of the Harrison files, she thought about what she'd jokingly told Gary. When it came down to it, for Marco Garibaldi she just might fill her mouth with marbles and sing about the rain in Spain. Because he was worth it.

Chapter 2

His landlady had legs. Killer legs. Eye-popping legs. Long, gorgeous, endless legs. How had he never noticed?

As Marco unfolded his body from the car he'd just parked on his side of the garage, he let his gaze travel the length of Gretchen Montgomery's legs to the simple black dress she wore, and he had his answer. He'd never noticed her legs because, before today, he'd never seen her hemline above her calf.

In his wildest imaginings, he'd never pictured her permitting said hemline to climb to thigh level, as it did now, or allowing the fabric of her dress to cling so tightly it looked as if it had been glued onto her. His mouth went dry when his gaze fastened on the low, square neckline. Not only did she have great legs, she also had cleavage. And one stunner of a figure.

"Wow," he murmured under his breath, thinking that it was about time Gretchen Montgomery broke out of her shell.

Leaning back against his car, he loosened his shirt collar. The weather might have cooled to a balmy eighty degrees, but looking at his landlady in that dress definitely had him hot under the collar. Uncomfortably hot.

Sometime, during the three-and-a-half weeks since their midnight conversation on the front porch, she'd undergone a complete transformation. It was incredible. She was the caterpillar who had emerged a butterfly, Cinderella after her fairy godmother had outfitted her for the ball.

She'd cut her hair, he realized. Now he would never get a chance to run his fingers through its lustrous length. Instead of feeling regret, he couldn't help admiring the appropriateness of the new style. Her now shoulder-length brown hair curled gently around her face, emphasizing her cheekbones, the curve of her chin and the elegant length of her neck. Should the occasion ever arise, her hair was still plenty long enough to run his fingers through.

She wasn't wearing her glasses, and he saw that her eyes were a rich, chocolate brown. They still gleamed with the intelligence she couldn't hide, but there was something else there, too. Amusement? Awareness of the effect she was having on him? As she leaned against her car, he saw that his landlady was inspecting him as closely as he was her.

Something was still up with her, that was for certain. Whatever it was, today Marco liked it a lot. After the day he'd had, she was a sight for sore eyes. Or, to take the trite analogy one step further, she was just what the doctor had ordered—he being the doctor in question.

It had to be a man, he decided, and wondered at the sour taste the thought left in his mouth. In his experience, no woman went to such trouble unless a man was involved.

"You like?" she asked.

It took him a beat to realize she meant her car. Expecting the aging, sedate Volvo, he did a double take at the sleek, black Dodge Viper that now graced his landlady's half of the garage.

Marco gave a low, appreciative whistle. "That is some car. When did you get it?"

"An hour ago. It has an 8.0-liter V10 engine, 450 horsepower and six-speed manual transmission. It can accelerate from zero to sixty miles per hour in 4.1 seconds."

To Marco, she sounded as if she were reciting painfully memorized facts, much like a second grader reciting her times tables.

"You know what all that means?" he asked. His heart skipped a beat when she grinned impishly.

"I haven't a clue. All I know is that the salesman made a big deal out of it, and that the car can go fast."

He laughed. "Mind if I look it over?"

She stood aside. "Be my guest."

Slowly he walked around the vehicle, running a finger over the sleekness of its gleaming curves. It was the kind of car he'd always dreamed of owning. Once he paid off all his school loans, that is. It cost a small fortune, he knew, more than most people earned in a year. More than he'd be able to afford for quite a few years to come.

How, he wondered suddenly, and with a start of concern, had his landlady afforded it? Now that he thought about it, she had spent a lot of money lately. That outfit didn't come cheap. Nor did the ongoing repairs to the duplex. Like the music that had kept him awake three weeks earlier, the way she was dressed today, not to mention buying a vehicle like this, seemed so out of character for her that he couldn't help wondering what was going on. Was she involved in something—or with someone—that, in the long run, would only bring her trouble?

Before he let his imagination run away with him, Marco decided a note of caution was in order. After all, what, if anything, did he really know about her? Maybe she'd scrimped and saved for years, just to savor this moment of ownership. As for the improvements to the house, it only made sense for a homeowner to keep up her property. Probably a tax write-off, as well.

And the new clothing? The answer to that one was also simple. She couldn't drive around town in a car like this wearing a three-piece suit. Could she?

"I removed the hardtop myself," he heard her say. "It was surprisingly easy."

"So I see," he replied, peering into an interior that was all cognac leather and fancy gadgets.

"Impractical, isn't it?"

Straightening, he returned his gaze to hers and smiled. "The most impractical thing I've ever seen. That's what makes it so great."

"It is great, isn't it?"

Was that a flicker of doubt in her eyes? Did she need him to convince her that she'd done the right thing?

"Sure is," he said with a heartiness he didn't feel, his own doubts resurfacing. "You don't see many cars like this around here."

"Which means," she said, surprising him with her candor, "you're wondering how I could afford it."

Again he thought of the improvements she'd made to the duplex. And to herself. As for the duplex, it was a comfortable, middle-class home. Nothing about it, or Gretchen Montgomery herself, had ever indicated she could afford to spend money the way she had been lately.

Had she won the lottery? Received an inheritance? Robbed a bank? He felt his lips curve at that last, fanciful imagining.

"The thought may have crossed my mind," he admitted, deciding to be as frank with her as she had been with him.

"Just think of it as creative financing," she replied. "I am a CPA, after all."

Which told him nothing, even though it wasn't any of his business in the first place. Whatever the source of her newfound wealth, it did seem to be accomplishing one thing. It was definitely pulling her out of her shell. And that was a good thing.

"Let me reassure you," she added with a smile. "I'm not going to lose the roof over your head."

"I'm happy to hear it." Relieved was more like it.

The conversation underscored how little he knew about her, even though he had been her tenant for two years. Was he really so shallow that a change in her looks, and a flashy car in her garage, were what it had taken to arouse his curiosity?

No. There was more to it than that. Part of the reason had to do with the fact that Gretchen Montgomery had always put up walls around herself. Now that she'd pulled them down, he should probably take advantage of the opportunity to learn more about her.

So long as he remembered that she was his landlady and nothing more, he cautioned himself.

"Would you like to go for a ride?" she asked.

He knew she meant the car, but he couldn't help thinking of a far different, exceedingly intimate kind of ride that, landlady or not, he'd like to take with her. "I don't know how to drive a stick shift," he said.

She maneuvered those long legs of hers into the driver's seat. Looking up at him expectantly, she replied, "That's okay. I do."

When he hesitated, she patted the creamy leather of the passenger seat with fingernails that had been painted a bright red. "Don't worry, Dr. Garibaldi. I promise I won't bite."

She might not, but he was afraid that if he was cooped up in close quarters with her for too long, he might.

"Marco," he said. "The name's Marco."

"Call me Gretchen."

"Very well, Gretchen." Swinging the passenger door open, he sank with a sigh onto the soft leather seat. Inhaling a heady breath of new-car aroma, he said, "Take me away from all my troubles."

"My pleasure."

When she started the engine and began backing down

the driveway, he glanced over at her. "Don't you need your glasses to drive?"

"Lasik surgery," she explained. "You are now looking at an emancipated woman. Twenty-twenty vision, both eyes."

She was emancipated all right, he thought, eyeing her body in that tight dress. Any more emancipated, and he might not be able to contain himself.

"Must feel good," he said, mentally adding the cost of the lasik surgery to the growing column of cash outlays she had made in recent weeks.

"You don't know the half of it," she replied fervently. "To have the weight of glasses off my nose is heavenly. And the exhilaration of waking up in the morning and being able to see—"

She broke off, looking embarrassed. "Sorry. I didn't mean to bore you with all the details."

Bore him? How could she bore him, when the light of pleasure gleaming in her eyes had his pulse rate accelerating like mad? How could she bore him, when all he could think of was how exhilarating it would be to wake up in the morning and see *her* lying next to him? He, Marco Garibaldi, who made love to women but who avoided sleeping with them.

He forced his gaze out the window and shoved his inappropriate thoughts to the back of his mind. "Trust me, I'm not at all bored."

Ten minutes later they were out on the open highway.

"Let's see what this baby can really do, shall we?" she said.

Marco felt the rhythm of the engine change as she shifted gears and the vehicle picked up speed. In fascination, and not a little trepidation, he watched the speedometer needle edge past sixty, to seventy, then eighty, until it finally rested at eighty-five.

Outside, the scenery rushed past, wildflowers and trees

melding together in one big blur. Thank goodness they were on a flat stretch of road and there wasn't another car in sight. Of course, that wouldn't help them if a deer darted out from nowhere, or an unseen patch of oil sent the car into an unexpected skid.

Tossing her head back, Gretchen laughed. It was the delighted, triumphant laughter of an explorer discovering a new land.

"Quite a kick, isn't it?" she said.

"Oh, it's a kick all right," he replied tensely. "A real boot to the backside."

"I've never felt so exquisitely free in my entire life."

And he'd never felt so exquisitely terrified.

"You do know that the posted speed limit is fifty-five, don't you?" he felt compelled to say.

Her hair blew wildly around her face, and she raised one hand to tuck a stray strand behind her ear. "I know."

"Just thought I'd mention it." He watched carefully until she'd placed her hand back on the steering wheel.

"Consider it mentioned." She glanced at him out of the corner of one eye. "Did you know that the top speed this car can reach is 189 miles per hour? That's why the manufacturer doesn't install anti-lock breaks. Without them, the driver can maximize the car's acceleration potential."

He hadn't known that, could have lived a long and happy life without knowing it, and prayed fervently she wasn't going to try to attain warp speed this outing.

"Let me guess. Part of the salesman's pitch?"

"Uh-huh."

Suddenly she turned to him again, and her eyes flashed with an emotion he could only describe as regret. There was a self-accusatory tone in her voice when she said, "Do you realize that I'm almost thirty years old, and I've never gotten so much as a traffic ticket? Worse, I've never even been stopped by a policeman. Isn't that a crime?"

Swiftly, and to his relief, she faced forward again.

"Well, I'm thirty-four," he said tautly, fingers clenched

against the dashboard, "and I've never had a traffic ticket or been stopped, either. You ask me, a lot of people would envy your record. I'm sure your insurance company appreciates it. Of course, if you keep traveling at this speed, you'll most likely discover the thrill of being stopped and ticketed. Any second now." If they were lucky.

She flashed him a look of surprise. "Am I making you nervous?"

He didn't know what scared him more: the speed at which they were traveling or Gretchen Montgomery herself. He'd never met another woman like her, one minute shy and quiet, almost reserved, the next vibrant and outgoing, and totally unpredictable. Talk about a paradox; he was looking straight at one.

"Terrified," he admitted.

"I'm sorry." She eased up on the accelerator. "I thought all men loved to go fast."

"Only with women, and only when they feel like they're in control," he muttered, watching in relief as the speedometer nosed its way back to a sedate fifty-eight miles per hour.

"What did you say?"

"Nothing."

"You don't have to worry, you know. I'm an excellent driver."

"I'm sure you are."

It was just that he had a thing about excessive speed. He'd seen its tragic aftermath too often in the E.R. not to respect that there were some things best left to the professionals. Traveling at a high rate of speed in an automobile was one of them.

Several miles flew by without either of them speaking. Relaxing at last, Marco leaned back against the seat, closed his eyes and wallowed in the feel of the fresh air washing over his face.

"Long day at work?" she asked.

"Long week," he said.

''You work at Bridgeton Hospital, right?''

''Yes. In the emergency department.''

''Been there long?''

''Three years as a resident. Three years now on staff.''

''You must find it very rewarding.''

''It has its moments. What about you, Gretchen? Do you enjoy your work?''

There was only a slight hesitation before she replied, ''Very much. It's quite challenging. If you're like most people, though, you think accounting, and CPAs in particular, are deadly boring.''

Eyes still closed, he smiled. ''I suppose I've fallen victim to that stereotype once or twice.''

''Who hasn't? By the way, you wouldn't happen to own a Harley, a leather jacket or have a tattoo, would you?''

He ranked Harleys up there with driving at a high speed: too dangerous. Leather jackets were okay—his brother Carlo practically lived in one—but tattoos were definitely out. Why subject himself to needless infection?

Bemused, he swiveled his head toward her and opened his eyes. ''No. Why?''

She shrugged. ''I just realized we've been next-door neighbors for more than two years now, and I really don't know very much about you.''

His thoughts precisely. ''What would you like to know?''

''For starters, why do you rent from me?''

''Is there a reason I shouldn't?''

''Only that you're a doctor. I assume you could afford a place of your own.''

He grimaced. ''You haven't seen the bill for my medical school loans.''

''I'm not the type of landlady who steams open her tenants' mail,'' she said lightly.

''For which I'm heartily grateful.'' After a pause he added, ''I suppose I could swing a house if I wanted to. I just don't want to.''

"Would you mind my asking why not?"

"It's simple, really. I have a job that demands a lot of my time. What little I have left over, I'd rather spend with my brothers and my sister, and not have to worry about the care and upkeep of a house."

"Makes sense to me," she said.

"Me, too. Anything else you want to know?"

She startled him by pulling to the side of the road. Car idling, she removed her hands from the steering wheel and placed them in her lap before turning in her seat to face him. She seemed oddly tentative.

"Are you involved with anyone?"

The unexpected question knocked him totally off balance. "Not at the moment," he replied carefully.

She digested that for a minute before asking, "Do you find me...attractive?"

"I think the answer is obvious."

"Is it?" She seemed to be holding her breath.

He ran his gaze hotly over her, paying particular attention to her legs and her cleavage. When he returned his attention to her face, he saw that her cheeks were red.

"Do you still doubt it?"

"No." She licked her lips. "In that case, what do you think of the idea of us having a wild, crazy affair?"

His heart surged into his throat. "An affair?"

She nodded. "No strings attached."

"And when it's over?"

"We go our separate ways."

"No hard feelings?"

"None."

"Now?"

Her lips curved. "I was thinking of someplace a little more private." She nodded at their surroundings. "Also, a little more romantic. And roomier."

He didn't smile back at her. He couldn't. He knew he was stalling, asking questions to put off having to give her an answer. The real question was, Why?

Because he would have staked his reputation on the wager that she was not a woman who entered into an affair lightly. Considering that they'd spoken to each other more today than they had in the sum total of their conversations over the prior two years, he was at a loss to explain why she had made the offer.

"Well?" she repeated. "What do you think?"

What did he think? That it was the best idea he'd heard all week. That it had been a long time since a woman had made him so aware of his maleness and her femaleness. That he'd be a fool to say no.

The best thing about it was that she was offering what every man dreamed of: a no-strings-attached, fleeting affair. She was offering what he offered every woman he got involved with. So why was he hesitating? It wasn't like him to be gallant.

Yes, she was his landlady, which offered up all sorts of potential complications. But there was more. Despite the come-on, he sensed a loneliness about her and an underlying tension. Something wasn't right here. She wasn't herself, and until he knew why, Marco couldn't take advantage of her vulnerability. He had no choice but to say no.

"I think," he said carefully, reluctantly, "that the timing isn't right."

She looked away from him, but not before he caught a flash of what he could swear was relief in her eyes. He had been right. Something was definitely going on here. If only he could figure out what it was.

"So you're saying no," she said flatly.

"Have you had an accident at work?" he asked.

"What do you mean?"

"Have you fallen, hit your head? Perhaps a reaction to a new medication? You're not acting at all like yourself today."

Her body went rigid. "Oh? And just how should I be acting?"

"This isn't you, Gretchen."

Her gaze met his, her eyes defiant. If relief was what he'd glimpsed in them a minute ago, it was absent now.

"What isn't me?"

"This." He swept an arm out. "The car, the clothing, the come-on. Especially the come-on."

She bit her lip and looked down at her lap. "So, what you're saying is that I look ridiculous."

"Not ridiculous," he replied gently. "Not even close. You just seem a little…well, uncomfortable."

For a long minute she didn't say anything. Then, with a rueful smile, she tugged at the hemline of her dress.

"You'd be uncomfortable, too, if you'd poured yourself into this thing. It's so tight I can barely breathe. It may fit like a second skin, but it feels like a tourniquet."

"For what it's worth, you look great."

"Not great enough to make you want me."

If only she knew how wrong she was. "I have my reasons, Gretchen."

"And I respect them. Don't worry. I won't bother you anymore with my unwanted attentions."

"They're not entirely unwanted," he admitted. "They're just…"

"Inconvenient?"

It was as good a word as any. "The dress really isn't you, you know."

"Why?" Her voice took on a bitter note. "Because it isn't practical?"

"Yes. No. I guess so," he ended lamely, not knowing what to say.

"And I'm a practical woman."

"I've always thought of you that way."

"Well, maybe I've decided to erase the word *practical* from my vocabulary."

"What's wrong with being practical?"

"Let me ask *you* something," she retorted. "When's

the last time you took a practical woman like me to your bed?''

When he didn't answer, she gave a hollow laugh. ''That's what I thought.''

Shifting, she pulled back onto the highway. At the first exit she turned around and headed for home. The sun was setting when she pulled into her garage.

''Thank you for the ride,'' Marco said, feeling awkward.

''Anytime.'' She wouldn't meet his gaze. ''Next time, though, I'll leave out the seduction scene.''

''Gretchen,'' he began.

She held up a hand. ''It's okay. You don't have to try to make me feel better. I'm a big girl. I'll be just fine.''

There was so much he wanted to say to her. That he thought she was the loveliest thing he'd ever seen. That he wanted her. That he regretted his clumsiness in his handling of the situation. That, under the proper circumstances, he would kill to have a wild, crazy affair with her. That he was there for her if she just wanted to talk.

The way she held her body, stiff and unyielding, told him the words wouldn't be welcome, so he remained mute. When they parted at their respective front doors, Marco felt more confused than ever.

She'd blown it. Big-time.

Bracing one hand on the edge of the kitchen sink, Gretchen pressed a frosted mug of root beer to cheeks that still burned with embarrassment. Outside her kitchen window the sun dropped below the horizon. A romantic scene if ever there was one, and she was watching it all alone. Which was a good thing, because she had never felt more mortified in her entire life.

How could she ever face him again?

She hadn't set out to try to seduce him. For one thing, she was in the middle of her period, which made things logistically difficult. The only purpose of the dress and the drive was to get his attention and to, hopefully, pique his interest. No one—except maybe Marco himself—had been more surprised when the words rolled out of her mouth. If she had piqued any interest on his part, it was whether or not she was playing the cards of life with a full deck.

What hurt the most was that she'd planned it out so painstakingly. For the past three and a half weeks, during which time she'd recovered from lasik surgery, had her hair styled and bought a whole new wardrobe, she'd been careful to keep out of his sight. She'd been especially careful to confine her piano practice to times when she was certain he wasn't home.

While she'd waited for the perfect time to put her plan into action, she'd read books on flirting, along with car brochures. She'd found herself listening for Marco and trying to ascertain his schedule. Then, when she was ready, she'd dressed herself up and shamelessly placed herself in his path.

The naked appreciation in his eyes had made her giddy. For the first time in what seemed forever, a man wasn't looking at her for just her mind. On the contrary, Marco had regarded her solely as a sexual object. Though she had known that officially she should be offended, she hadn't been able to summon up any indignation. The look in Marco's eyes was heady stuff for someone who was used to having men's glances slide away from her to more attractive women.

Never before had Gretchen felt such confidence, such an incredible sense of her power as a woman. And it had all fallen apart the minute she'd thrown caution to the wind rushing through their hair and propositioned him.

She heaved a heavy sigh. What had every flirting book instructed? Dress your best. Be mysterious. Play hard to get. Keep him off balance.

If Marco's reaction was anything to go by, she'd gotten the dressing-her-best part down pat. The mysterious part was harder to judge. As for being hard to get, what a laugh. She was the mouse who had baited its own trap.

She had kept him off balance, though. She'd driven him to the middle of nowhere at a speed that had shaved a year or two off his life. Then she'd pulled to the side of the road and ambushed him. He hadn't even seen it coming.

No wonder the poor man had seemed so terrified. Had they been any closer to home, he probably would have jumped from the car and run.

Which all went to prove that she was no good at seduction.

She'd kept her promise, and that was all that mattered, she told herself. She'd asked, and he'd said no. What more could she do? Besides, with Marco out of the picture, she could now concentrate on the piano competition, which was only a little more than three months away. She should be relieved. Why, then, did she feel so disappointed? So empty. So…restless.

Gretchen drank deeply from the mug, then placed it in the sink. "So Marco Garibaldi turned you down," she said to her reflection in the window. "Big deal! Is the world going to end? Sure, your pride's a little dented, but you'll recover. The condition isn't terminal."

Like Jill's had been.

Jill. Gretchen drew herself up straight. The revelation that came to her was like a flash of lightning in the darkest night. What was the one lesson she should have learned from Jill's untimely death? That life was short, precariously short. And that she, Gretchen Montgomery, was wasting precious time.

When all was said and done, after the makeover and all the new clothes, what had really changed? Nothing. She was still the same Gretchen inside that she'd always been.

The one promise that Jill had extracted, and which didn't cost a cent, was the very promise Gretchen had overlooked entirely. By dutifully spending a huge sum of money on a flashy car and a new wardrobe, she'd carried out the law of her promises, but not the spirit. She'd adopted the outward appearance while ignoring the inward attitude.

This wasn't about seducing Marco Garibaldi. It wasn't about seducing any man. It most certainly wasn't about buying a flashy sports car and blowing her inheritance on impractical things.

It was about living and enjoying life. It was about appreciating every moment in a way she never had before.

What was it Jill had said to her? *Remember that line from* Auntie Mame? *"Life is a banquet, and most poor suckers are starving to death." I want you to feast, Gretch, feast like no one has feasted before.*

Jill was right. She'd been going at it all wrong. No book, no wardrobe, no flashy car, and certainly no *man* was going to teach her how to get the most out of life. That had to come from inside of her. Just as a wild, crazy affair had to happen spontaneously. It couldn't be planned. She knew that now.

Gretchen recalled the exhilaration of flying down the road at eighty-five miles per hour. That was the way she wanted to feel every day of her life. That was the way she wanted to feel when a man took her into his arms.

It was all so clear now. Why had it taken her so long to see it, to understand what Jill had really been doing when she'd extracted all those promises from her? Life *was* too short. Too short for regrets, too short for fears, too short for embarrassments, too short for not doing all the things she'd always wanted to do.

Sometime, between now and the end of her life, she *would* have a wild, crazy affair. But not with a stranger, no matter how much he made her toes curl. She'd have that affair with the man who ultimately ended up owning her heart, the man who would love her and cherish her as much as she did him.

Until that time, though, Gretchen was done being timid. She was done being hesitant. She was done living her life for her career and ignoring everything else. She'd keep the car and the wardrobe, and she'd use them to bring *her* pleasure. From now on, she was going to live as if there was no tomorrow.

"How's it going?" Gary asked.

"Fine." Gretchen sank down into a chair and crossed her legs. "I should be wrapping up the Harrison account today."

"Good to hear. By the way, I like your dress. It's very flattering."

She glanced down at the camel-colored silk coatdress. Though not as tight as the black dress she'd worn the day before when she'd taken Marco Garibaldi for a ride, it was just as short. She was growing accustomed to the length of leg it exposed. Just as she was growing accustomed to, and even enjoying, the admiring glances the outfit garnered from the other men in the office.

"Thanks. I like it, too."

Leaning forward, Gary placed his elbows on his desk and steepled his fingers. "Can I ask you something I've been wondering about, but never quite had the courage to ask?"

She shrugged. "Sure."

"Why is it you had to come to me for advice on how to attract a man? Why didn't you already know these things?"

It was a subject she'd given a lot of thought recently. "I was an only child. My parents were older when they had me, and they were very old-fashioned in their behavior and their dress. I guess it rubbed off on me."

"You never rebelled? Not even as a teenager?"

"No. You see, I wore the label 'smart' all through school. It wouldn't have mattered how I dressed or behaved. The popular kids just looked right through me. Besides, I was too busy studying and taking care of my mother when she got sick. Then, in college, when my dad got sick, I took care of him, too. It wasn't that I was unaware of the way my peer group dressed and behaved. I just didn't have time to join them."

"Do you regret it?"

She thought for a minute. "No. The only thing I regret is that Jill didn't have more time."

"So, this is your time," he said.

"Yes." She smiled. "I plan on making the most of it."

"Good to hear." He drew a breath. "How's the seduction campaign going?"

"Oh, that." She waved a hand airily. "Dead in the water. He turned me down flat."

Gary peered closely at her. "You don't seem upset about it."

"I'm not."

"Why not?"

"Because I know now it wasn't meant to be. Actually, that's why I came to see you. I know it's short notice, but I need to take next week off."

"The whole week?"

She nodded. "Every single day."

"I'm not sure we can spare you that long."

"It's not like it's busy season, Gary. April fifteenth is still a whole eight and a half months away. The Harrison account will be wrapped up, and Laura and Jack will easily be able to take up the slack."

"It's that important to you?" he asked.

"It's that important," she confirmed. "You know I wouldn't ask if it weren't."

"What are you planning to do?"

"All the things I've never done."

"*All* of them?"

"Well," she amended, chuckling, "as many of them as I can cram into one week. The rest I'll just have to get to as I can."

"Sounds like fun."

"I'm looking forward to it." Rising, she headed for the door.

"Just because he turned you down, it doesn't mean you have to give up," Gary said.

She glanced at him over her shoulder. "I know. But you see, I realized something. *I'm* the one who's not ready for a wild, crazy affair. Not yet. But I will be someday."

"Maybe after the week off," he said.

"Maybe. I'll know when the time is right."

"Have fun," Gary said.

She flashed him a smile. "Thanks. I intend to."

Chapter 3

He had to stop thinking about her.

Marco knotted and cut the fifth of six required stitches on an eight-year-old's chin and tried to make his mind blank. It was a waste of effort. If he didn't know better, he could swear he was suturing Gretchen Montgomery's image to the viewing screen of his mind, instead of closing a little girl's cut.

He snipped the thread from the last suture and stood back to survey his handiwork. Neat. Clean. Although the cut had been a wide one, the scar should barely be noticeable.

It was the child's silky brown hair that had him thinking of his landlady. This time. Over the past three days since her unexpected proposal, any variety of sights and sounds had served to bring her to mind. A woman's laughter. A glimpse of a slender leg. Anyone with brown eyes. The sound of a car engine. It was driving him crazy.

The fact that they were having an uncharacteristically slow day in the E.R. wasn't helping, either.

"All done, Taylor," he said, after applying a bandage. "So, did I keep my word? Did it hurt?"

Taylor rewarded him with a wide, gap-toothed smile. "It didn't hurt at all, Dr. Marco. Just like you promised. Thanks."

"No thanks necessary. You were a very brave girl. But you might want to think twice the next time you decide to see if you can fly. I think you should leave that to birds and airplanes."

"Okay," she agreed readily, making Marco chuckle. The child was a good-natured imp. She was also, according to her mother, somewhat of a daredevil. Add inquisitive and extremely bright to the mix, and it was a given that this wouldn't be her last trip to the pit, as everyone who worked there called the emergency room.

Still smiling, Marco turned to Taylor's mother. "How are *you* doing?"

The woman gave a wan smile. "Honestly? She scared me half to death."

"Well, you have my word that Taylor will be just fine."

Once again, as Marco gave cleaning instructions and soothed the worried mother's fears, thoughts of Gretchen Montgomery invaded his consciousness. They continued to bedevil him as he moved on to his next patient and throughout the remainder of his shift.

"I have to stop thinking about her," he said out loud, hours later, as he stared unseeingly at a television drama. He'd been watching for twenty minutes, and he hadn't the faintest idea what the story line was.

He couldn't figure out his sudden fixation on a woman he barely knew. It wasn't as if he hadn't had his share of relationships. According to Brian, he'd had more than his fair share. And when they'd ended, he'd never looked back. So why, when he hadn't had so much as a date with his landlady, let alone a relationship with her, was she all he could think about?

Maybe that was the problem. Maybe if he had a brief affair with her, he would be able to get her out of his mind. After all, she *had* offered. Maybe this was his subconscious's way of telling him that he'd been a fool to turn her down.

Fool or not, he knew his decision had been a wise one. Something just hadn't seemed right about her unexpected proposition. Heaven forbid he should become entangled with her, only to discover she was some sort of psycho stalker, the way it often happened in movies where men were propositioned by women they didn't know.

To show just how addled he'd become over her, his first thought when his doorbell rang at ten o'clock was that it was his landlady, coming to repeat her offer. Which was ridiculous. Other than to bring him a casserole the day he moved in, Gretchen Montgomery had never come to his door. If she needed to communicate with him, she left a note in his mailbox or a message on his answering machine.

But then, he reminded himself, prior to three days ago she'd never taken him for a car ride, either. Or propositioned him. She had been acting out of character lately. Was it so far-fetched to think she might be standing on his doorstep?

"This is getting ridiculous," he muttered, climbing to his feet and walking out into the hallway. Mentally he vowed to put her out of his mind once and for all. Enough was enough.

"Hey, buddy," Brian said when he opened the door.

Marco stood stock-still while he took in the sight of his best friend with a baby tucked in one arm and a diaper bag hanging from the other. Thoughts of Gretchen Montgomery fled as a sense of foreboding filled him.

"What's wrong?" he asked urgently. "Is Kristen sick?"

Brian's smile seemed forced. "Kristen's fine. Can't a guy drop in on his best friend, without his motives being suspect?"

"Not when he has his baby in tow. It's ten o'clock, Bri. Rather late for the two of you to be out for an evening stroll. Isn't it past her bedtime?"

"A little," Brian agreed.

"Where's Val?"

Brian looked over his shoulder to where a late model SUV idled at the curb. "Getting some things from the car. She'll join us in a minute."

Marco expelled an impatient breath. "Do you plan on keeping me in suspense forever, or are you going to tell me what's going on?"

"You going to invite me inside?"

He stood aside while his friend filed past him into the hallway. "Okay, spill it," he demanded.

Brian avoided eye contact. "In a minute. First, I need you to answer a couple of questions. Are you on your off stretch?"

One of the perks of working in the pit, other than not being tied to a patient list, was that he worked for three weeks straight, then had one week off. Yes, the nineteen days in a row he did work were grueling, but the nine days that he had free gave him ample time to recover. It also gave him time to spend with his family.

"As of four hours ago."

"That's what I thought." Brian peered into the living room, where the television blared to an absent audience. "No date?"

"No date," Marco replied with exaggerated patience.

"Okay, I'll get to the point." Brian drew a deep breath. "Since you're free, I was wondering if you could do me a favor. A huge favor, actually. I was wondering if you could watch Kristen for Val and me."

Marco felt his eyebrows climb. "Kristen? As in the baby in your arms? As in six months old?"

"Seven."

"What?"

"She's seven months old."

Marco couldn't quite grasp the importance of that distinction, but he supposed he could humor his friend. "I could watch her for an hour or two."

Brian bit his lip. "Well, see, that's the problem. I need you to keep her for the weekend. Actually, I kind of already told Val you would."

The shock momentarily robbed Marco of speech. "The entire weekend?"

"My back's to the wall here, buddy. Val and I have plans to spend the weekend together at a bed and breakfast in Maryland. We need the time alone to try and patch up our marriage. We had a baby-sitter all lined up, but a family emergency forced her to cancel at the last minute. I've called everyone on my Rolodex. No one is available."

"But me."

"But you," Brian confirmed.

"I don't know anything about taking care of babies, Bri."

"You're a doctor, Marco."

Marco spread his arms. "So?"

"So, you should know all about babies."

"And you of all people should know that what my being a doctor means is that, in medical school, they taught me how to deliver a baby. They taught me how to examine one medically. They never touched on day-to-day care. Perhaps, being a pediatrician yourself, you've forgotten all that."

"You're an uncle," Brian said. "Surely you've been around babies."

"I am, and I have. But my brother Roberto had his kids when I was in medical school, so I didn't pay all that much attention. And the only time I hold my sister, Kate's, baby is when she's happy and gurgling. The minute she starts crying, I hand her back."

"There's nothing to it," Brian assured him. "Kristen's a good baby. All you have to do is feed her, change her diaper and keep an eye on her when she's crawling around, so she doesn't get into trouble.''

Marco felt his lips twist. ''Really? Is that all?''

Brian tossed a quick glance over Marco's shoulder, and his voice took on a new urgency. ''Val's coming. Please, Marco. I'm begging you. This might be the last chance I have to convince her that we can make our marriage work.''

Marco heaved a weary sigh. Brian was his best friend. And he truly did seem desperate.

''Okay. I'll watch her. But only if you think I can really do the job.''

Relief filled Brian's eyes. ''You can do it. I have faith in you. Thanks, Marco. I owe you big-time.''

''Don't think I'm going to let you forget it, either.''

Val breezed through the door. ''Sure you really want to do this?'' she asked, depositing what looked like enough gear to furnish a small room on his living room floor.

''I wouldn't have volunteered, if I didn't,'' he replied.

Raising up on tiptoe, she kissed him warmly on the cheek, then moved to take Kristen from Brian. Her voice was noticeably cooler when she spoke to her husband.

''Could you bring in the car seat, the portable crib and the swing from the porch? I need to go over a few things with Marco before we leave.''

With a nod Brian disappeared outside. When Val turned to face Marco, her smile seemed forced. The strain was taking its toll on her, he realized, noticing for the first time how thin she'd grown.

''Diapers and clothing are in the diaper bag,'' Val instructed, ''along with the phone number where you can reach us in event of emergency. Formula, baby food and bottles are in the brown bag, toys in the blue. Kristen takes a bottle every four hours and a jar of baby food at mealtime. You can heat the bottle in the microwave, as long as you test it first, but the baby food is okay at room temperature. If she gets fussy, just put her in her swing, and she usually calms down right away.''

Having deposited the items she'd asked for behind the sofa, Brian moved to his wife's side and ran a hand down her arm. Marco almost winced when Val flinched away from the caress.

"It's time to go, honey," Brian said firmly.

Val bit her lip, then gave her daughter a final hug and kissed her on the forehead. "You be a good baby for Marco, okay?''

"She's going to be a sweetheart, aren't you?" Brian said, taking Kristen from Val and handing her to Marco.

"She really likes it when you sing to her at bedtime,'' Val said quickly, as, taking her by the arm, Brian dragged her into the hallway. "And she loves sleeping with her little pink pillow. Oh, and she's crazy about stairs, so you're really going to have to watch her around them.''

At the door she turned back, indecision written all over her face. "Maybe we shouldn't go. This is too much to ask of you.''

"Go," Marco said firmly. "Kristen and I will be just fine.''

"We have to go, honey," Brian repeated. "Now.'' To Marco he added, "We'll be back around six o'clock Sunday night.''

"We'll be here," Marco assured him. "Have a wonderful time.''

The whole way down the sidewalk, Val kept her head turned over her shoulder and her gaze on her daughter. She looked as if she might be going to protest some more when they reached the SUV, but Brian finally coaxed her inside. After practically running to the driver's side, he gave Marco a final wave before speeding off.

Marco closed the front door and looked down at the child in his arms. Kristen gazed unblinkingly at him for the space of ten seconds before screwing up her tiny face and wailing at the top of her lungs.

* * *

Gretchen could swear she heard a baby crying. Raising up on her elbows, she cocked her head and listened carefully. Yes, there it was again. A cry, faint but unmistakable.

It couldn't be a baby, she told herself, shaking her head. The only family with an infant on her block were the Ericksons, and they lived five houses away. Her windows were closed, and the air-conditioning was on full blast. A baby's cries just didn't carry that far. No, it couldn't be a baby.

Sinking back into the cocoon of pillows she'd piled against her headboard, Gretchen crossed her ankles and focused on the schedule she'd painstakingly filled out with all the activities she planned on accomplishing over the following week. Counting both weekends, she only had nine days, and she wanted to use her time as efficiently as possible. She had a lot of lost time to make up for. Before she found herself chained to her desk again, she wanted to experience everything she could.

A shiver of anticipation raced up her spine as she reread the list of her planned activities. She really was looking forward to doing all of the things she'd never been allowed to do as a child, or gotten around to doing as an adult. It was going to be such fun.

Tapping the lid of her pen against her teeth, she decided that she definitely needed to make room for a trip to Kennywood Park and a ride on its premier roller coaster, The Phantom's Revenge. That was a must. It was also imperative that she walk barefoot through her local park. That should be easy to squeeze in somewhere. Her brow furrowed in concentration. Had she forgotten anything else?

The sound she'd heard earlier distracted her again, and Gretchen lowered the schedule to her lap. Sure did sound like a baby was crying somewhere.

It was probably just a pair of amorous cats out in back by the garage, she finally decided. Their cries often mimicked those of an infant. Although this particular pair of cats seemed to be enjoying themselves for an unprecedented length of time.

Gretchen felt her lips twist mockingly. It was a sorry state of affairs when the neighborhood cats' love lives were far more exciting than her own. But then, hadn't that always been the case?

Maybe it wouldn't be for much longer, though. If she opened herself up to experience all that the world had to offer, who knew? She could stumble across Mr. Right tomorrow. Crazier things had happened.

The peal of her doorbell shattered a fantasy of Gretchen and a Mr. Right, who looked suspiciously like her tenant, floating together amid a shower of rose petals down an aisle toward a smiling priest. With a sigh and a rueful glance at her schedule, she shrugged into her robe and slippers. Who could be ringing her doorbell at this time of night?

As she descended the stairs, the wails that had puzzled her for the past few minutes grew in intensity. This time there was no mistaking it. This wasn't a pair of amorous cats. The sound filling her ears was definitely a baby's cries. Could the Ericksons be in some kind of trouble and need her help?

Rushing to the door, she flung it wide. Her mouth dropped open when she saw Marco Garibaldi on her doorstep with a squalling infant in his arms. As her gaze ran from one to the other, she couldn't decide who looked more miserable: Marco, with his weary eyes and tousled hair, or the baby, whom, by the pink romper she wore, Gretchen assumed was a girl.

"Yours?" she asked quietly.

Marco grimaced. "A loaner."

Gretchen continued to stare at him in bemusement. "I've heard of borrowing a cup of sugar. I've even heard of borrowing someone's car. But I have to tell you, I've never heard of borrowing a baby."

"She's my best friend's child. He and his wife are away for the weekend, trying to save their marriage."

"And you volunteered to baby-sit."

"In a roundabout way." He looked pained. "As you can see, I'm not doing a very good job."

All Gretchen could see was that he'd never looked more virile than he did at that moment, with his shirttail pulled loose from his jeans, more than a hint of five o'clock shadow on his cheeks and the light of panic in his gorgeous brown eyes. Was there anything more appealing to a woman than a big, strong man who was helpless in the face of a crying baby?

That he was a doctor only enhanced that appeal. Gretchen knew without a doubt that, had the infant been a patient in the emergency room, Marco would have handled her cries with confidence. But because she was in his care and because he obviously knew little about babies outside of an examining room, he was at a total loss.

"You do look like you're having a bit of trouble," she said.

"She won't stop crying," he replied, his frustration obvious. "I was hoping you could tell me what I'm doing wrong."

Reaching out, Gretchen plucked the wailing infant from his arms and cradled her close. "What's her name?"

"Kristen."

"Hey, Kristen," Gretchen crooned, swaying from side to side. "What's all this crying about? You don't want to cry anymore, do you? Crying just makes a lady's face all red and splotchy. Very unappealing to the opposite sex."

After a couple of hiccups and sniffles, Kristen quieted and gazed up at Gretchen with curious eyes.

"There," Gretchen said, smiling. To her delight Kristen smiled back. "That's better, isn't it?"

"How did you do that?" Marco sounded so thunderstruck, it was hard for her not to laugh.

"It's all in the way you hold them," she explained.

"Babies can sense when you're uneasy around them. It makes them nervous."

"And when they're nervous, they cry," he murmured.

She nodded. "At the top of their lungs."

"Tell me about it." He thrust a hand through hair that looked as if it had seen the motion often in recent minutes.

Gretchen's heart melted. "It was hard on you, wasn't it?" she said sympathetically.

"I'm not used to crying like that."

No, she conceded, he probably wasn't. Most females were undoubtedly putty in his hands. Truth was, if he smiled encouragingly at her, *she'd* be putty in his hands. She gazed at Kristen with new respect.

She moved back into the hallway, and he followed her inside. "You were holding her all wrong," she said.

"What was wrong with the way I was holding her?"

Gretchen chuckled. "Nothing, if she was a piece of porcelain you were afraid of breaking. But she's not a piece of porcelain. She's a flesh-and-blood baby. You were holding her away from you, and babies like to be cuddled close. They need to feel the warmth from your skin, to hear your heartbeat and be encircled in your arms. They need reassurance that your only concern is for them alone."

Babies weren't the only ones who needed that reassurance. Where Marco Garibaldi was concerned, the words could have just as easily applied to Gretchen herself. What was it about him that made it impossible for her to look at him without her knees going weak? Why did he fascinate her so? In the end it didn't really matter, since he'd plainly shown her, in both word and deed, that he would never hold her the way she was instructing him to hold Kristen.

Shoving her disturbing thoughts aside, she said, "Pick them up with authority and cuddle them close. If they still cry, usually one of three things is wrong."

"What are the three things?"

"They're either hungry, tired or wet."

"How do you know which is which?"

"Process of elimination. Start with changing her. If that doesn't work, feed her. Then, after that, if she's still crying, put her to bed." She held Kristen out to him. "Want to give it another try?"

He looked terrified, but he took the child in his arms. This time he cuddled her close to his heart. After a minute, when Kristen didn't protest, he looked over at Gretchen with wonder in his eyes.

"She's not crying."

"No," Gretchen said gently, feeling her heart thump, "she's not."

"Maybe I can do this after all."

"I know you can."

The expression on his face changed. "Uh-oh."

"What?"

"She might not be crying, but this child is definitely wet."

"Let me guess," Gretchen said wryly. "You've never changed a diaper."

He shook his head. "Not even in med school."

"Do you have any diapers?"

"Upstairs."

She nodded to the door. "Lead the way. Who knows? If you're nice to me, I might even show you how to make formula."

She hadn't meant the words to sound so provocative, but she knew by the look Marco tossed her that they did. When he passed by her without comment and went out onto the porch, she didn't know whether to be thankful or disappointed.

Curiosity got the better of her, and she found herself avidly studying her surroundings when she followed Marco inside his half of the duplex. To her left, the living room was furnished nicely with a leather sofa and love seat and a big-screen television. A beautiful oriental carpet in varying shades of brown sat in the middle of the floor. If the open book on an end table and the mail scattered across the surface of the coffee table were anything to go by, this was where Marco spent most of his time.

Down the hallway she caught a quick glimpse of mahogany furniture in the dining room and a butcher-block table in the kitchen. The place was neat and clean, thanks, she knew, to the service that came weekly.

Though all the furnishings were of good quality, and she all but drooled over the oriental carpet, as a whole the apartment lacked…something. It came to her in a flash as he headed into the living room. There were no paintings hanging on the walls, no framed pictures of family members gracing side tables.

It needed a woman's touch, Gretchen decided, and felt a stab of regret at the realization that she was obviously not the woman who might one day bring these rooms to life.

"The diaper bag is over here," Marco said, heading for the far side of the leather sofa and the mound of baby supplies piled there.

Gretchen pulled out a diaper and a rubberized mat. After spreading the mat protectively across the sofa, she waited for Marco to place Kristen on it. It took less than two minutes for her to swiftly change, powder and snap the baby into a clean romper.

Standing, she handed Kristen back to Marco, carefully rolled the soiled diaper into a neat ball and nodded toward the kitchen. "Let me dispose of this, wash my hands, and I'll show you how to make formula."

His mouth widened in a decidedly lethal smile. "I thought I had to be nice to you in order to get that instruction."

Gretchen went hot inside. Drat her and her big mouth! And drat Marco for remembering.

"I'll let it slide. This time." She hoped the words sounded light and carefree, although she was fairly sure the heat in her cheeks was a dead giveaway that she was feeling anything but.

Five minutes later Gretchen sat at the kitchen table. Directly across from her, Marco held Kristen in his arms while the infant suckled happily on a bottle of formula.

"And that's all there is to it," she said. "Any questions?"

Marco gazed at her with obvious admiration. "Where did you learn all this?"

She shrugged. "I worked part-time in a day-care center during college."

"You're very good at it."

"Thank you." She drew a deep breath. It was time to clear the air between them. "About the other day. I'm sorry for ambushing you like that."

His brow furrowed. "Ambushing me?"

"Putting you on the spot. Propositioning you."

"Oh, that. You didn't ambush me."

It was gallant of him to shrug it off. Still, she couldn't let the subject drop until she'd had her say.

She stuck out her chin. "Oh, yes, Marco, I did. We both know I did."

"It's okay." In a low voice he added, "You don't know how hard it was for me to say no."

Gretchen clutched at the table. Her senses reeled as the implication of his words whirled around in her brain. To know that he'd actually been tempted left her dizzy and weak. And the look in his eyes took her breath away.

"It was hard for you to say no?" Her voice came out in a high squeak, and she cleared her throat. "It was hard for you to say no?" she repeated in a more normal tone.

"I'm a man, Gretchen. When a beautiful woman makes an offer like that, it's always tough to say no."

Beautiful? He thought she was beautiful? She swallowed and forced herself to remain focused.

"But you did say no," she pointed out.

"Just chalk it up to a feeling I had."

"What kind of feeling?"

"That something wasn't right. That your heart didn't seem to be in what you were doing." He paused as if rethinking his actions. "It wasn't, was it?"

What was she to do here? If she admitted that the only thing she'd ever wanted since laying eyes on him two years ago was to ravish him, how would he react? Would he suddenly take her up on her offer? How would she feel if he did?

Gretchen glanced down at her robe and nightgown. She didn't have to look in a mirror to know that her hair was as tousled as Marco's. This definitely wasn't the moment. When and if she repeated her offer, she at least wanted to look a little more presentable.

Besides, it wasn't as if they could do anything about it now, even if he was amenable. Not with Marco babysitting. Truth was, she needed time. Time to think with a clear head, away from his overwhelming presence.

"I had mixed emotions," she admitted.

He nodded as if that explained everything. "Like I said, you weren't yourself. I didn't want to take advantage of that."

"A man of honor," she murmured.

"Is that bad?"

Oh, it was bad all right. It made him utterly irresistible.

"No," she replied. "Of course not."

"You want to tell me what that was all about? The other day in the car, I mean," Marco said.

"It's a long story," she demurred.

He glanced down at the baby in his arms. "I've got time."

"I suppose you do." She paused for a moment while she decided just how much she should tell him. "My best friend died last March."

"I'm sorry," he said, with obvious sympathy.

"Me, too. Anyway, she left an audiotape behind for me to listen to. On the tape she asked me to make several promises. One of the promises was to have a wild, crazy affair.''

"And you chose me."

"Yes."

"Why?"

She could hardly tell him the truth, that he made her feel wild and crazy just looking at him. After all, he had said no to her offer. Her pride wouldn't let her forget that.

"Proximity, I guess." She shrugged. "My boss is gay, and almost everyone else in my office is either married or in a committed relationship. The only men I've seen lately are clients, which would be bad form all around."

"Totally unadvisable," he agreed.

"Totally."

"I make it a practice to never date anyone from the hospital."

"A wise move on your part."

"So you picked me," he said.

"Yes."

"Because I was convenient."

"Yes."

His lips curved in a sardonic smile. "You're devastating my ego."

"I should think you'd be relieved," she retorted, trying to ignore the way her toes were curling in her slippers.

He arched an eyebrow. "Why should I be relieved?"

"Fewer complications for you. You don't have to deal with the unwanted attentions of a landlady who's besotted with you. And who also has a key to your apartment."

"That could get awkward," he agreed.

Gretchen tried to turn the whole embarrassing experience into a joke. "Think of the subterfuge, the sneaking around to avoid running into me. The cost of having the locks changed."

"The horror," he said, chuckling.

"Eventually, of course, you'd probably have to move out just to get away from me. And then I'd have to go to all the bother of finding a new tenant. All things considered, I think I've done us both a huge favor by not having a crush on you."

Liar. She still had a crush on him. A major crush.

"In that case," he said solemnly, although she thought she caught the flicker of amusement in his eyes, "I am forever in your debt."

"Can I hold her again?" She nodded toward Kristen, who, after finishing the bottle, looked as though she would fall asleep any minute.

"Be my guest."

Kristen nestled her head into Gretchen's shoulder, and Gretchen lowered her face to nuzzle the hairs on the back of the child's neck. When she looked up, she surprised an odd expression on Marco's face.

"They smell good, don't they?" he said softly.

"What?" she asked breathlessly, uncomprehending in the face of his intent regard.

"Babies' heads."

She tore her gaze away to stare down at the infant in her arms. "Yes, they do," she replied. "If you really want to know the truth, I'd take a mixture of formula, baby shampoo and baby powder over Chanel Number Five anytime."

"You'd make a wonderful mother."

Instead of being flattered, Gretchen felt her lips twist. Looking up at him, she said, "So I've been told."

"By whom?"

She gave him a pained smile. "By men who ran as fast and as far from me as they could, the minute after they uttered the words."

He looked curious. "Why did they run?"

"They never actually told me, but if I had to hazard a guess, I'd say they were terrified I'd expect them to father the children they said I'd be so good at mothering."

"Oh."

"'Oh' is right."

He spread his arms. "I'm not running."

"*We're* not involved."

"I suppose you're right," he conceded.

She'd do well to remember that. "And since we never will be, you don't have to plan on running a marathon anytime in the near future."

"Why would you think that?" he asked.

Now she was totally confused. "Think what?"

"That we will never be involved."

Hadn't they just covered that ground? "The other day," she said with exaggerated patience. "Remember? You looked me straight in the eye, and told me I sucked at seduction."

"I said no such thing."

"Not in those exact words, maybe, but the implication was clear. You looked at the way I was dressed and at my new car and told me they weren't me. You turned me down when I propositioned you. Face it, Marco. If the seduction police had been anywhere near at the time, I would have received a lengthy citation."

He shook his head. "You misunderstood me, Gretchen."

"What was to misunderstand?"

"Everything. Seducing a man is a far different thing from propositioning him. What I meant the other day was that you're not the type of woman who goes around propositioning strange men. If you had it in your head to really seduce a man, however, he'd stand little chance. Trust me. That aside, I don't see where you go from my saying you aren't that type of woman to our never becoming involved."

Her heart thumped unevenly. "I...just assumed..."

Marco pushed his chair back from the table and moved to stand directly in front of her. "Perhaps I haven't made myself clear. The truth is, Gretchen, if I hadn't thought there was something a little...well...off about your behavior the other day, we'd be in the middle of a wild, crazy affair as we speak."

Chapter 4

For a long, breathless minute, Gretchen was aware only of the weight of the child in her arms, the wild thundering of her heart and a desire that left her giddy.

Now she knew how she would have felt if Marco had said yes to her proposition. Terrified. And thrilled beyond all measure.

"What are you saying?" she finally managed to ask.

He took a step toward her. "Exactly what you think I'm saying. That if you got it into your head to *really* seduce me, right here and right now, no ambivalence about it, I wouldn't say no."

"Oh," she said weakly, taking a step back.

"Oh, is right," he replied.

Clutching the baby like a lifeline, Gretchen took another backward step. "Even though it wouldn't be a wise move for either of us?" she asked.

"Even then."

A third step brought her smack up against the wall. "As we speak?"

"As we speak," he confirmed.

"It would be kind of hard to accomplish with a baby in my arms, don't you think?"

She tried to sound nonchalant, a not inconsiderable feat given that she was fighting an incredibly strong impulse to run next door to her bedroom, don one of her recently purchased—and as yet unworn—negligees, light some candles, open a bottle of wine and seduce the living daylights out of him.

"Trust me," he said softly. "I'd find a way."

He would, too, she thought, swallowing hard. She could tell by the way he gazed at her so intently, and the way her knees felt so wobbly. When Marco Garibaldi set his mind to something, it was obvious that he would let nothing stand in his way.

All at once she needed to sit down. But to do so would be to betray just how much his announcement had thrown her. Resolutely Gretchen locked her trembling knees together. As she did, she couldn't suppress the irreverent thought that the action was not exactly what Jill had had in mind when she'd extracted that fourth damnable promise of hers.

"You're not going to, are you?" he asked.

"Wh-what?"

"Seduce me."

Was that regret she saw in his eyes? "No," she replied, trying to inject some determination into her voice.

"Is that no just for tonight or for forever?"

She wished she knew herself. "Definitely for tonight, and probably for the future."

"You do have a promise to keep, you know," he reminded her.

If ever she'd lost sight of exactly how virile the man was, and how susceptible she was to that virility, it was brought home with the force of a hurricane. "I know."

"Proximity not enough anymore?" The question sounded idle, but the look in his eyes was anything but.

She drew a long, bracing breath. "It wasn't enough then," she said quietly. "Why should it be enough now? Isn't that why you turned me down?"

"Yes," he said ruefully, "I guess it was."

"Nothing's changed, Marco. My ambivalence, as you call it, is still alive and well." And growing by the second.

Why *was* she fighting it? she wondered. Especially now that Marco had admitted he was ready, willing and able. Was it simply because she was no longer dressed in the outfit that had given her so much courage, and that, without it, she had no faith in her powers of seduction? Maybe it was because there was a baby present, a baby who needed Marco's undivided attention. Or maybe it was something as simple as that she was an out-and-out coward.

No, she finally decided. No matter how hot and bothered he made her feel, what she wanted was a wild, crazy affair of the heart. Nothing Marco had said so far had led her to believe that he was offering anything more than a one-night stand. She fully intended to keep her promise: when the time, the place and the man were right. The whole point of the promises she'd made to Jill was to avoid regret, not create it. Until she knew better, she had to think of Marco Garibaldi as one walking, talking hunk of regret.

"Isn't it time to go to bed?" she asked. A rush of heat colored her cheeks. "What I meant," she amended quickly, "is that it's time for you to put Kristen to bed. She can barely keep her eyes open."

She handed the sleepy child back to him and nearly ran to the door. "See you later."

"Wait!" he called after her.

Reluctantly she turned to face him. "Yes?"

"Before you leave, could you help me with a problem?"

"What kind of problem?" she asked warily.

"It's about Kristen's sleeping arrangements."

On this topic, at least, she felt as if she were on safer

ground. "I think I saw a portable crib in that pile in your living room. Just set it up in your bedroom. It should only take a few seconds."

"But what if she wakes up in the middle of the night?"

To Gretchen, the answer was obvious. "You change her diaper, give her a bottle and put her back to bed."

He shook his head. "That won't work."

It worked for 99.9 percent of the population, she thought. Why was he so certain he was the exception to the rule?

Folding her arms across her middle, Gretchen arched her eyebrows. "Why not?"

"I'm a sound sleeper. I sleep through everything. And I do mean everything."

She stared at him in amazement. "You're a doctor, and you're that sound a sleeper?"

"Believe it or not. Doctors come in light sleepers and sound sleepers and those who are in between, just like every other occupation."

"Don't you ever sleep at the hospital?"

"Of course. When you work sixteen-hour days, catnaps are a must."

"When you take these catnaps of yours, don't you have to keep one ear open, in case of an emergency?"

"Ideally, yes."

She didn't understand what the problem was. "Well, just consider this an emergency. Sleep with one ear open. If you hear her fuss, take care of her."

"You don't understand, Gretchen," he explained carefully, as if addressing a person who was extremely dim-witted. "In case of emergency, the hospital knows better than to beep me. Instead, they send someone after me. Even then it can take several minutes to rouse me."

"You must be a very good doctor," she murmured, "for them to go to the trouble."

"I am," he stated with quiet confidence.

"You couldn't sleep through my pi...CD music last month," she pointed out.

"That's because I hadn't fallen asleep before the music started. Remember that earth tremor we had a couple of years ago? The one that rattled the dishes in the cupboards and left paintings hanging sideways?"

"Of course," she said.

"Slept right through it."

"I suppose this means alarms don't work for you. Just how do you manage to get up in the morning?"

"I have an internal alarm clock that wakes me up at precisely 5:00 a.m., regardless of the time I go to bed the night before."

She tilted her head and studied him. "Tell me, Marco. Why didn't you think of this *before* you agreed to baby-sit?"

"It was a last-minute thing. I didn't think that far ahead."

Neither had she, when it came to him. "I see."

There was something going on here, Gretchen realized. Something more than just his concern about Kristen waking in the middle of the night.

"You're terrified of being alone with her, aren't you?" That's why he hadn't commented on her Freudian slip; why he'd tried so hard to keep her from leaving.

"Yes," he admitted. "Wouldn't you feel the same, if you were me? Look at the way I handled her earlier. A lawyer could easily build a strong case against my being left alone with her."

She gazed at the child in his arms. Kristen had given up the battle for wakefulness and was sleeping peacefully, her head on his shoulder.

"You're doing just fine now."

"What about when she wakes up? What about the rest of the weekend?"

"You could consider it practice for future fatherhood," she offered.

"I don't need the practice."

She felt a shaft of irritation. Was he being deliberately obtuse? "You just admitted that you're terrified of being alone with her, Marco."

"You didn't let me finish," he replied. "I don't need the practice because I'm never going to be a father."

Gretchen just stared at him. This was turning into the strangest conversation she'd ever had with a man.

"Accidents do happen, you know," she felt compelled to point out.

"Not if the women I choose to be intimate with don't want children, either. We both take precautions."

For some reason the remark set her teeth even more on edge. And here she'd started to feel sorry for him and the predicament he found himself in. What she couldn't understand was how she could be aroused by his mere presence at the same time that he irritated her to the point where she wanted to throttle him.

"Does that include your future wife?" she asked sweetly.

"No," he replied.

"Then how can you guarantee you will never be a father?"

"A lot of women react like I've sprouted two heads whenever I answer that question honestly."

"Women who were thinking of getting involved with you, you mean," she said.

He nodded.

"Well," she said briskly, "since I'm not thinking of getting involved with you, you needn't worry about my reaction. So tell me, Marco. How can you guarantee you will never be a father?"

"That's easy. I'm never getting married. There is no future wife. I believe that a child needs two parents, and I'm what, in polite circles, they call a confirmed bachelor."

His words drove home how right her earlier caution had

been. Marco Garibaldi had nothing to offer her beyond the brief pleasure of being held in his strong, capable arms. Unfortunately, she wasn't totally put off by that realization. She would just have to work on it some more.

"I've always wondered what it meant," she quipped, "when a man says he's a confirmed bachelor. Does it mean he's joined a secret club? Do you have an induction ceremony, like they do in most religions, when young men and women come of age?"

Instead of answering, he looked from one shoulder to the other.

"What are you doing?" she asked, her irritation growing.

His expression was deadpan. "Searching for my other head."

She couldn't help herself; she burst out laughing. With the arrival of her laughter, her tension melted away. Why was she so prickly around him tonight, so quick to take offense, so hasty to look for hidden meanings beneath every word? It really was foolish of her to behave so idiotically. There was nothing between them. She shouldn't be upset that he wasn't the paragon she'd built him up in her mind to be. He'd done nothing to her. He certainly hadn't led her on. If anything, she was the one who had led him on.

"I'm sorry," she said. "I guess I'm feeling a little on edge this evening. So tell me. Do you give your confirmed-bachelor speech to a woman before you go out on your first date with her?"

"I believe in being up-front and honest," he explained.

"Is that what you call it?" she murmured.

He looked closely at her. "What would *you* call it?"

"An easy out."

"Why?"

"Because that way you can always lay the blame at the poor woman's feet when she becomes too demanding." She tilted her head back and placed the back of her hand across her forehead. " 'I'm sorry,' you'll say, in very dramatic fashion, of course, 'but I did tell you in the beginning that I was a confirmed bachelor.' "

She lowered her arm and leveled her gaze at him expectantly. "Am I right, or am I right?"

He laughed. "Let me guess. You've heard the speech before."

She hadn't personally. But she'd known quite a few women who had. Instead of answering, she asked, "I assume, way back in the dark ages, when this conversation started it had a point?"

"Before we got sidetracked, you mean?"

"Yes."

"We seem to be doing that a lot tonight, don't we? I wonder why."

"I haven't the faintest idea," she lied. She knew exactly why. They were both wondering how it would be between them. She suspected that it would be pretty darn terrific, better than anything she'd experienced so far, anyway. Which was probably why she couldn't let it go. And why she felt disappointed in him when he acted like the person he really was—a flesh-and-blood man, with all his inherent foibles—instead of the icon she'd imagined him to be.

The Marco Garibaldi she'd built up in her mind was the perfect gentleman, the perfect lover and the perfect friend. And, once he married, he would also be the perfect husband and father. Small wonder, as she learned more about him, that he fell short of her expectations. The pedestal she'd created for him was so high off the ground, it was a wonder he didn't get a nosebleed.

Gretchen sighed. Maybe a little honesty *would* clear the air.

"It's all my fault. I was the one who put sex between us. Now it won't go away, no matter what we think, do or say. It's always there, like this invisible wall."

He nodded in agreement. "It's practically all I can think about."

"Me, too," she admitted.

"What should we do about it?"

"Nothing."

"Doing nothing hasn't helped so far," he said.

"Maybe not. But if I indulged my every craving for chocolate, I'd be as big as a house. Some things are just best left alone."

"And you think this is one of them."

"Don't you?" she asked. "Seems to me I recall this conversation where we both agreed that the sanctity of the landlady-tenant relationship should not be breached."

He gave a reluctant sigh, then grinned at her unrepentantly. "You can't blame a guy for trying, can you?"

No, but she could blame him for being too blasted sexy for her own good. "I'll give you an A for effort."

He looked disappointed. "Just an A?"

Once again she couldn't help laughing. "Okay, an A-plus."

She was flirting with him, she realized. And he was flirting back. The amazing thing was how good it felt. How easy. How right. If she let it, flirting with Marco Garibaldi could become as addictive as smoking.

Come on, she cautioned herself. She was almost thirty years old. It wasn't as if he was the first man she'd ever flirted with. Or the second. Or even the third.

But if she were such an accomplished flirt, why had she had to go to Gary Curtis for advice? She certainly didn't call it flirting, the way she'd propositioned Marco the day she'd taken him for a ride in her car. That was still, and would always be, in her mind an ambush.

The sad truth was that all of her previous relationships, and that included her engagement, had been as staid and businesslike as she herself had been. Probably still was. How boring. It would probably have done her a world of good if, somewhere along the way, a heartbreaker like Marco had given her his I'm-a-confirmed-bachelor-and-I-don't-want-to-get-involved speech, and she'd gone ahead anyway and thrown caution to the wind. Maybe if she'd had her heart dashed a time or two by a totally unsuitable man, she wouldn't be so tempted to do so now, when she was old enough to know better.

"Weren't we trying to get back to the original point of our conversation?" she said.

"What kind of sleeper are you?" he asked.

She blinked. "Average, I guess."

"Do you sleep through thunderstorms?"

"I usually wake a time or two. Why?"

"Do you think you'd notice if a child stirred in the night?"

Normally she was much quicker on the uptake. But tonight, in the presence of the one man who possessed the power to scramble the connections between her brain cells, she was amazingly slow.

"You want me to watch Kristen for you this weekend," she said flatly.

"Not exactly. I know I have no right to ask you this, but I was hoping you would stay here and help me with her."

Gretchen felt a brief flare of pleasure that he had so much confidence in her abilities as a nurturer. On its heels came doubt. If she agreed, she'd be spending the entire weekend with him. Kristen would be there, but it would still be like living together—without the sex, of course. They would be bound to find out a lot about each other, both good and bad. Come Sunday night, she'd either be panting with desire or ready to kill him. Probably both. Either way, deep down, she wasn't sure she was ready to totally obliterate the pedestal she'd put him on. He'd been knocked close enough to the edge as it was.

"You want me to stay here?" she repeated.

"Unfortunately, I turned the second bedroom into an office." He nodded to the living room sofa. "I thought maybe I'd sleep there, and you could sleep with Kristen in my room."

She couldn't sleep in his bed. That would be just too…intimate.

"Tell you what," she suggested. "Why don't I take her to my apartment at night and bring her back here in the morning? Wouldn't that work just as well?"

He shook his head. "I can't let you do that."

"Why not?"

"I just can't."

He was trying to spare her feelings, she realized. "I guess it wouldn't look good if you gave your best friend's daughter to someone else to watch."

"Put it this way," he said. "*I* trust you. But Brian and Val don't know you. And, despite how this might look, Val is the most protective mother I've ever seen. For her to actually agree to leave Kristen with me says a lot about her state of mind. And the state of their marriage."

"You think there's a good chance they'll turn around and come back, don't you?"

"Yes, I do. But I hope they don't. They need this time together. You're not offended are you, that I won't let you keep Kristen at night?"

She made her voice brisk and businesslike. "Not in the least. She's your best friend's daughter. And I'm practically a stranger."

"You're not a stranger, Gretchen."

"Yes, I am," she contradicted. "After all, what do we really know about each other?"

"I know one thing," Marco said. "Kristen likes you, and you're very good with her. For her sake, if not for mine, could you possibly find it in your heart to stay? If you do, you'll earn our undying gratitude. Besides, it's not like you'll be far from home. Everything you need is just next door."

Everything she needed was here, was the thought that wouldn't be denied. All she had to do was find the courage to reach out and take it.

With a pang Gretchen recalled the schedule she'd so painstakingly created, and everything she'd planned to accomplish that weekend. Her week of living was slated to begin first thing in the morning. She'd put off doing the items on that list for too long, a lifetime, really. How could he expect her to turn her back on it now?

He was just feeling overwhelmed, that was all, she told herself. A little more time in Kristen's company, and he'd relax. Besides, no one could be as sound a sleeper as he claimed to be. They'd get along just fine without her.

"I'm sorry," he said at her continued silence. "I've been thoughtless. You probably have plans. Please, don't worry about us. We'll get by."

She made the mistake of looking at him. Though his words were sincere, he couldn't hide the misgiving he still felt. It would take someone with a far harder heart than Gretchen's to resist the appeal in Marco's eyes.

She gave one last, longing thought to her schedule, then dismissed it from her mind. She supposed she could start living on Monday. A little creative juggling, and she still could accomplish most of the things she'd intended to do.

The bottom line was that she was a woman who needed to feel needed. Wasn't that why she'd made all those promises to her family over the years? Marco definitely needed her help. Or, at least, he believed he did, which amounted to the same thing. She'd also promised to live for each moment, to treat life as an adventure. If spending the weekend with Marco Garibaldi—even with a baby to chaperone their behavior—wasn't an adventure, she didn't know what was.

"Okay, Marco, I'll stay," she said. "But on one condition. That I sleep in here with Kristen. For the next two days just consider me yours."

Gretchen nearly groaned out loud. She'd done it again: opened her mouth and inserted her foot. Closing her eyes, she uttered a silent prayer for fortitude and waited.

"Something wrong?" he asked.

"Just bracing myself for the inevitable," she told him.

"The inevitable what?"

"The remark you're going to make about my slip of the tongue."

"Oh, that," he said easily. "Hey, you just agreed to help me out here. I wouldn't touch that slip of the tongue with a ten-foot pole."

She opened her eyes and smiled at him. "Smart man."

He smiled back at her. "Thank you." Gratitude replaced the entreaty in his eyes. "And thank you, also, for agreeing to help me out. I don't know how I'll ever repay you."

Her heart swelled. "I'll think of something," she said lightly.

"Just in case you were worried," he said, "with Kristen by your side, you'll be safe from any unwanted attention from me. In fact, if you'd like, we could place a moratorium on seduction for the weekend."

Wasn't he the one who had said he'd find a way, even if she was holding the baby in her arms? Not that she was about to remind him.

"No need for the moratorium," she said. "I already know I'm safe."

That piqued his curiosity. "How do you know that?"

"I don't have any birth control," she explained. Okay, that wasn't strictly a lie. She had bought a package of condoms before her abortive attempt at seducing him. But she didn't have them with her. They were safe next door, at the bottom of her sweater drawer, out of sight from prying eyes. "And I want children. Oodles of them."

"Touché," he said with that endearing lopsided grin of his that made her heart thud. "In that case, you're safer here than in a nunnery."

She didn't know why the thought depressed her. "You don't watch much Monty Python, do you?" she muttered.

"What?"

"Where do you keep your linens?"

* * *

Marco held a still sleeping Kristen while Gretchen put the portable crib together and made up a bed on the living room sofa.

"You're supposed to put her on her back," she said, when he lowered the child to her stomach. "They think it helps prevent SIDS," she added at his questioning look.

"See how much I need you?" he commented as he gently turned the little girl over.

Kristen gave a soft cry, and her eyelashes fluttered. They both held their breaths until her body stilled and her breathing grew deep once more.

See how much I need you? Marco's words echoed in Gretchen's ears. What she needed, she decided, was a good, stiff drink. Because she now knew two things without a doubt.

The first was that, despite never being treated by him, she knew exactly what kind of doctor he'd be. The way he'd handled Kristen said it all. He'd be tender, caring, thoughtful; the patient's comfort uppermost in his mind at all times.

He was every bit as good a doctor as he'd claimed, probably better. Could a man who gave so much of himself to his work have anything left over for anyone else? For her?

The second thing she knew was that the minute she closed her eyes, she was going to picture the way his strong, capable hands, with their long, lean fingers, had gently handled the sleeping child. And then she was going to torment herself mercilessly by imagining how those very same hands would feel on her.

Unfortunately alcohol and baby-sitting didn't mix. Also out were sleeping pills and tranquilizers, not that she had any. She'd just have to rough it alone. And count sheep anytime an unwanted thought or image invaded her mind.

"I hope your friend and his wife reconcile," she said, searching for a topic that would take her mind off of him.

''Me, too.''

''You don't sound overly optimistic.''

''Why do you think I'm a confirmed bachelor?''

He sure was going out of his way to remind her of that. She manufactured a yawn.

''I think I'll go to sleep, too. Who knows what time Kristen might wake up. I'd better be rested. Goodnight, Marco.''

''Goodnight, Gretchen.'' In the doorway he gave her one last look. ''Thanks again. For everything.''

''You're welcome.'' For everything.

Though she'd been convinced that sleep would be impossible with him so close by, the minute her head hit the pillow Gretchen fell into a dreamless slumber.

Chapter 5

With only the predawn light to illuminate his way, Marco descended the stairs in his bare feet and crossed to the living room doorway. Thrusting his hands deeply into the pockets of his robe, he gazed silently at the woman asleep on his sofa.

She looked like an angel. His own personal angel come to Earth.

But what kind of angel was she really? A guardian angel, sent to help him with Kristen? Or a fallen angel, sent to tempt and torment him beyond all human endurance? At the moment it was a toss-up.

She lay on her left side, her right arm stretched protectively across the railing of the portable crib that, sometime during the night, she'd moved to rest against the sofa. The sight was the most alluring thing he'd seen in years. She was a born mother, he realized, and had to remind himself why that was a bad thing.

Had Kristen awakened in the middle of the night? Had she been fretful and fussy, crying for the comfort of her mother's arms? Had it taken Gretchen a while to calm the child and then for the two of them to fall back to sleep? Was that why they both slept so soundly now, neither of them moving, neither of them aware of his presence?

If indeed that was what had taken place, Marco hadn't heard. He hadn't exaggerated when he'd told Gretchen that he was a sound sleeper. When he'd climbed into his bed the night before, he remembered hoping that she'd be comfortable enough on the sofa, and had felt a stab of guilt that he would be sleeping on his own comfortable mattress. They were the last conscious thoughts he'd been aware of until his eyes popped open ten minutes ago, at exactly five o'clock.

Gretchen's tousled brown hair rayed out on the pillow like a halo. In sleep, her face looked serene and untroubled. Innocent. At some point she'd kicked off her covers, and her nightgown had inched up, exposing her legs from the knee down.

Instead of finding the view provocative, Marco surprised himself by wanting to reach down and pull the sheet back up over her sleeping form. He couldn't understand the need. She'd revealed much more leg in that tight black dress she'd worn four days ago.

Perhaps it had something to do with the design of the nightgown itself. Made of a soft, pink, no-frills cotton, it covered her thoroughly from the neck down without so much as hinting at the figure it concealed. He had no doubt that it had been fashioned—and purchased—with modesty in mind.

Even had the gown not revealed her innate modesty, Marco knew he had no right to stare at her like this while she was unaware of his regard. If she wanted him to look at her legs, she'd have to be the one, with full knowledge of the action, to lift her gown, so to speak. And he'd better shepherd his thoughts into a different direction, pronto.

Tiptoeing to the sofa, he bent over and retrieved the sheet that she'd kicked aside, then carefully smoothed it over her still form. When he stood back, he saw with satisfaction that she was now chastely covered from her shoulders on down. The only body parts exposed to his view were her head and her right foot.

He'd never noticed a woman's feet before. He had pretty much focused his attention and efforts on her face, her breasts, and that infinitely fascinating and mysterious juncture between her thighs. Feet hadn't even come close to making his short list of erogenous zones.

Gretchen had nice feet, he decided, inclining his head for a closer look. Very nice. Because she was so tall, her feet were larger than average, her toes long, slender and well shaped.

What, he wondered, would it feel like to wrap his hand around her ankle, to run his thumb across her instep, over her heel and to knead the ball of her foot. How would it taste to draw first one toe, then all five, into his mouth?

Appalled at the turn his thoughts had taken, Marco drew back and stifled a moan of dismay. What was wrong with him? Surely he couldn't be developing a foot fetish this late in life.

It was time to walk away, he told himself. Time to leave this room. Now.

Still, for untold minutes he simply held his position and stared at Gretchen Montgomery while a strange yearning not even remotely related to a foot fetish or breasts or mysterious thigh junctures grabbed hold of his heart. Snippets from their conversation the night before echoed in his mind.

She'd said she wanted children. Oodles of them. If that wasn't enough to dash cold water on the flame of his desire for her, he didn't know what was.

He wasn't surprised that she wanted children. She was wonderful with Kristen. And from the day he'd moved in here, he'd pegged her as the maternal type. Wasn't that why he'd turned her down when she propositioned him? It certainly wasn't because he hadn't found her desirable.

He'd told her he'd said no because he'd sensed her ambivalence, that he hadn't wanted to complicate their relationship as landlady and tenant. But that wasn't the complete truth. Subconsciously he'd also been protecting himself from himself and the unexpected, and amazingly strong, sway she held over him.

She'd also said she didn't have any birth control. How long, he wondered, had it been since she'd last made love with a man? How many men had she been with? Had any of them been able to tap the well of passion he sensed was centered deep inside her? Could he?

He'd assured her she was safe from him. But she wasn't safe at all. Because he wanted to make love to her. Badly.

He'd never been more awake, or more aroused, in his life. Kristen or no Kristen, if Gretchen woke this minute, he knew he wouldn't be able to trust himself not to reach out for her. How was he ever going to make it through the rest of the weekend with his sanity intact?

It was too early to fetch the newspaper. He couldn't turn on the television without waking his house guests. Even something as simple as brewing coffee might make too much noise. Stifling his need to simply lie down beside Gretchen so he could feel her next to him, Marco did the only sensible thing he could under the circumstances. He turned on his heel and went upstairs. Then he took a cold shower and, shivering, climbed back into bed.

Kristen in her arms, Gretchen approached Marco's closed bedroom door. "Marco, we're awake," she called.

No response.

A roll of thunder shook the house. Gretchen waited till it passed. "Marco?"

Still no response from the other side of the door.

One good thing about the early-morning storm, she reflected. She no longer had to regret that she'd put off doing the items on her list in order to help Marco out this weekend. When she'd been filling out her schedule, which centered mainly around outdoor activities, she'd neglected one tiny thing. The woman who often had a To Do list for her To Do list had forgotten to take into account the weather.

"Rain, rain, go away, come again some other day," she sang to the child in her arms. "Little Kristen wants to play. Rain, rain, go away."

Kristen smiled and burbled at her.

Gretchen raised a fist to rap sharply against the closed wood door, then halted abruptly. What was that sound? It definitely wasn't thunder.

Recognition came, and a slow smile spread across her face. The devastatingly handsome Dr. Marco Garibaldi snored. Not only did he snore, but if the noise he was making was any indication, he was felling the entire rainforest in there.

A wave of nostalgia washed over her. Her father had snored like that. This morning, listening to Marco snore, she felt oddly comforted. A feeling of well-being made her heart swell. All was right with her world.

She was half tempted to nudge the door open and peer inside. He was such a sound sleeper, he'd never know. Her hesitation had nothing to do with a sense of propriety, or of what was right and wrong. She had the feeling that the image of Marco, sound asleep in his bed, was one she wouldn't easily forget. There were already too many unforgettable images of him in her mind, and they kept cropping up at the most inconvenient times. She didn't need to add another one.

"Hey, sweetie," she said softly, to the child in her arms, "what do you say you and I get dressed and make breakfast?"

Marco opened his eyes to the crashing of thunder, the pelting of rain on the roof and the aroma of freshly brewed coffee. His stomach rumbled. A glance at the clock told him it was nearing nine. How had he slept so late?

As fast as he could, he threw on a pair of shorts and a

shirt, splashed water on his face and brushed his hair and teeth. Then, feeling halfway presentable, he made his way downstairs.

A glance into the living room showed that Gretchen had folded up the linens she'd used on the sofa and placed them neatly on the coffee table. He found her in the kitchen, at the stove. Barefoot, she wore a faded pair of cutoff jeans and a shapeless T-shirt. Her hair was pulled back into a ponytail, and her face was free of makeup. She was the total antithesis of the woman who had lured him into her car several days ago.

If she was trying to make herself unattractive to him, which Marco had the niggling suspicion was exactly what she was up to, she failed miserably.

Barefoot and pregnant was the thought that claimed his mind as he gazed at her. What would she look like with her belly swollen with child? It was a thought that none of the other women in his life had ever inspired. But then, he'd rarely spent the night with them. And he'd *never* let them cook him breakfast.

He hadn't spent the night with Gretchen, either, he reminded himself. Yes, she'd stayed in his apartment, but while he had slept solo in his lonely bed, she'd slept chastely on the living room sofa.

Still, the thought of her round and heavy with child wouldn't leave his mind. It was all her fault, damn her. If she hadn't put sex between them in the first place, he'd never be having these ridiculous thoughts about her. His gaze roved over the figure her baggy T-shirt couldn't quite hide. Yeah, right.

Kristen cooed to him from the makeshift highchair Gretchen had fashioned out of an oak captain's chair and some blankets. He crossed the room to chuck the child gently under her chin.

"Good morning," he said.

"Good morning." Turning from the stove with a spatula

in her hand, Gretchen glanced pointedly at the clock on the wall. "Alarm on the fritz?"

"I beg your pardon?"

"It's after nine. I thought your internal alarm clock always aroused you at 5:00 a.m. sharp."

She aroused him more than any alarm clock ever could. So did his memories of the way she'd looked earlier, fast asleep on his sofa.

"It did. Since I don't have to go into work, I shut it off and went back to sleep."

A long roll of thunder made her grimace. "It's definitely a good morning to sleep in."

"You can say that again. I don't think we'll be taking a long stroll in the park."

"Canoeing is more like it," she agreed. "According to the weatherman, we can expect this to continue until well into tonight."

Which meant they'd be stuck inside the entire day. Damn. He'd counted on some outdoor activities to keep some space between them.

"How's your back?" he asked.

Her brow wrinkled in confusion. "My back? Fine. Why?"

"I just thought sleeping on the sofa might aggravate it. I hope you weren't too uncomfortable last night."

She turned back to the stove and expertly flipped a pancake. She must have heard him moving around upstairs to time it so perfectly with his arrival.

"To tell you the truth," she replied, "I was quite comfortable. Although I have an extra-hard mattress on my bed, I didn't even notice I wasn't sleeping at home."

Hard or soft, he didn't want to think about the mattress on her bed, because his thoughts inevitably flew to how she would look on that bed. Specifically flat on her back, her eyes slumbrous with desire, and her hair a wild halo around her head because the thrusting of his fingers through it had made it that way.

Too many more thoughts like these, and he'd be as hard as that damn mattress of hers. Again. He was beginning to understand why moratoriums usually failed. It was like telling a person not to think about purple elephants. Once the suggestion was planted in the brain, of course that's all the poor sap could think about. He could mutter, "No purple elephants, no purple elephants," all he wanted, and still it would be all he could think about. Certainly telling himself, "No sex, no sex," was having absolutely no effect where Gretchen was concerned.

"How did Kristen sleep?" he asked.

"Like an angel." Gretchen flipped another pancake. "She didn't wake once."

"Good."

"I understand now why you wanted me to sleep with her. We knocked on your door this morning, but you didn't respond."

"I told you so."

"Yes, you did." She glanced over her shoulder at him. "I hope you don't mind me making myself at home in your kitchen."

He should mind, he knew. She looked like she belonged there.

"Not at all. Feel free to help yourself to anything you need." *Including me,* he amended silently.

"I also hope you don't mind that I took Kristen next door with me while I changed."

"Why would I mind if you did that?"

She shrugged. "You seemed concerned last night that if I took her with me to my apartment to sleep, your friends would show up and be upset to find her not with you. I figured if they showed up while I was changing, I'd just whisk her up the back stairs, and no one would be the wiser."

"It wasn't necessary, but thanks for the concern."

She slid three pancakes onto a plate and placed it on the

table. "Would you like some breakfast?" she offered with a smile.

He was only hungry for her. He also found himself wishing that she could greet him this way every morning, a wish that was definitely disconcerting to a man who had convinced himself that he was a confirmed bachelor.

"Breakfast sounds great."

"Dig in, then." She nodded toward the plate.

He sat down at the table, and she picked up the coffee-pot. "Coffee?"

"Yes, please. Black. Mmm," he added appreciatively as she placed a steaming mug at his side. "These are from scratch."

"I wouldn't ruin that pure maple syrup of yours by serving anything less." She gave an impish grin. "Plus, there was no pancake mix in your cupboards."

Heart thudding madly, he found himself unable to look away from her. Why did she fascinate him so? She was striking, yes, but he'd known and been intimate with women more beautiful than Gretchen. None of them had affected him the way she did. None of them had constantly occupied his thoughts when they weren't together.

The answer came to him in a flash of understanding. She was fresh and open and honest. There was no artifice about her. She truly cared for people. And she gave of herself without stopping to consider what she might gain in return. That was the difference between Gretchen Montgomery and most of the women he'd had relationships with.

Until that moment Marco hadn't realized just how jaded and self-centered the women he had dated the past few years had all been. They had definitely been beautiful, and they had definitely been sophisticated and accomplished in their careers, not to mention highly entertaining and sexy as hell. But not one of them could hold a candle to Gretchen when it came to generosity of spirit. And, beautiful as each woman had been, as accomplished in the art of lovemaking as each had been, the aftermath of their coupling had never left him feeling that they'd joined together on a more spiritual plane.

To them, as well as to him, lovemaking had been a release of pent-up energy, a passing, fleeting pleasure. He had no question that, as far as Gretchen was concerned, lovemaking would mean much, much more: a giving, a sharing, a belonging that was hard to find in a day and age where casual sex had become as commonplace an act as the brushing of one's teeth.

That was why she'd been so ambivalent the day she'd offered herself to him. She'd wanted to fulfill a promise, but fulfilling it with him meant she would be violating the tenets of her inner self. She would be violating an act that was both physical and spiritual to her.

She was getting under his skin, he realized. If he wasn't careful, he'd find himself doing the unthinkable. He'd find himself renouncing his confirmed bachelor status and trying to find a way to make her his in a manner far more permanent than the temporary, no-strings-attached affair she had once offered him.

For his peace of mind, and for Gretchen's safety, he'd be better off spending the rest of the weekend focusing more on Kristen, and less, much, much less on his other unexpected house guest. And he would start now, this very minute.

A woman learned a lot about a man, Gretchen decided, when she watched him play with a child.

With Kristen, Marco had infinite patience. He helped her pull all the pots and pans out of his cupboards, then fetched a couple of wooden spoons so they could bang on them in an endless, cacophonous concert. He put her up on his shoulders and charged around the living room like a bucking bronco, yodeling at the top of his lungs. He crawled around on his hands and knees—getting rug burns for his troubles—and chased Kristen around the dining room table. After a while, it became a game between them to see who could elicit the most smiles from the child.

Of course, he did go a little green around the gills when confronted with his first messy diaper, and Gretchen had had to step in and take charge. But that was only to be expected.

Now he was lying on the floor while Kristen climbed all over him, her chubby fists pulling at his cheeks and hair. He looked as though he was loving every minute of it.

This was a man who didn't want children? Or maybe it was marriage that was his sole objection.

"You're wonderful with her," Gretchen said softly.

Kristen got a handful of leg hair, and Marco winced. "That's only because you're here to help me out if I get into trouble. I can relax and not worry that I'm going to screw up."

If he relaxed any more, she'd be tempted to shoulder Kristen out of the way and jump him where he lay.

"Did some woman break your heart?" she asked. "Is that why you've decided not to marry?"

"I was engaged once," he acknowledged as Kristen climbed onto his lap. "But that has nothing to do with my decision not to marry."

She didn't know why that surprised her so—that at one time he *had* let a woman close enough to his heart to ask her to marry him. After all, it made sense.

"You were engaged?"

"Way back in medical school," he told her.

"Who broke it off?"

"She did."

Another unexpected revelation. "Why?"

"She said if she spent so much time alone when I was still in school, she could just imagine how alone she'd be when I became a full-fledged doctor. She was right, of course."

"That must have hurt," Gretchen observed.

He spread Kristen's arms wide, then clapped them shut in a silent game of patty cake. "At the time, yes. But I got over it. It made me do a lot of thinking."

"What happened to her?" Gretchen asked.

"Last I heard, she'd married a banker. Someone who works strictly from nine to five. By all accounts, they're very happy."

What about Marco? Gretchen wondered. Was he happy? Did his heart still ache all these years later for the woman who got away? Since he wasn't looking at her, it was hard for her to read the emotion on his face.

"Is that when you decided to become a confirmed bachelor?"

"Shortly afterward."

"Based on one bad experience?"

"There were a couple of other factors influencing my decision."

"Do you mind sharing them?"

While Kristen played with the buttons on his shirt, Marco propped himself up on his elbows and leveled his gaze on Gretchen. "Mind telling me why you're so interested?"

Because everything about him fascinated her, the way an unexcavated site fascinated an archaeologist. Of course, there was no way she was going to admit that to him.

"We've got a long weekend ahead of us. We have to pass the time somehow."

"I see."

She studied him a little more closely. "Does this discussion make you uncomfortable?"

"Why should it?"

"You just don't seem…comfortable talking about it."

"I'm very comfortable talking about it. The other factors influencing my decision were Brian. And my parents."

"Brian?"

Lying flat again, he propped Kristen on his lower legs,

raised them in the air and bounced her up and down. The baby crowed her delight.

"Brian and dozens of men and women just like him," he said. "Doctors. People devoted to a career that demands all that we have to give. Physicians are not noted for having the most stable marriages in the world. Those who do have children usually miss the greater part of their developing years."

"You mentioned your parents having a significant impact on your decision," Gretchen said. "What does your father do for a living?"

"He's retired now. But when I was growing up, he was a cop."

"Was he too busy with his job to spend time with you?"

"No. When I was small, he was always there for my mom and us."

Gretchen took Kristen from him, raised her up in the air and rubbed her head into the little girl's tummy. "Correct me if I'm mistaken," she said, smiling at Kristen's laughter, "but don't cops work long hours, too? Don't they work double shifts, as well as weekends and holidays?"

"Yes." A defensive note had crept into his voice.

"And still your father was there?"

The defensive note intensified. "Yes."

"Maybe because he made the time?" she suggested.

"Maybe," he allowed.

"What about your mother?" Gretchen asked. "Did she work outside the home?"

"No. She was a homemaker. She was devoted not only to my father, but to me and my five brothers and my sister."

It sounded like the ideal childhood to her. Why wouldn't Marco want to replicate it with a family of his own?

"Is their marriage not a good one?"

"They had a wonderful marriage. I've never seen another relationship to equal it."

He was speaking in the past tense, she realized. "You said 'had,' Marco. Are your parents divorced?"

He climbed to his feet and crossed the room to peer out the window at the falling rain. "No. My mother died."

Now they were getting somewhere, she thought. Picking up a rattle, she handed it to Kristen. The little girl shook it vigorously.

"When?"

"I was fourteen. Roberto, my oldest brother, was nineteen and newly married. Kate, the baby, was ten."

Gretchen had lost her own mother at eighteen. As awful as that had been for her, it must have been doubly devastating to a young boy on the brink of manhood. And for a little girl of ten? She shuddered at the thought.

"I'm sorry," she said. "It must have been a very difficult time for all of you."

"Want to know the truth?" he asked, his voice heavy with his memories. "It was hell. I've never seen my father the way he was then. He was a different man after my mother died, lost somehow."

"As you said, he loved her very much."

"I often wondered, if he hadn't had us, whether he would have willed himself to join her."

"But he didn't."

Marco shook his head. "No, but for a long time he was a broken man. My brother Carlo, who was only seventeen, stepped into the breach. He sacrificed a lot to make sure we all got the attention and the direction we needed. I don't know how we would have survived if he hadn't."

The pain in his voice made her heart ache for him. "I'm sorry, Marco. I didn't mean to resurrect such sad memories."

He turned to face her. "And I'm sorry for being so maudlin. The whole point of my mentioning my parents was, if I can't create the kind of home life they did, I won't create one at all. With the way things are with my job, the

way they're going to continue to be, I don't see me changing my mind on that issue.''

"Don't you have a full week off every month?" she
asked, unwittingly betraying how much she knew about
his schedule. "Seems to me, if you wanted to, you could
pack a lot of husbanding and parenting into that week.''

"One week a month isn't enough, Gretchen. If it was,
Brian and Val wouldn't be having the problems they're
having. The other three weeks are just as important. Children need both of their parents, every day. When they
don't have them, their whole world falls apart.''

The way his had when his mother died?

"Maybe now you'll understand a little better why I'm
a confirmed bachelor.''

Oh, she understood all right. The question was, did he?

He was a man who specialized in transient affairs, yet
he'd refused to have one with her. If she believed him, his
refusal had nothing to do with his not being attracted to
her, but to his being sensitive enough to sense her inner
hesitation. That, coupled with his revelations today, told
her a lot.

Whether Marco knew it or not, there was more to his
decision to never marry than the demands of being a doctor. It all dated back to his mother's death, and to his
feelings of abandonment by both of his parents.

"How's your father doing now?" she asked him.

"Wonderfully. He remarried a couple of years ago.''

At least one Garibaldi had gotten the courage to risk
loving again.

"So, you're determined to never marry," she said
softly.

"Yes.''

"Isn't that a lonely way to live?''

"I don't think so. My work, my family and my relationships, temporary though they may be, give me everything I need.''

Why was she so concerned? Gretchen asked herself. It

was his decision to make, after all, not hers. A thought struck her. Surely she wasn't still trying to mold him into the man with whom she could have a wild, crazy affair. Was that what this was all about? Was that why she was giving him the third degree?

If so, she had to banish the foolish notion from her mind. Now. This very minute. Before she opened herself up to a world of hurt. Because, whether or not he understood the truth behind his decision to remain a bachelor, the one thing she believed was that he definitely intended to stay that way. He fully intended to shield his heart from emotional involvement with any woman.

Which meant that, no matter how fast he made her heart beat, or how tightly he made her toes curl, Marco Garibaldi was not the man for her.

Chapter 6

"Like I already told you when you called earlier," Marco said into the telephone receiver, "Kristen's doing just fine."

"But I can hear her crying," Val protested.

"That's because the ringing of the phone woke her from her nap."

"Oh. I'm sorry. I guess it is that time of morning."

Marco looked over to where Gretchen was pacing the room with the still-sleepy, and understandably fussy, child. "See, she's quiet now. She's even smiling at me. Trust me, Val, please." The "please" had a pleading note to it. "Your daughter is doing just fine."

"If you're sure." Doubt filled Val's voice.

"I'm positive. Look, is Brian available? Can I speak to him for a minute?" After a brief pause Marco said, "Hey, pal. How's it going?"

"Okay." Brian sounded cautious, and Marco wondered if his friend was censoring his comments because Val was standing there.

"You getting much talking done?"

"Not much."

That's what he'd thought. "How's the weather where you are?"

"It's pretty gray out, but it's not supposed to rain."

"Good. Could you stand a word of advice from a concerned friend?"

"Sure."

"Get her out of there. Take her for a long, and I do mean long, walk. You two will get a lot more talking done if she doesn't have access to a telephone."

"I see your point."

"Good. Now go commune with nature, and your wife."

With a sigh Marco hung up the phone. For long seconds he stared into space.

"Not going so well, huh?"

Gretchen's question brought him back to reality. "No."

Shrugging aside his worries for his friend, he looked from the portable crib to the stairs. "I've got an idea. Why don't we put this thing in my office? I'll disconnect the phone in there. At least when Kristen goes down for her next nap, and Val calls, there'll be no sudden noises to wake her."

"Sounds like a plan to me."

Marco lugged the crib upstairs and reassembled it in the darkened alcove on the far side of his office. At one o'clock, Gretchen placed Kristen, along with the pillow she seemed to adore so much, inside. Together they hovered anxiously over the little girl, until, lulled by the dimness and the soft drumming of the rain, she closed her eyes, and her chest rose and fell in an even rhythm.

Putting a finger to her lips, Gretchen plugged in the baby monitor Val had provided and quietly backed out of the room. It wasn't until they had descended the stairs and entered the living room that Marco realized they were alone together for the first time since he'd gone with her for a ride in her new car.

An awkward silence settled between them as Gretchen picked up a few scattered toys before taking a seat on the edge of the sofa. Earlier, when Kristen had been asleep in the room, he'd expected, even welcomed, the silence. Not that it had lasted all that long. Val had phoned a scant fifteen minutes into Kristen's nap. And he had spent that time cleaning up in the kitchen. Now, with the child no longer in the room with them and with no breakfast dishes to attend to, Marco felt compelled to find a way to fill the silence.

Not knowing what else to do, he sat down in an armchair. He crossed and uncrossed his legs and twiddled his thumbs, before moving on to more productive pastimes, like looking around the room, down at his lap, up at the ceiling, anyplace but at Gretchen. Suppressing the nervous urge to whistle aimlessly, he studied a cobweb in the corner that the maid service had missed. And a dust bunny under the television set. He'd have to speak to them about both items.

Right about now, he decided, a phone call from Val would be a welcome interruption. He glanced over to the end table where the phone sat and willed it to ring, but it remained stubbornly silent.

"How long do you think she'll sleep?" he finally asked.

Gretchen shrugged. "From my day-care experience, anywhere from thirty minutes to three hours."

Three hours? What on earth were they going to do to pass the time for three hours?

Marco knew what he wanted to do, had wanted to do ever since he'd seen her in that tight black dress. It was an activity most eminently suited for consenting adults on rainy afternoons just like this one. He hadn't exaggerated when he'd told Gretchen that making love to her was all he could think about.

She'd said it was all she could think about, too. Did that mean she was thinking about it now? Was that why she couldn't meet his eyes?

If so, why wasn't he making his move on her? The reason had nothing to do with his self-imposed moratorium or the ambivalence he still sensed in her. Marco wasn't making his move on Gretchen, because he couldn't meet her eyes, either. He was the one who had practically gone down on his knees and begged her to stay with him this weekend; yet, all of a sudden, without Kristen in the room to keep them both otherwise occupied, he was feeling extremely wary around her.

"Maybe I should run the vacuum cleaner," he said.

Gretchen shook her head. "Too loud."

"That's what I thought." Plus, it wouldn't take anywhere near three hours to vacuum rugs that had already been tended to—in this case, quite thoroughly—by his cleaning service. And, when he was through, he'd still have to think of something to fill the remaining time.

They could always sit around and talk, he supposed, then had to suppress a grimace when he remembered their last conversation. Had he really blabbed all that personal information to her? Why had he told her so much about himself?

She was a good listener, and she'd seemed truly interested. Funny, now that he thought about it, how most of his recent girlfriends had been more interested in their clothing, their figures and their careers than in the formative events of his life. Funny, too, how he hadn't thought about those events for such a long time now.

He hadn't thought about them, he told himself, because they were from a time he didn't care to remember. Losing his mother was one of the most painful episodes of his life. He didn't see any point in dredging it up all over again. Resurrecting those memories only served to stir emotions that were better left unstirred. What was past was past. It couldn't be changed. No useful purpose could be served by reliving it.

At least now he understood the real reason why he was having so much trouble looking Gretchen in the eye. Like

some women he'd known—marriage-minded women—
she'd challenged his reasons for remaining single. Unlike
those very same women, he was afraid he would find himself listening to her. If he let her, he was terrified she'd
have him second-guessing—and maybe even revising—a
decision that had served him quite well so far, thank you.

But had it? Had it really?

Yes, he told himself firmly, it had. So what if he felt
lonely now and then? Didn't everyone, at some point or
another in their lives? Why couldn't Gretchen just accept
that after carefully weighing the alternatives he'd made a
choice, that he was confident it was the right one for him
and his lifestyle and that he was perfectly happy with it
and had no intention of changing it?

Because to women like Gretchen, a man who professed
no interest in marriage and fatherhood was an abomination
to be obliterated in any way possible. Well, he had news
for her. He was one abomination who would not be obliterated.

Without question, she unnerved him in a way no other
woman had. First she'd made him physically uncomfortable. Then she'd made him emotionally uncomfortable.
From the moment of that unexpected proposition, she'd
knocked him off balance and kept him there. It was an
unaccustomed and most uncomfortable place for him to
be. He didn't like it at all. He felt like a tightrope walker
getting ready to span a wire stretched across the Grand
Canyon. And he was afraid of heights.

No, talking with her was definitely out. For the time
being, anyway. Because he never seemed able to have a
conversation with her that didn't end up with the tables
being turned on him.

"We could always watch TV," he offered.

She looked relieved. "Couldn't hurt to check and see
what's on."

When he turned on the television, he wasn't surprised
to discover that the baseball game had been rained out. In

its place the station was airing an infomercial on rotisseries. The offerings on the other two major networks were equally unpalatable: another infomercial, this one about flattening your abs, and a fifties sci-fi thriller that he might have been tempted to watch, had they not missed the first half. As a last-ditch attempt, Marco switched to PBS. What he got was an incredibly graphic eyeful of the mating habits of the African black rhinoceros. Quickly he turned the television off.

"Let me guess," Gretchen said. "You don't have cable."

He shook his head. "Seemed like a waste of money, when I'm hardly ever home."

"Sure would come in handy right about now," she murmured.

He agreed with her.

"Do you have a VCR?" she asked.

He nodded. "But I only have one tape. I use it to record sporting events. You into baseball?"

"Not really."

"What about you?" he asked. "You have any tapes?"

"Nothing I haven't seen a dozen times already. Like you, I guess I don't watch much TV."

He really was pathetic, Marco decided. Surely he wasn't *that* unnerved by being alone with her. After all, what did he think she was going to do? Tie him to a chair, call a priest and somehow have them married before nightfall? In a state that not only required blood tests but also a three-day waiting period? How ridiculous could he get?

He could always ask her to go home—at least until Kristen's bedtime tonight. But a part of him wanted her to stay. And another part of him felt hopeful that, with continued exposure to her, he'd finally grow immune to the unease she made him feel and put it to bed, so to speak. Then, once that was nicely tucked in, maybe he could seriously reconsider putting Gretchen to bed, too.

"We could read," he said.

"Okay," she agreed. "Let me run home and get a book."

Five minutes later she was curled up on his sofa, and he was stretched out in his armchair with his legs propped up on the ottoman. Yes, he thought with satisfaction, this was a great idea. Opening the latest offering in the adventures of Spenser, his favorite detective, Marco drew an anticipatory breath and began reading.

When thirty minutes had elapsed and he couldn't begin to recall the content of the ten pages he'd managed to read, Marco closed the book. It wasn't because the story wasn't riveting. It was because his gaze kept straying across the room. To *her.*

He knew one thing. When the antics of Spenser couldn't keep him pleasurably occupied for a good hour or two, he was definitely in trouble.

The trouble was sitting less than five feet from him. He hadn't realized, until she'd stretched them the length of his sofa, exactly how long and lean Gretchen's legs truly were. How finely shaped her feet were. How beautifully crafted her toes—

He brought his thoughts to an abrupt halt. He couldn't believe that he was actually fixating on her toes. Again. He had to stop looking at her toes. He had to stop looking at *her.*

But instead of looking away, he found his gaze running the length of her body. Big mistake. Her skin seemed creamy and soft, her eyelashes lush and thick, her lips full and kissable. For long moments he found himself staring at the soft rise and fall of her chest, until his awareness of her charged the air around him like the storm still raging outside.

Surely she had to feel it. Surely she couldn't be as oblivious to his presence as she seemed to be. But if she did and if she wasn't, he couldn't tell. From where he sat, she seemed totally absorbed in the romance she was reading.

Damn her.

Marco shifted uncomfortably. Would Kristen never wake up?

Activity was definitely the key. Unfortunately, because of the weather, his options were severely limited. What he needed was something mindless to occupy him, something not as challenging as a book, but consuming nonetheless.

In an act of desperation, Marco lurched from his chair. After a brief search through the shelves of his hallway closet, he hauled out a jigsaw puzzle and placed it in the middle of his rarely used dining room table. A thousand-piecer. Surely that should keep him busy enough.

"She isn't going to sleep that long," Gretchen drawled, her tone wry.

He looked up and saw her framed in the doorway. "I know. But I've been meaning to put this together for months, and today seemed as good a day as any to start. My brother, Roberto, gave it to me for Christmas."

After a brief pause, he added needlessly, "It's a picture of the Gateway Arch in St. Louis."

"Very pretty." She angled her neck to study the picture on the lid. "Mind if I join you?"

"Is your book boring?"

"I'm just not in the mood to read this afternoon."

Boy, could he relate. "You like puzzles?"

She moved to the table and took a seat across from him. "I used to."

After a moment's hesitation, Marco decided not to ask her what she meant. "Do you prefer to put the border together first, or are you one of those people who just dumps the whole thing out on the table and sets to work?"

"The border first," she said.

"Me, too."

This was much better, he decided as, ten minutes later, in companionable silence, they searched through the pieces for all the straight edges. So far he'd only been distracted by her presence a time or two, and then only because their fingers had accidentally brushed together.

Yes, he thought in satisfaction, this he could do. There was only one thing that would make it better.

"Do you think it would disturb Kristen if I put on some music?" he asked.

"Not if you keep the volume low. What sort of music did you have in mind?"

"I have mostly instrumentals. Bach, Beethoven, Gershwin, that sort of thing."

It was the music he'd listened to all through medical school because there were no vocals to intrude on his studies. He supposed, now that those years were behind him, it might be time to expand the range of his collection.

"Do you have anything else?" Gretchen asked.

When he'd entered college, he'd given the bulk of his rock and roll collection to his younger brother, Antonio. "Don't you like classical music?"

"I love it. I've just been listening to a lot of it lately. It would be nice to have a change of pace."

Marco glanced over at her, and his heart started thudding unevenly. It was probably a trick of the lighting, but her eyes seemed impossibly big and luminous. Maybe something a little intrusive would be a good idea. When he'd given his collection to Antonio, he had held back a few of his most treasured recordings.

"I have several Van Morrison CDs."

Her eyes lit up. "I adore Van Morrison. You wouldn't happen to have 'Moondance,' would you?"

He pushed back his chair. "Coming right up."

He really should have given a second thought to the lyrics, Marco thought, when Van's voice, singing about stars and romance and making love, softly filled the room. This much intrusion he hadn't bargained for. Carefully avoiding Gretchen's gaze, he sat back down and continued sorting through puzzle pieces.

"Why did you become a doctor?" she asked.

He looked at her blankly, thrown by the unexpectedness of the question.

"Just making polite conversation," she said with a smile. "Of course, if you prefer, we could always return to the awkward silence. Personally, I'd like to avoid it if at all possible."

He grinned. "It was uncomfortable, wasn't it?"

"Put it this way," she told him. "If I had to choose which was more comfortable, a bed of nails or that silence, I'd take the bed of nails, hands down."

"Me, too."

She stared at him expectantly. "So, why *did* you become a doctor?"

Marco had a stock answer whenever anyone asked him that particular question. He always replied that he found the workings of the human body fascinating and that he'd dedicated his life to studying those workings.

So no one was more surprised than he when he opened his mouth and said, "When my mother was sick, I hated how helpless I felt. I wanted to be able to do something, anything, to make it better for her, but I couldn't. It damn near killed me."

Dismay filled him, and he forgot all about awkward silences and the disturbing lyrics of "Moondance." He bit down hard on his lower lip to keep from saying more. How *did* she do it? How did she manage to crawl under his defenses and make him open up to her the way she did?

"So you became a doctor to help other people, the way you couldn't help your mother?"

"Yes," he grudgingly agreed.

Okay, she wanted to talk. Then talk they would. This time around, though, *he* would be in charge. This time *he* would dictate the direction their conversation would take. Besides, right now she knew more about him than he knew about her. It was time to even the scales. Not to mix metaphors, but maybe he could even turn the tables on her.

"Why did you become an accountant?" he asked.

She took another mound of pieces and started sorting through them. "Because of a promise I made to my mother."

Marco felt his eyebrows arch. "Your mother made you promise to become an accountant?"

"Not in so many words. What she made me promise was to choose a solid, stable career. Accounting more than fit the bill."

Put that way, it sounded calculated and bloodless. Emotionless. He'd always, at least until she'd taken him for that car ride, thought of Gretchen as a highly practical woman. But not emotionless. Never emotionless. At least he'd based his choice of career on several criteria, one of which happened to be a deep-seated emotional need, the fulfillment of which gave him a great deal of satisfaction. But if he understood her correctly, Gretchen had made her choice based solely on one criterion: financial security.

Was she satisfied to tote up numbers, day after day? Was she content to sit at a lonely desk for hours on end, while the rest of the world passed her by? He remembered the way she had looked, with the wind blowing through her hair and her face alight with the sheer joy of being alive, and he just couldn't picture it.

"Was there something else you were thinking of doing, before you made that promise to your mother?"

All of a sudden, she seemed terribly interested in gathering up all the straight edges that would form the border of the sky. Marco finished sorting through the last of the mixed pieces and waited patiently.

"Quite a few things, actually," she finally said. "Like any adolescent, I imagined myself in a variety of careers. When I was ten, I wanted to be an astronaut. When I was twelve, I was certain I would be the first female president of the United States. Of course, maturity put things in their proper perspective."

"And you chose to be an accountant."

"Yes."

He wasn't going to let her off that easily. "But was there one thing that stayed with you longer than a month or two, one dream that filled you with so much excitement you couldn't sleep at night?"

She kept her gaze fastened on the puzzle piece between her fingers. When she spoke, her voice was barely audible. "Yes."

"What was it?"

Slowly, she lifted her gaze to his. Her eyes were bigger and more luminous than ever.

"I wanted to be a concert pianist."

"You took piano lessons?"

"From the time I was five years old until I was sixteen."

"That's a long time," he said. "You must have enjoyed it."

"I lived for it. I must have practiced two to three hours a day. Sometimes more on weekends. There were times my incessant playing drove my parents crazy."

The reflective light in her eyes and the dreamy quality in her voice told him she was in a place that was far, far away from his dining room table.

"If you loved it so much," he said, "why did you stop taking lessons? Why did you give up your dream?"

She seemed to snap back to reality. Reaching for a few more puzzle pieces she said, "Because of the promise to my mother."

"Your promise to choose a solid, stable career."

"Yes."

"Couldn't you have done both? Couldn't you have had the career and continued to study the piano?"

She wouldn't look at him. "When you work sixty hours or more a week, it doesn't leave time for much else."

No, it didn't, he acknowledged. He sat back in his chair and stared at her.

"So you gave up your dream because your mother asked you to."

Her back went ramrod straight, and a defensive note

entered her voice. "You make her sound like an ogre, but she wasn't. Far from it. I was her only child, and she loved me very much. My welfare was her main concern. She had her reasons for asking me to make that promise. I understood and respected them. I probably wasn't good enough to be a concert pianist, anyway. It was an impossible dream."

The last statement was said with a wistfulness that tore at his heart.

"You don't know that for sure."

"No," she admitted before turning her attention back to the puzzle. "I suppose I don't. Not 100 percent, anyway."

Marco gathered up the pieces that would form the puzzle's lower border and began fitting them together. He tried to imagine what he would have done if someone had tried to talk him out of being a doctor. He didn't have to imagine long. He would have laughed in that person's face.

But what if his father had been the one making the request? What would he have done in that case? He supposed it would have depended on the reasons put forth to him.

"You said your mother had her reasons for asking you to make that promise. What were they?"

"My father was a steel worker. When the steel industry all but died in Pittsburgh, he was one of the thousands of men who suddenly found themselves unemployed. I was eight years old when he lost his job. It took him almost three years to find another one. My mother had never worked outside the home, but she took whatever work she could find to help out. Of course, nothing paid all that much. The only reason we didn't lose this house was because the rent our tenant paid helped my parents meet the mortgage."

No wonder she'd always seemed so serious. "That must have been a tough time for you."

"It was awful," she replied. "I don't like to think about it much."

He certainly understood that. He had his own painful memories. "I guess you had to give up piano for a while."

She shook her head. "I offered to, but my parents refused to let me because they knew how much pleasure it gave me. They made many sacrifices during that time to try and keep my life as normal as possible."

"Let me see if I understand properly," he said. "Your mother knew how much you loved the piano, refused to let you give it up when she couldn't afford to pay for your lessons, and still she made you promise to give it up when you told her you wanted to be a concert pianist?"

Gretchen reached past him for a puzzle piece. "Number one, she didn't make me promise to give up the piano, she made me promise to choose a stable career. I made the choice to stop playing. And number two, it wasn't immediately after I told her I wanted to be a concert pianist. She spoke to my piano teacher first and found out what being a concert pianist entailed. Then she asked me to make that promise. She didn't want me to struggle the way she and my father had."

"So," he said, "she equated your being a concert pianist with the years your father was without work. Why?"

"Because of what my piano teacher told her. Only a handful of musicians, like Van Morrison here, actually make a living from their talent. The rest of them pretty much live hand to mouth. If they're lucky enough they get steady work in seedy bars. If they're not, they work two or three jobs just to keep on playing. It's a tough life."

"I see. So you kept your promise to your mother."

"After everything she sacrificed for me, making a few promises in return seemed like the least I could do."

That caught his attention. "There was more than one promise?"

"Yes. Not all at once. They were spaced over many years."

"Do you remember all of them?"

"Of course."

"Mind sharing them with me?"

This time she sat back in her chair and stared at him. "Why are you so interested?"

He used the same words she had earlier. "Just making polite conversation. Plus, I'd do anything to avoid that awkward silence."

She gave an indifferent shrug. "It's no huge secret. The first promise I remember making was when I was five. I'd just been diagnosed with asthma, and my mother made me promise not to overexert myself."

"Let me guess," he said. "No sports. No riding bikes. No roller skating. No running."

"That pretty much sums it up."

He wondered if she realized that her interest in the piano coincided with the time her physical activities were curtailed. "I didn't know you had asthma."

"I don't anymore. I outgrew it."

"What else did you promise?"

"When I was a teenager, I promised to be practical when it came to boys."

He had to smile at that one. "To steer away from boys like me, you mean."

She smiled back. "Most definitely. My mother also asked me to promise to keep an eye on my father. I was eighteen, and she was dying."

He felt a surge of sympathy. "So you lost your mother at a young age, too."

"Yes. My father also."

"I'm sorry."

"Me, too."

"How long did you live here with your father?" Marco asked.

"Seven years."

So, during a time when most of her contemporaries were out forging independent lives, she'd stayed home. "You didn't mind spending those important years with him, instead of being out on your own?''

"It was an honor being with him," she stated simply. "Besides, it's not like I didn't have a life. I went to college. I dated. I even got engaged. I did everything all the kids I went to high school and college with did. I just did them while living at home.''

He couldn't hide his surprise. "You were engaged?"

Amusement flickered in her eyes. "Is that so hard to believe?"

"Of course not," he said quickly.

He didn't know why he was so surprised. She was in her late twenties, after all. By that time most women had had more than just a brush with serious romance.

It was just that until recently she'd seemed so consumed by her work he'd assumed she'd rarely made time for romance. Was he subconsciously hoping that she'd saved herself for…him? Not only was that mode of thinking macho drivel, it had gone out of fashion years ago, when the first feminist burned her bra.

And if she had saved herself, only a man who was willing to treasure and cherish her forever would deserve the privilege of that gift. It was the only kind of man who deserved her now.

"What happened?" he asked.

"He was offered a job in Philadelphia, and I had to stay here.''

If the memory caused her any pain, he couldn't tell. "Chose to stay here, you mean.''

"My father was sick by then. Of course I chose to stay here. Since neither my fiancé nor I wanted a long-distance marriage, we parted ways. We still keep in touch, although he married someone else.''

"That was quite a sacrifice you made," Marco said.

"Are you saying you wouldn't have done the same thing for a member of your family?"

There were times when all he wanted to do was throttle

the lot of them. Despite that, if asked, he would gladly lay down his life for each one of them. Without hesitation.

"I would have done the same thing," he told her.

"I thought so."

He thought about everything she'd sacrificed for her family. "You're a very special person, Gretchen Montgomery."

"So are you, Marco Garibaldi," she replied. "Whether you know it or not."

After a brief pause she added, "I think I'm ready to link up to you now."

Chapter 7

Marco's heart faltered, and he began to sweat. "Wh-what did you say?"

"I said," Gretchen repeated, "that I'm ready to link up to you."

That's what he'd thought she'd said. Then she nodded at the puzzle pieces that he'd fitted together, and he belatedly understood.

"Oh."

Feeling like a fool, and hoping his face didn't reflect that feeling, he slid the lower border toward her. Of course it fit perfectly with the pieces she'd assembled. The way he knew *they* would fit together.

Marco gnawed on his lower lip and gave himself a mental shake. He had to get his mind out of the gutter.

"Are you okay?" Gretchen asked, peering at him. "You look kind of funny."

She'd look kind of funny, too, if all the blood in her body had, without warning, rushed to a certain part of her anatomy.

''I'm fine.'' To take her focus off him, he added, ''Any promises we haven't covered?''

''Just the promises to Jill.''

Thankfully, his blood flow seemed to be restoring itself in a speedy fashion. ''I already know about the wild, crazy affair you're supposed to have. What other promises did she ask you to make?''

Gretchen counted off on her fingers. ''To live each day to the fullest, to spend every single cent of the money she left me, and to enter a piano competition.''

At least now he knew where all the money was coming from. And, of course, why she'd been spending it so freely and acting so out of character.

''I'm beginning to see a pattern here,'' he said.

''Me, too,'' she agreed. ''It took a while, but I finally realized that every promise Jill asked me to make is in direct opposition to a promise I made to my mother.''

''And Jill knew all the promises you'd made.''

She nodded. ''We were best friends. Of course she knew.''

''Do you regret making them?''

''Which promises? The ones to my mother, or the ones to Jill?''

''The ones to your mother.''

She seemed to ponder the question. ''No. Those promises, and others like them, formed the person I am today. But I guess in some ways they have limited me.''

''Which is why Jill made you promise to do the things she asked.''

''That's my conclusion.''

And, being a person who always kept her promises, she had wasted no time buying a fancy car, a whole new wardrobe and propositioning him. ''Have you entered a piano competition yet?''

''Yes. In Morgantown, West Virginia, in early November.''

''That doesn't give you much time to prepare.'' A sudden thought occurred to him. "Wait a minute. That was *you* I heard playing the piano the night I came to your door and asked you to turn down the music?"

She looked embarrassed. "Guilty as charged."

"Jill was right. You need to enter a piano competition. You're very good."

Her embarrassment changed to pleasure. "Thank you. And thank you for not saying my mother was wrong."

"What's past is past," he told her. "You can't change it, so why dwell on it?"

He regarded her for a moment. "Why haven't I heard you playing since that night?"

"I didn't want to disturb you."

"But the competition is only three months away. You need to be putting in all the time you can."

She looked amused. "I do practice, you know."

"When?"

"When I'm sure you're not home."

"Practice whenever you want," he told her. "Anytime, day or night. If it bothers me, I'll let you know."

"Thank you."

He drew a breath. "So, you intend on keeping the promises you made to Jill?"

"Yes, I do."

"Does this mean you're still looking for a man to have sex with?"

She gave him a patient look. "It's not just about sex, Marco."

"Sure sounded like it to me."

"No. If it was only about sex, I could wander out into the middle of the street, pick up the first man I saw and have sex with him. If it was only about sex, I could make love to you, right now, here on this table. But that's not what Jill wanted. It just took me a while to figure that out."

He was having some difficulty breathing after the

making-love-with-him-on-the-table part. "What did she want?" he finally managed to say.

"What a wild, crazy affair symbolizes."

"And that is?"

"Letting go of all preconceived notions, of all inhibitions. Losing myself completely in another person, to the point where I don't know where he ends and I begin. You can't do that with a stranger."

He got his breathing under control. Barely. "Or a tenant," he supplied.

She nodded. "Or a stuffed shirt."

"Stuffed shirt?"

"Jill's term for all the men in my life to date."

"Does that include your erstwhile fiancé?"

"Especially my ex-fiancé," she said.

"No wild, crazy affair with him?"

"He wasn't the wild, crazy affair type."

At least she thought *he* was, or she wouldn't have propositioned him. That was some consolation, anyway. "Serious guy, was he?"

"Deadly."

"So who can you have this affair with?"

"I don't know." She shrugged. "What I do know is that up until now I've been going about finding him the wrong way."

"Including the way you came on to me?" he asked.

"Absolutely." Her voice rang with her conviction. "You know how it is when you have something you need to do, but deep down inside you don't really want to do it, so you just decide to get it over with?"

"Biting the bullet," he said flatly.

She nodded. "Well, that's the way I initially approached the wild-crazy-affair thing."

He took the hit square in his ego. "That's why you propositioned me? So you could get it over with?"

"Yes." She gave a faint smile. "Not really in the spirit of things, was it?"

"That's the only reason?" he pressed, his ego still smarting.

"Why do you ask?" Suddenly she sounded wary.

"Well, I figured you can't have a wild, crazy affair if the person you plan on having it with doesn't make you at least feel *something*. Can you?"

She stared at him. "You're asking if I'm attracted to you."

Her honesty surprised him. "Yes, I guess I am."

"Then let me ask you something," she retorted. "Have you ever really let yourself go with a woman? Have you lost yourself so completely in her that you didn't know where she ended or where you began?"

He'd had mind-blowing sex a time or two. He'd even had what he'd considered deep, thoughtful conversations, but which had, upon reflection, never been about anything too important. After each type of encounter, he had never experienced the intimacy, the closeness, that Gretchen was referring to and that other men seemed to feel.

The only time he'd come close to losing himself in another person was back when he was engaged to Tess. Thank goodness he hadn't lost himself to the point of submersion, because when she broke it off, where would that have left him?

He had no business letting his ego get in the way of his dealings with Gretchen. Hadn't he already decided that?

"No," he said.

"And you don't want to, either, do you?" she replied, surprising him yet again with her insight.

Treating her question as rhetorical, he said instead, "Does this mean you're withdrawing your proposition?"

"I thought I'd already made that perfectly clear." After a brief hesitation, she added, "Do you mind that I've withdrawn it?"

He was off the hook. She wouldn't be weaving any impossible fantasies around him. His life could go on just the way it always had, the way he had designed it. Why wasn't he happier about that? And why was he feeling envious of the man she would ultimately choose?

"Of course not."

"I didn't think so. Just for the record, I don't know who I'm going to have this affair with. What I do know is that I'm going to open myself up to new experiences, to new people. I'm going to get to know them and let them get to know me. When the time and the person are right, there will be no ambivalence on either part. We'll both be ready."

"And then you'll fulfill that promise to Jill," he said dully.

"Yes. The sooner each promise is filled, the sooner my life can get back to normal."

Did normal mean she'd revert to her old way of dressing and living, that she'd be like a caterpillar who, once it had emerged from the cocoon, was so terrified of the outside world that it climbed back inside, never to reemerge?

It really was none of his business, or his concern, Marco told himself. He certainly couldn't offer Gretchen what she wanted—needed—from a relationship.

Still, after her revelations to him, and his to her, he couldn't help feeling closer to her than he'd been to any other person in quite some time, including his brothers and his sister. The rain outside pattering softly against the roof, the soft lighting inside, her presence across from him at the table, the soothing voice of Van Morrison in the background, all combined to create a comforting feeling of intimacy.

They both reached for the same puzzle piece, and their fingers brushed together. The soft catch of Gretchen's breath was his undoing. Unable to resist the impulse Marco leaned forward and placed his mouth on hers.

It was a kiss that started with the slight pressure of two pairs of lips brushing together, and ended with them both out of their chairs, his hands framing her face to pull he as close as the width of the table would allow, her hands clutching his shoulders and their tongues entwined.

As the kiss continued and grew deeper, Marco felt something shift deep in his soul, like a boulder rolling away from the entrance to a cave. He sensed he was about to cross a boundary he had never crossed before. One he wasn't ready to cross just yet. Abruptly he broke the kiss.

For a long moment they simply stood there, staring at each other and breathing hard. There was a stunned looked in Gretchen's eyes that Marco knew she saw reflected back at her from his own eyes.

"That was certainly a new experience," she murmured, sounding dazed.

"Oh, it was a new experience all right," he said.

Well, he'd done it, he told himself. He'd accomplished what he'd set out to do. He'd turned the tables on her. The only problem was, he'd turned them on himself, as well.

"I think I've had enough puzzles for one day," she said.

"Me, too."

As if on cue there was a cry from the baby monitor. In unison Marco and Gretchen raced for the stairs.

"You don't have to cook dinner for me, you know," Gretchen said. It was five o'clock, and the rain was still falling steadily.

"I know," he replied, reaching up to pull some pans off the overhead pot rack and placing them on the stove.

She watched while he opened a drawer and selected a paring knife. From a second drawer he pulled several pot-holders, which he placed on the floor in front of Kristen. The little girl cooed with delight.

As if by unspoken agreement, neither of them had mentioned the kiss. Gretchen supposed he didn't want to analyze it any more deeply than she did. Why waste time thinking about it, anyway? It was just a kiss. It didn't mean anything.

But if it didn't mean anything, why had she responded

the way she had? Why had she practically climbed up onto the table in her haste to get as close as possible to him? Why, for just the briefest of seconds, had she felt as if she'd finally met the one man with whom she could abandon her inhibitions?

Because her imagination had run amok on her, that was why. And because, without question, Marco Garibaldi was the most accomplished kisser she'd ever encountered. It was all that practice he got. But she couldn't abandon her inhibitions with a man who didn't believe in committing himself to anything but his work, no matter how good a kisser he was. Could she?

"We could always order out," she said.

"I don't want to order out. I eat enough cardboard food at the hospital cafeteria." He plucked a cutting board from a shelf and began chopping up vegetables. "Tonight I want a home-cooked meal. And I'm the one who's going to cook it."

"Seems a lot of trouble to go to for one dinner," she said.

He stopped chopping long enough to raise an eyebrow at her. "You think you're going to get food poisoning, don't you?"

She was willing to concede that the notion might have crossed her mind. None of the men she'd known had been any good in the kitchen. Her father had been the worst. He was the only person in the world who truly could burn water.

"Well…"

"It's either that," he said, "or you think I'm going to burn the food to a crisp."

"Maybe," was all she would say.

"That's quite sexist of you, you know. I'm officially offended. Need I remind you that all of the best chefs are men?"

Her chin went up. Talk about sexist. "That comment deserves only two words. Julia Child."

"Okay, so there's an exception to the rule."

He grinned, and she knew he had been teasing her. And that she had deserved it.

Gretchen looked around the room.

For a bachelor, he certainly had an amazingly equipped kitchen, a fact she'd easily discovered while cooking breakfast. The room had a hominess to it that was missing in the rest of the apartment.

Face it, she told herself as she eyed a copper espresso maker with an emotion akin to lust, it was far better equipped than her own. And he certainly looked like he knew what he was doing. If she tried chopping vegetables at that speed, she'd probably lose a finger.

Fascinated, she watched his long, lean fingers as they moved the length of a carrot. He sure knew his way around a cutting board. She remembered how it had felt to have those very same fingers cradle her face, and shivered. He sure knew his way around a woman, too.

"What can I do to help?" she asked.

"You prepared breakfast and lunch. It's my turn now." He waved the hand holding the knife. "Just sit back, put your feet up and relax."

Fat chance of her relaxing in the same room with him. Scooping Kristen from the floor, Gretchen headed for the living room. "We'll get out of your hair, then. Call if you need anything."

An hour later she nearly groaned aloud when she took a bite of the chicken he'd prepared. It all but melted in her mouth. "Where did you learn to cook like this?"

He cupped a hand to his ear. "Hark, is that an apology I hear?"

Gretchen laughed. "It is indeed."

After another bite she said, "I have never tasted chicken this yummy in my life."

"You really like it?"

The pleasure in his eyes warmed her. "I more than like it. This is wonderful, Marco."

"Thank you. My oldest brother, Roberto, owns a restaurant. I worked in his kitchen when I was a teenager. He taught me a thing or two."

"He taught you well."

"He'll be happy to hear it."

She speared another piece of chicken with her fork and stared at it. "I suppose a confirmed bachelor needs these skills."

He nodded. "They do come in handy at mealtime."

"Tell me more about your family," she said.

"Oh, no, my family." He clapped a hand to his forehead. "I totally forgot."

"What did you forget?"

"I'm supposed to have brunch with them tomorrow."

"What's stopping you?"

He nodded at her and Kristen. "I can't just abandon you to go have brunch with my family."

"You wouldn't be abandoning us. Trust me, Kristen and I can fend for ourselves just fine for a couple of hours." She tilted her head. "Or is it that you still don't trust me enough not to run off with her?"

"It's not that," he denied.

"Then what is it?"

He looked like he was searching for the proper words. "I made a promise to Brian. Like you, I always keep my promises."

"And that promise was?"

"That *I* would watch Kristen."

"Need I remind you that *you* asked *me* to help?"

"I never promised not to bring in reinforcements."

Sometimes, Gretchen thought, the man could be downright infuriating. She took another bite of chicken. Good thing he was such a good cook.

"Then don't go," she said.

"That's not an option," he replied.

"Why not?"

"You don't know my family. If I don't show up, they're going to assume something terrible happened."

"And?" She waited patiently.

"And the next thing you know," Marco said, "we'd have the cops and the fire department at the door, along with my five brothers and my sister. If we're lucky, we'd get to them before they chopped the door down."

"I have an idea," she said. "Let me know if it's too radical for you. You could take Kristen with you."

He shook his head. "After everything you've done to help me out this weekend, it wouldn't be fair to leave you behind. You'll just have to come, too."

As invitations went, it wasn't the most heartfelt one she'd ever received. "Worried I'll embarrass you?" she asked sweetly.

"Of course not."

The promptness and the sincerity of his denial soothed her somewhat. "Then what's the problem?"

"The problem is my family," Marco said. "If I bring you with me, they're going to put two and two together and come up with five."

Suddenly everything grew crystal clear. "Meaning they'll assume something is going on between us."

"Exactly," he said.

"Can't you just explain the situation to them? Surely they'd understand."

"One might think that. Unfortunately, all they would understand is that I went to you for help, not them. That understanding would then lead them to jump to some interesting conclusions."

"Two plus two equals five?" she asked.

He nodded.

Gretchen laid down her fork and stared at him curiously. "Don't they know you're a confirmed bachelor?"

"Of course."

She spread her arms. "Then what's the problem?

They'll just assume I'm another of your temporary flings. I don't mind.''

''You don't understand,'' Marco said. ''We Garibaldi brothers don't bring temporary flings to family functions. Last November, my brother Carlo, a confirmed bachelor if ever there was one, brought a woman with him to Thanksgiving dinner. He told us that they were just friends. They were married six weeks later.''

''Happily?'' she asked.

''Deliriously.''

''How lucky for them.'' And she'd thought her conversation with him last night had been odd. ''So what you're saying is, you're afraid that if you take me with you to brunch tomorrow, we'll end up getting married?''

''Of course not.'' He sounded appalled at the thought. ''But my family might think that.''

''So?''

''So I don't want them thinking that.''

''Marco,'' she said.

''What?''

''Take a deep breath.''

He just looked at her.

''I'm waiting.''

With an expression on his face that told her he was indulging her only because she was his guest and it was the polite thing to do, he drew a deep breath and slowly let it out.

''Good.'' She nodded her satisfaction. ''Feel better?''

''I guess so. Why did you ask me to do that?''

''You needed to relax. For a minute there I thought you were going to have a full-scale panic attack.''

He gave a rueful grin. ''I was that bad, huh?''

''You were that bad,'' she agreed. She waited a beat before saying, ''If I make you a promise, will you trust me to keep it?''

''Of course.''

''Then I promise you this. Neither now, nor anytime in

the future, will I try to deprive you of your confirmed-bachelor status. No matter what your family thinks. You have my solemn vow.''

At three o'clock in the morning, Marco was still wide awake. He'd tried everything he could think of to fall asleep: reading until his eyes nearly crossed with the effort, counting sheep, lying rigidly still with his eyes tightly closed, repeating a mantra over and over again to rid his mind of all thought. Nothing had worked.

Maybe a good, old-fashioned remedy was what was called for. When he was a child and he couldn't sleep his mother had always made him a glass of warm milk.

In the kitchen, he took the milk out of the refrigerator and a glass from the cabinet. Opting to use the stove instead of the microwave so as not to disturb his guests, he poured some milk into a saucepan and placed it on a burner.

It wasn't long before it was ready. Marco took a sip and grimaced. Warm milk didn't taste nearly as good as he remembered. Now that he thought about it, he never had liked it much. What he had enjoyed were those moments, rare in a family as large as his, that he'd had alone with his mother. She'd had a way of zeroing right in on his problems and listening until he'd worked the solutions out for himself.

Even if a miracle occurred, and she materialized before him this very minute, his mother wouldn't be able to help him tonight. How could he confide his troubles to her, when he himself didn't know what was keeping him awake? With a sigh he placed the now-empty glass in the sink and headed for the stairs.

On impulse he stopped outside the living room. Maybe he should check on Kristen. If she was awake and getting ready to fuss, he could save Gretchen the effort. Especially since he was wide awake.

Marco didn't know whether to be relieved or disappointed when he bent over the crib and found the child fast asleep. Of course, once he'd assured himself that his charge was resting peacefully, he couldn't keep his gaze from wandering to the woman who slept less than a foot away.

Tonight there was no need to cover her, as the sheet wrapped around Gretchen's body protected her chastely from both the artificially cooled air and his regard. With a sudden tightness in his chest, Marco studied her sleeping face. She was so achingly lovely.

He was about to turn away when Gretchen opened her eyes. There was no surprise or alarm in her expression when her gaze unerringly met his. It was as if she had known, before she woke, that she would find him standing there.

Wordlessly they stared at each other for endless, breath-stealing minutes. In the darkness Gretchen's eyes seemed bottomless, like eternity. Marco found himself wanting to kiss her again. Desperately. He also found himself consumed by a yearning that had nothing to do with his need to kiss her.

"Marco," she said softly.

"I was just checking on Kristen," he said, backing away. "She's fine. Good night."

Heart beating like a jackhammer, and his hands clenched into fists at his sides, he turned on his heel and went back to his lonely bed.

Brunch was high atop Mt. Washington at Roberto Garibaldi's restaurant. The view of downtown Pittsburgh from its floor-to-ceiling glass windows took Gretchen's breath away. Due to all the rain they'd had the day before, the city, looking clean and refreshed, literally sparkled in the sunlight.

After a flurry of introductions, and many openly speculative glances, she found herself seated at a circular table for fourteen. Marco was to her left, with Kristen sandwiched between them in a high chair. To her right was Marco's youngest brother, Antonio.

"I hope you're all prepared for a feast today," Roberto Garibaldi announced as two white-jacketed waiters placed glasses of ice water on the table.

"You think every meal you prepare is a feast," Antonio teased.

"That's because it is," Roberto said seriously.

Leaning behind the high chair, Marco murmured into Gretchen's ear, "I hope you're hungry. Whenever it's Roberto's turn to host Sunday brunch, he always serves a traditional Italian meal. Get ready for a lot of food."

Gretchen couldn't ever recall seeing this number of people at the duplex. "Do you ever host Sunday brunch?" she murmured back to him.

"Of course," he replied. "We all take turns."

"I've caught a glimpse of a brother from time to time, but I don't ever recall seeing your whole family arrive at once."

"That's because I always hold my Sunday brunch at a Chinese restaurant."

"Always?"

"Always," he confirmed. "It's tradition."

"What about your other brothers and your sister?" she asked. "Do they have a tradition?"

"Let me see. Carlo is Greek cuisine, Bruno is German, Franco is French, Kate is Mexican and Antonio is strictly American."

Gretchen smiled. "Quite a cosmopolitan group. How often do you do this?"

"Once every other month or so."

"On your week off," she guessed.

"Yes."

"So, despite their busy lives, and your hectic schedule, everyone makes the time for this. *You* make the time for this."

"Yes."

"Interesting," she said, raising the glass of water to her mouth.

"What's so interesting?"

Only that, despite his protest that he had no room in his life for a wife and family, he did find time to maintain his ties with his brothers and his sister.

She replaced the glass on the table and met his gaze. "Just that your family is important to you."

Marco looked as if he wanted to say something. Then, with a shake of his head, he seemingly changed his mind.

"What have you prepared for us today, Roberto?" Kate asked.

"I don't wish to toot my own horn, but—" assorted boos and catcalls had Roberto smiling sheepishly "—today I have outdone myself. Our first course will be a perfect Insalata Caprese…"

"Salad with vine-ripened tomatoes, basil, mozzarella and olive oil," Marco translated for Gretchen's benefit.

"…followed by a delicious Schiaffi and an exquisitely tender Pollo alla Griglia."

"Grilled chicken and ravioli made with prosciutto ham and spinach," Marco said.

"We'll finish up with Torta Mantovana and, of course, my favorite, cappuccino."

Marco was leaning so close to her she could smell the minty scent of his toothpaste. His breath pulsed warmly against her earlobe, sending her nerve endings into a flurry of activity.

"Dessert," he said, in a low voice that had goose pimples breaking out on her skin, "is a cake made with butter, peeled almonds and pine nuts that is dusted with powdered sugar."

"My mouth is watering already," Gretchen murmured, and told herself she was speaking about the food.

"With good reason," Carlo told her. "Roberto has the only five-star restaurant in Pittsburgh."

She looked around the crowded room. There wasn't a

spare chair to be found, and the waiting area outside the main dining room was filled to capacity.

"I can tell," she said. "He sure does seem to love his food."

"Besides his wife, Louise, and his kids, it's his life."

Another Garibaldi who was devoted to his chosen profession. Gretchen wondered how it would feel to have a job that she loved so much. While she enjoyed her work, and often found it challenging, she'd never approached it with half the relish and enthusiasm she saw on Roberto Garibaldi's face. Or on Marco's, when he spoke of medicine.

"I'm amazed," she said pointedly, "that the demands of this restaurant leave Roberto any time to spend with his family."

Marco's face took on a closed look. "Louise works here with him. As do the kids during the summer. It helps."

The expression on his face told her he wasn't willing to entertain the notion that he could have everything Roberto did. Gretchen decided it was time to drop the subject. She didn't know why she kept pressing the matter. It wasn't going to get her anywhere to harp endlessly on a subject he'd already made up his mind about. He'd certainly made that more than clear.

"Before we begin," Antonio said, "I have to tell you about what happened to me this week." He launched into a story about his work as an undercover cop and an encounter with a particularly inept drug dealer that had the whole table laughing.

Because she'd never had brothers and sisters, as the meal progressed Gretchen found the interplay between Marco and his siblings fascinating. It was obvious that everyone knew everyone else's business. They teased each other mercilessly, but with genuine affection. Marco's turn came just as the waiters had begun clearing away the dishes from the chicken and the ravioli.

"How long have you known my brother?" Bruno asked.

"Two years." At Marco's warning glance, she amended quickly, "Well, we really haven't known each other that long. I'm his landlady, you see."

Suddenly, thirteen pairs of eyes sharpened on her.

"That's why you look so familiar," Franco said. "I must have seen you when I dropped by Marco's to visit."

"Something's different about you," Antonio said thoughtfully. "I just can't figure it out."

"She got a haircut," Marco supplied in a curt tone that discouraged further conversation. "Anything else you want to know?"

"What I want to know," Bruno said, "is why you've never mentioned Gretchen to us."

"Bruno," Kate warned.

"What? He brought her with him to Sunday brunch. Surely that must mean something. Besides, if I had a landlady who looked like Gretchen, you'd have all heard about it by now."

"Well I'm not surprised he hasn't said anything about her," Franco said. "Marco always was the secretive sort. Remember when he witnessed that bank holdup? Never said a word about it to us, even though the guy had held everyone at gunpoint. The only reason we ever found out was because he had to go testify in court and Dad had to skip work to accompany him to the courthouse because he was still a minor."

Marco held up a hand, and conversation ceased. "I don't understand how my witnessing that bank robbery has anything to do with my never mentioning Gretchen to you. Like I told you all before, I agreed to watch Kristen this weekend as a favor to Brian. Because Gretchen helped me out of a tight spot with Kristen, I invited her to join us here this afternoon. That's all there is to it."

Dessert was served, along with a large helping of skepticism, if the expressions on the faces of the Garibaldi clan were any indication.

"Practicing?" Roberto asked, nodding at Kristen.

Gretchen couldn't help herself. "According to Marco, he doesn't need any practice."

Marco shot her a dark look. "That's right, I don't."

"Of course you do," Carlo told him. "What do you know about raising children?"

"He's a doctor, isn't he?" Bruno said.

"That doesn't mean a thing," Kate interjected. "All they teach you in medical school is how to deliver a baby and how to diagnose illness. They never touch on feeding and diaper changing and all the day-to-day care that goes into raising a child."

"Which is exactly what I told Brian, when he asked me to watch her," Marco said.

"How is Brian?" This was from Franco.

"Not so good. He and his wife are having marital difficulties. That's why they went away this weekend, to hopefully sort it all out."

"I'm sorry to hear that. Brian and Val are good people."

"Yes," Marco said quietly, "they are."

"Actually, that's where I come into the picture," Gretchen said, hoping to take the spotlight off Marco. "After Brian left, Marco asked if I would help take care of Kristen. You know what a sound sleeper he is."

Gretchen had never realized that you could actually hear stillness. But after her announcement, and despite the murmured conversations of the other diners, she could actually hear how still her table mates had grown. All except Kristen, who gleefully banged on the high chair's tray with a spoon.

"I knew that," Roberto said softly. "I just didn't know that *you* knew that."

Gretchen felt her cheeks heat. Damn. She'd tried to help,

and instead had only succeeded in making matters worse. Astronomically worse.

"It's not what you think," she said. "Marco was afraid he'd never hear Kristen if she woke in the middle of the night. So I slept with her in the living room. On the couch."

"You don't have to justify yourself to them," Marco said stiffly.

Carlo's wife, Samantha, gave her a sympathetic smile. "Marco's right. Don't let these overgrown bullies intimidate you. They can be a bit overwhelming at first meeting, but deep down they're all pussycats. If you need any moral support, you can always look to Steve—that's Kate's husband—Louise, or me."

"Thanks," Gretchen said with a grateful smile.

"See what you did?" Louise chided her husband. "You've made our guest uncomfortable."

"You're right, and I'm sorry, Gretchen," Roberto said, sounding genuinely contrite. "That was inexcusable of me."

"How's he doing with Kristen?" Carlo asked Gretchen.

"He's doing a great job."

"Good, 'cause he needs the practice."

"I don't need the practice," Marco grated from between clenched teeth, "and you all know very well why."

Carlo waved a hand in the air. "Yeah, yeah, we know. You're never going to get married."

"Just because you changed your mind, it doesn't mean I'll change mine."

"You will if you meet the right woman." Carlo looked directly at Gretchen. "Who knows, maybe you already have."

Chapter 8

They drove home in silence, Marco staring straight ahead as he maneuvered through traffic. In the back seat Kristen was sound asleep in her car seat.

Gretchen watched his hands on the steering wheel: strong, capable, sure. A lock of hair fell forward onto his forehead, making him look like a devilish imp getting ready to raid the cookie jar. In contrast, there was nothing of the mischievous child in the set of his mouth, which looked so taut and grim she found it hard to believe it was the same mouth that had kissed her with such devastating thoroughness just twenty-four hours earlier.

"Did you really witness a bank robbery?" she asked when the silence, and the force of his presence, finally got to her.

"When I was fifteen I witnessed an attempted robbery," he replied, without taking his gaze off the road.

"And you didn't tell your family about it?"

"I told my father."

"But not your brothers and your sister?"

"No."

"Why not?"

"They have a tendency to blow things out of proportion."

After her experience with them at brunch, she had no trouble at all believing that statement. "Must've been scary."

He shrugged. "Not really. He wasn't much more than a kid himself. The gun shook in his hands even more than his voice did when he ordered us all to hit the floor. It was fairly obvious, at least to me, that he didn't want to hurt anybody, that he just desperately needed some money. At the trial I learned the gun wasn't loaded. I also learned that his father had just died, that his mother had seven other children to feed and was facing a mountain of unpaid medical bills and that the bank was threatening to foreclose. The same bank he tried to rob."

"How sad," she said.

Marco nodded. "He spent five years in prison. When he was released, he put himself through college by working two and three jobs at a time. He now works as a counselor for troubled kids, and has a wife and three children."

Gretchen stared at him, amazed.

"We keep in touch," Marco said in answer to her unspoken question.

She felt a rush of admiration. How many crime victims forgave their victimizers, let alone befriended them?

"Did his mother lose the house?"

"No. My father was on the Pittsburgh Police Force then. He and some fellow officers got a fund going and collected enough money to keep the bank at bay. Because of all the publicity and the public sympathy surrounding the case, the hospital agreed to forgive a huge chunk of the debt."

Sometimes, Gretchen mused, the system actually did work. "About brunch," she said, deciding it was time to broach the subject they'd both been avoiding. "Thank you for not saying, 'I told you so.'"

His smile held no humor. "I told you so."

"It really wasn't that bad," she felt compelled to say.

He spared her a disbelieving glance before turning his attention back to the road. "Wasn't it?"

She looked out the rear window. "So far as I can tell, we're not being tailed by a mad group of vigilantes intent on rounding us up for a shotgun wedding. We're still footloose and fancy-free, as our grandparents' generation was fond of saying. We escaped unscathed."

"We may be footloose and fancy-free," he replied, "but we didn't escape unscathed."

"Why do you say that?"

"Because we left thirteen people back there who, thanks to you, are totally convinced we're sleeping together."

She felt her eyebrows climb. "Thanks to me?"

"The minute you told them you knew what a sound sleeper I was, it was clear what they were all thinking."

Her chin went up. "I can't help what they think."

"I know that."

"I was only telling the truth."

"I know that, too."

"Did you want me to lie to them?"

"Of course not."

And just a minute ago she'd actually been wishing that he would kiss her again.

"I see," she said. "Then you wanted me to be a good little girl and keep my mouth shut. Is that it?"

A nerve throbbed in his jaw, and his knuckles whitened around the steering wheel. "No."

"What did you want?" she asked.

"To have a nice, quiet, uncomplicated brunch with my family."

Gretchen had a feeling that nothing was uncomplicated where the Garibaldis were concerned. Or quiet.

"As the song goes, Marco, 'You can't always get what you want.'"

Frustration gleamed in the depths of the eyes he turned her way. "I didn't get what I needed, either."

What did he really need? Did he even know? Gretchen was curious to find out.

"And what was that?"

"For my family to believe that we are uninvolved."

Gretchen stiffened. She knew she wasn't the most beautiful woman in the world. Nor was she the most charming and sophisticated. But did he find her so undesirable that it actually horrified him to have his family believe they were having an affair? If he found her so repulsive, why had he kissed her the way he had?

She turned in her seat to face him. "Can I ask you a question?"

He gave a curt nod.

"Up until this morning, has your family believed you were leading a celibate lifestyle?"

"Of course not." He sounded impatient.

"So there have been times in the past when they thought you were sleeping with a woman."

"I suppose so. It wasn't something we discussed."

"But you were pretty certain they were thinking it."

"Yes."

"Did it bother you?"

"No." His impatience had turned to reluctance.

"But it bothers you now," she said softly. "Because they think you're sleeping with me."

"Yes," he said, "it does. Doesn't it bother you?"

"Should it?"

"I think it should."

"Why?"

He shot her a glance. "Because I always thought you were the type of woman who would mind if people thought you were sleeping around. Your reputation is important to you, isn't it?"

She had no idea what he meant. "Of course it is."

"Well, then..."

She spread her arms in a helpless gesture. ''Well, then, what?''

''It should bother you that they think you're sleeping with me.''

''Because I'm not,'' she said.

''Yes.''

Gretchen was so amazed, for a minute she didn't say anything. He wasn't ashamed of her. He was trying to protect her, or rather, her reputation.

It was a new millennium, the sexual revolution had long ago freed women from the chains of endless years of child-bearing if they so chose, and Marco Garibaldi—even though he had done nothing to compromise it—was trying to protect her reputation. As unbelievable as it seemed, there was still a man left in this world who thought that way. Gretchen didn't know whether to be flattered or offended.

Even though this protective instinct of his was macho as all get-out, and even more out of date than beehive hairdos and fishnet stockings, it generated a warmth inside her. She'd been alone for so long, and now Marco had come along, and in his own way he was trying to take care of her. She'd almost forgotten how good that felt.

Of course, she had to put a stop to it. Right here and right now. She might not have been the most progressive person around before she'd made those promises to Jill, but she wasn't back in the dark ages, either. She didn't want a man to take care of her. When she allowed a man to enter her life, it was always as an equal partner.

''I'm not a virgin, Marco,'' she said. ''I'm an adult woman fully capable of making my own decisions where my sex life is concerned. I don't need anyone's approval, nor do I care if they disapprove. And I don't need you to protect my reputation from what people might or might not think about me, although I appreciate the thought.''

''I didn't say I had to,'' he said.

No, but his actions spoke louder than his words. An

even more interesting question was why it had bothered him when his family thought he was sleeping with her, but not when they thought he was sleeping with any of the other women he had been involved with. There was only one answer to that question that Gretchen could figure, and the implication left her dizzy.

Whether he wanted to or not, he had feelings for her. And those feelings were different from any he'd felt in his previous relationships. They had to be, otherwise he wouldn't be so afraid of having an affair with her. And he was afraid of having an affair with her. That was obvious to her now.

Before she let her imagination run amok with crazy hopes and dreams, Gretchen cautioned herself, it was time she remembered one basic fact: if she was right, and he really did have feelings for her, he was going to fight them—was already fighting them—with every breath he took. Life was too short for her to wait around to see who would win the battle. Jill's death had taught her that, at least.

"Did you think less of me when I propositioned you?" she asked him.

He blinked. "Of course not."

"You still respected me. As a fellow human being, I mean."

He looked confused. "Of course."

"Correct me if I'm wrong," she continued, "but didn't you tell me that you were actually tempted to accept that proposition?"

"Yes." He sounded wary again.

"And that if you hadn't sensed any ambivalence on my part, we would, in all likelihood, have slept together that day?"

She could tell that he wanted to lie, but his innate honesty wouldn't allow it. "Yes."

"Then, what your family is thinking would actually be true."

He gave a grudging nod. "Yes."

"Would you still be upset about it?"

"Yes. No." He thrust a hand through his hair. "Hell, I don't know. I don't even know what we're talking about anymore."

She knew, though. It had taken her a while, but she had finally figured it out. This whole thing with his family had nothing to do with his outmoded chivalric response to their assumption about her and Marco. It had nothing to do with his trying to protect her reputation. It had everything to do with his fear of commitment.

Of course, if she were to voice her thoughts aloud, he'd simply deny them.

"I'm not going to lose sleep over what your family might or might not think about me," she said.

"I'm glad to hear it."

"You shouldn't, either."

"I'll do my best."

His forced politeness was starting to grate on her. All questions of his fear of commitment aside, did he even begin to realize how fortunate he was? So what if his family was pushy and butted their noses in where they didn't belong? At least they were there. And they obviously loved him and had his best interests at heart. Did he even begin to have the faintest notion of how many people would gladly change places with him in a heartbeat, herself included?

"You really are lucky to have each other," Gretchen said.

"So they keep telling me," he grumbled, although he sounded relieved that she'd changed the subject.

"They didn't mean any harm," she said.

"Maybe not, but subtlety is not exactly their strong suit."

"Still, it was obvious how much they really care about you."

After a minute he said quietly, "Yes, they do."

''That's not something to be taken lightly.'' She paused, then added, ''Or to be tossed aside on a whim.''

''No, it isn't.'' At a red light he turned to meet her gaze. ''I've been an insensitive fool, haven't I? You miss having a family, don't you, Gretchen?''

Without warning, she felt the sting of tears behind her eyes and had to look away. ''More than I ever thought possible,'' she replied, her throat thick with emotion.

When she felt composed enough to meet his gaze again, the light had changed and he was staring straight ahead.

''I hope you get that family of yours someday,'' he said as the car moved forward. ''You deserve it.''

His sincerity was clear, as was the implication of his words. While he wished her all the best, he had no intention of helping her form that family. But then, hadn't she already known that?

''I hope so, too,'' she said softly.

Brian and Val arrived shortly after a very quiet and subdued dinner, during which Marco tried very hard not to make eye contact with Gretchen. His friends didn't look rested, nor did they look all that happy, although their pleasure at reuniting with their daughter was real enough.

There were hollows under Brian's eyes that Marco felt fairly certain had nothing to do with the hours he devoted to his profession. And, although she smiled, Val's mouth had a pinched look to it that made her appear older.

Marco had a feeling that, after the weekend he'd just spent, if he peered at himself in the mirror this very minute, he'd find he looked much the same. His emotions were in a turmoil. They were so churned up he felt like a washing machine stuck on the spin cycle.

''Who's the babe?'' Brian murmured, his gaze on Gretchen as, after a brief introduction, she and Val oohed and aahed over Kristen's attempts at standing.

''My landlady.''

Brian gave him a look brimming with curiosity. "You never told me your landlady looked like that."

First his family. Now his best friend. Would it never end?

"She's just a friend, Bri. A friend who very graciously agreed to help me out with your daughter after you all but dumped her in my lap."

Brian had the grace to look ashamed. "Remind me to thank her before we leave."

"How'd it go?" Marco asked.

Brian's face took on a haggard look. "Not well."

"Did you talk things out?"

"We did a lot of talking."

"Things any better between you two?"

"We're still married, if that's what you mean."

It wasn't exactly the joyful news Marco had hoped for.

"How'd everything go here?" Brian asked.

A loaded question if ever Marco had heard one. But then Brian was asking about his daughter, not Gretchen Montgomery. At least the answer to that question was fairly simple.

"Everything went just fine."

The next ten minutes were spent gathering up Kristen's belongings, loading up Brian's car and accepting his friends' thanks. Then Marco was alone with Gretchen again, the two of them standing shoulder to shoulder on the sidewalk, arms raised to shield their eyes against the brightness of the sun as they watched the Newcomes' car turn the corner and disappear.

"This may sound funny," he said, "but I'm really going to miss her."

"Me, too," Gretchen replied softly. She dropped her arm and turned to face him.

"I'm not ashamed to admit that she pretty much had me wrapped around her little finger."

He smiled. "I could tell."

Gretchen gave him a pointed look. "She had you wrapped, too, Marco."

If he wasn't careful, Gretchen would have him wrapped even tighter than Kristen did. His stomach started churning again.

"Yes, I suppose she did."

Gretchen brushed an errant strand of hair from her eyes. "Well," she said, sounding awkward, "I guess it's time for me to go home, too."

"I guess so," he said.

She turned and made her way up the sidewalk and onto the porch. Marco followed her, unable to take his eyes off the length of her legs and the gentle sway of her hips.

At her door she turned to face him. "Was it as awful as you thought it would be?"

"What?"

"Your brief stint at fatherhood."

"It's not fatherhood I object to, Gretchen."

She held up a hand. "It's marriage. I know. Believe me, Marco, I know."

He thrust his hands into the pockets of his jeans. "I guess I've mentioned that a time or two."

"Over the past two days I've heard about twenty variations on that theme."

"Sorry."

She tilted her head to study him. "To tell you the truth, you do seem a little paranoid about it."

Defensiveness straightened his spine before he relaxed and gave her a weak smile. "Maybe I am."

"Why?" She sounded genuinely curious.

Why was he so paranoid about it? Usually, with every other woman, he had the confirmed-bachelor discussion once, and that was it. But with Gretchen, he felt bound to bring it up every other second.

She'd been honest enough to tell him about the promises that had shaped her life. Wasn't it time he was honest with her, as well as with himself?

"Something my brother said at brunch pretty much sums it up."

"Which brother?" she asked. "As I recall, you have five of them."

His lips twisted. "Carlo. When he said that I might already have found the woman who would end my confirmed-bachelor status, it was easy for me to picture you in that role."

She let out a long breath. "And you've never pictured anyone else in that role before?"

"Only once."

"Your former fiancée."

"Yes."

"So I was right," she murmured.

"About what?"

Her gaze met his. "You do have feelings for me."

His heart gave a jolt before settling into an irregular beat. He should have expected that she wouldn't evade the issue.

"The same way you have feelings for me," he replied.

She nodded, then bit her lip. "But you haven't changed your mind about remaining a confirmed bachelor."

"No," he said, his gaze unwavering from hers.

"And you're not going to."

"The same way you're not going to stop searching for this person with whom you'll have a wild, crazy affair. A person who isn't me." The words tasted bitter in his mouth.

"That's why you walked away last night, when I woke up and found you watching me."

Her words took him back to that moment, and the same emotions of longing and wanting washed over him. He swallowed hard.

"Yes."

"And why you're going to let me go home right now."

"Yes."

Her eyes seemed to peer into the depths of his soul.

"And the real reason you didn't sleep with me when I propositioned you."

For the first time, he understood the truth of that statement. "Yes."

"Well," she said, flashing him a quick smile and sticking out her hand, "I guess it's goodbye, then. If Brian and Val go away for another weekend, you know who to call."

She really was like no other woman, he thought. No protestations. No use of her feminine wiles to get him to change his mind.

"Yes, I do."

He took her outstretched hand in his. Instead of shaking it, he turned it upward so that her palm faced the sky. Without even realizing he intended on doing so, he began swirling his thumb across the soft skin of her palm. He could tell the effect the motion had on her by the way her remarkable brown eyes darkened and the tenor of her breathing increased.

"Thank you, Gretchen, for all your help. I appreciate your giving up all your free time for me this weekend."

"You're welcome," she replied in a husky voice. "But I didn't give it all up."

"I beg your pardon?"

"I still have a lot of free time left. I took next week off from work."

He stared at her. "You're on vacation? You mean I ruined your vacation plans?"

Her smile was understanding. "You just modified them a little. I would have had to modify them, anyway, because of the weather. Remember the promise I made to my mother when I was diagnosed with asthma?"

He nodded.

"Well, this week I'm going to make up for a lot of lost time. For the next seven days, weather permitting, I'm going to do everything I didn't get to do when I was a kid. I'm going to have an adventure."

"Sounds like fun," he said.

"I really should go, Marco." She looked pointedly at the hand he still held captive.

"I know."

Instead of releasing his hold on her as she so obviously wished, with his gaze fixed firmly on hers, he slowly drew her palm to his mouth and pressed his lips to the soft skin. To Marco, the gesture felt more intimate than if he had taken her mouth. With great reluctance he let go of her hand.

"Have a good adventure, Gretchen."

"Have a good week off." Her voice sounded as shaken as he felt.

At her door she turned and waved one last time before disappearing inside.

When Marco walked into his apartment, it had never seemed so quiet. Or so lonely.

It was the perfect day for an adventure. Not too hot. Low humidity. An occasional passing cloud. Birds singing in the trees and crickets chirping from the bushes.

Filled with a sense of anticipation, and with her backpack settled squarely on her shoulders, Gretchen walked out onto her porch shortly after eight o'clock. She crossed to the railing, wrapped her hands around the wood, closed her eyes and inhaled deeply. Immediately her senses swirled with the aromas of roses and wildflowers and newly mown grass.

This was what summer smelled like, she told herself, tucking the scent memory away. She raised her face to the warmth of the sun.

Opening her eyes, she released her hold on the railing, turned toward the steps…and found herself staring straight into Marco Garibaldi's amused brown eyes. Clad in a pair of navy blue shorts, a striped polo shirt and tennis shoes, he leaned against a pillar, legs crossed at the ankles, a steaming mug of coffee cradled in his hands.

"G-g-good morning," she stammered.

"Good morning," he replied.

She didn't know whether her heart beat so fast because he'd taken her by surprise or because he looked so wonderful.

"You startled me."

"I didn't mean to."

"And I didn't expect to see you out here so early."

"Actually," he replied, "I was waiting for you."

She blinked. "You were?"

"Yes, Gretchen, I was."

After their discussion last evening, she'd assumed their relationship would revert to the status quo, meaning they would only occasionally cross paths.

"Why?"

"I'm in the mood for a little adventure myself," he said. "I was hoping you wouldn't mind if I joined you on yours."

"You want to join me?" she echoed dumbly.

Uncrossing his legs, he straightened to his full height. "I used to think that you were the serious one. But I'm the one who's taken everything too seriously for far too long. Myself. My work. My family. The world. It's been ages since I've taken the time to enjoy each day for the wonder it brings. To look at it the way a child would. I need to loosen up. I need to play, Gretchen. And since, coincidentally, I also have this week off…" He gazed at her expectantly.

"You decided to play with me," she finished, then felt a rush of heat to her cheeks. She'd be darned, though, if she'd give him the satisfaction of explaining that she didn't mean those words the way they sounded.

His lips twitched. "Yes."

He'd said it was a coincidence that they both had this week off, but was it really? She'd been aware of his work schedule for some time now. Had she subconsciously chosen this week for her adventure, knowing that it was also Marco's week off? Had she hoped that, being around the duplex at the same time he was, she would get to see him more often?

If he accompanied her on her adventure, she'd be seeing a lot of him. That realization was enough to make her mouth go dry.

She licked her lips. "I thought we decided last night that we wouldn't be spending any more time together."

"We did," he agreed. "But I thought, since we're both on vacation, we could treat each other like two strangers with the same itinerary who just happened to meet."

She should have known better than to hope he might have changed his mind about them. "And who just happen to keep running into each other," she said.

He nodded. "For just this week, Gretchen, let's forget about all our promises, except the first one you made to Jill. Let's live in the moment, enjoy whatever comes our way and take whatever happens at face value."

What a seductive idea. What a seductive man.

"And at the end of the week?"

"We go on with our lives, the way we always have."

Was it wise? Already, after just one weekend with Marco, Gretchen cared for him more than she thought possible. Could she spend a week with him and just walk away with her heart still intact?

On the other hand it sure would be nice to have some company.

Uncertain whether or not she was deluding herself, or setting herself up for the biggest fall of her life, she shrugged. "Sure. Why not?"

Marco set his coffee mug on the porch and gave her a smile that threatened to knock her socks off. "Great. What are we going to do first?"

She didn't know about him, but her first order of business was to restore her wildly galloping heartbeat to normal. "We're going to climb a tree."

His smile died. Something flickered in his eyes, an emotion she couldn't define. Maybe it was a trick of the sunlight, but she could swear he paled.

She took a step toward him. "Are you okay?"

He drew a deep breath and summoned another smile. It wasn't quite as bright as the first one, but it still packed a heck of a wallop.

"I'm just fine, Gretchen. Lead the way."

Chapter 9

When they drew even with the Japanese maple at the edge of Gretchen's yard, Marco came to a halt.

"This looks like a good climbing tree," he said, patting the trunk and trying to force some enthusiasm into his voice.

Gretchen barely spared it, or him, a glance. "Not a chance."

"Why not?"

"It's too short. The highest we could climb would be about ten feet off the ground."

Ten feet sounded plenty high to him. "What's the matter with that?"

She settled her hands on her waist and shook her head reprovingly at him. "The word for the week is adventure, remember? You can't have an adventure when you're only ten feet off the ground."

"Is that so?" he challenged. He lowered his voice seductively. "I guarantee you, Gretchen, that we could have

one doozy of an adventure if we were under this tree, flat
on our backs.''

For a second or two her eyes turned slumbrous. Then
she gave him a look that said she should have expected
such a comment from him.

"Do men think only about sex?" she asked.

"Do women think only about marriage?" he countered.

"It doesn't matter either way," she replied, "since we
agreed last night that both sex and marriage are out of the
question where we're concerned."

That wasn't exactly the way he recalled it. Gretchen
made it sound as if they were totally indifferent to each
other, which they both very well knew was not the case.

"We agreed that marriage was not for me, and that in-
discriminate affairs were not your style."

She spread her arms. "There you have it. You're not
about to marry me, and I'm not about to have sex with
you."

He knew he should have kept his mouth shut. "We
could still have quite an adventure in that tree, if we put
our minds to it," he insisted.

"You know how it feels, Marco, when you're on a Ferris wheel and you stop at the very top?"

He hadn't ridden a Ferris wheel in years, but he had no
problem recalling that nauseating feeling. His stomach
plunged as he nodded.

"Well," she said, "that's how I want to feel when I
climb a tree. I want to look down and have my breath
catch in my throat at the wonders laid out before me."

If his breath caught any further in his throat, he'd pass
out from lack of oxygen.

Gretchen set off down the street, and Marco realized he
had two choices. He could either follow her, or he could
climb back into bed and pull the covers up over his head.
While the latter sounded more than appealing, he didn't
think he was up to the inevitable questions that would
follow if he carried out that impulse. He was, after all, the

one who had insisted on joining her. Besides, when he looked into her eyes, he saw a light of expectation that he hadn't seen in his own for so very long now. He didn't want to do anything to extinguish it.

Not that he thought she'd be devastated if he changed his mind about accompanying her.

"Do you have a particular tree in mind?" he asked when he caught up with her.

She nodded. "In the park. In the middle. Near the swings."

Marco hadn't thought it possible, but his stomach plunged even further. He knew exactly which tree she had in mind. At least one hundred years old, it had twisted and gnarled branches that seemed to stretch a thousand feet into the sky. He knew the tree couldn't be that tall, but it seemed that way to him, whenever he looked at it.

He tried to remain calm. He was going to climb a tree. He, Marco Alonzo Garibaldi, was really going to climb a tree. A big tree. What *had* he been thinking?

It had all seemed so clear last night, when he was lying awake in bed. All he'd been able to think about were Brian and Val and their troubles, and everything at work that had been getting him down lately. Not to mention Gretchen and the unsettling way she made him feel.

That was when he realized he couldn't go on the way he had been. He needed a break, not just from the stresses of his job, but from his old, repetitive ways of thinking and behaving. He needed to find something to do that would free his mind from the cares and worries that had weighed so heavily on him recently. It didn't matter what that something was, only that it resulted in him refilling his well.

Gretchen was planning on doing that very thing, his tired brain had whispered. Why not join her? Of course, he could refill his well all by himself. But, he figured, since she already had everything planned out, why not play Jack to her Jill?

The bonus was she knew how things had to be between them, and she accepted that. Without complaint. It wouldn't be a problem.

Funny how when he'd told himself that palling around with her would be a great way to relieve his stress, he'd failed to take into consideration that some of the items on her itinerary might involve heights. And he had a thing about heights.

He could always tell her the truth, but a man had his pride. Besides, how hard could it be to climb one little tree? Okay, one big tree. With any luck, Gretchen would go up a branch or two, look down, decide she'd seen enough, and they could move on to bigger and better land-locked things.

When they reached the tree, Marco had to tilt his head way back to see the top. He swallowed hard. At least the branches looked sturdy enough. They weren't likely to break under his weight. He thought.

"Ready?" she asked.

Without waiting for his response, which she seemed to take for granted, Gretchen wrapped her arms around an overhead branch, braced one foot against the trunk and glanced at him over her shoulder. "Would you mind giving me a boost?"

The pose reminded him of everything he'd forgotten since her startling announcement: how long, slender and graceful her arms and legs were, how the fabric of her shorts molded to the curve of her backside. Maybe if he concentrated solely on Gretchen and the way the sight of those long legs and that curvy body of hers made him feel he just might make it through this ordeal.

Maybe.

Grasping her around the waist, he gave her a boost.

"Thanks," she said with a smile when she was crouched atop the branch. "See you at the top. Last one up is a rotten egg."

For someone who'd never climbed a tree before, he

movements were fast and surefooted, even with the backpack strapped to her back. Gretchen grasped each branch with the eagerness of a mountain climber approaching the top of Mt. Everest for the first time. There was an unmistakable athleticism in her every move that gave Marco a regretful pause. What, he wondered, could she have accomplished had she not made that promise to her mother?

Before he could refill his lungs with the air that had suddenly rushed out of them, she had already disappeared into the far reaches of the tree, blocked from his view by the proliferation of leaves. Gritting his teeth and praying they didn't both break their fool necks, Marco followed.

Halfway up he spotted her backpack, looped around a short, stubby branch. For one crazy, heart-stopping second he thought she'd fallen. He let out a shaky breath when he heard movement above him and spied a flash of leg. Evidently the backpack had grown cumbersome and she'd decided to leave it behind. The way she had him, he reflected wryly.

They were somewhere near the top when Gretchen plopped herself into the vee formed by two branches and turned a face lit with excitement to him. "Isn't this glorious?" she asked in a voice filled with awestruck wonder.

A bit more tentatively Marco settled onto a branch. The view was dizzying.

"Oh, look," Gretchen cried, pointing, "I can see the courthouse. And over there is the pool. They've got quite a crowd today. I never realized how small everybody looked from up here. It's almost like being in an airplane."

It had to be his imagination, but the air definitely seemed thinner up here. Marco wanted to reach a hand up to loosen the collar of his shirt, but didn't dare break the death grip he had on the branch. Sweat broke out on his forehead, and his hands trembled so alarmingly he feared he would lose his balance and go crashing to the ground.

For a while by concentrating on Gretchen's animated

face, the strong pull he felt toward her overcame his fear.
Then he made the mistake of looking down again.

"Gretchen?" he finally managed, his voice strained.

"What?"

"I don't want to alarm you, but I don't think I can
move."

She was still busy studying the view. "What's the matter?" she asked, sounding distracted. "Are you stuck?"

"Not exactly." He paused. "You see, I have
this…thing about heights."

Her gaze flew to him. "Why didn't you tell me this
when we were still on the ground?" she asked softly.

"It's not something I'm proud of. Plus, I was kind of
hoping I'd outgrown it."

"How long have you had this fear?"

"Since I was a kid." He grimaced. "I'm probably the
only thirty-four-year-old in this country who hasn't flown
in an airplane."

"That's not true." An impish light gleamed in her eyes.
"I'll bet there are plenty of thirty-four-year-old Amish
men who've never flown in an airplane, either."

He surprised himself by grinning. "Thanks for trying to
make things easier for me."

"Is it helping?"

"Not really. But I appreciate the effort."

She peered closely at him. "You do look a little pale.
You're not going to pass out on me or anything, are you?"

"I'll be fine, so long as I don't look down. I'm just not
sure how I'm going to *get* down."

"The same way you got up. I can talk you down,
Marco."

He shook his head. "I don't think it'll work. I really
can't move."

"I'll be right back," she said. With the same surefoot-
edness she'd shown climbing up, she began her descent.

"Gretchen," he called after her. It cost him, but he managed to add, "Don't leave me. Please."

"I'm not leaving," she called back. "I'm getting my backpack."

A minute later, backpack in hand, she stood on a branch beneath him. After unzipping a side compartment, she pulled out a cell phone. Marco watched in bemusement while she punched in a number, then held the phone to her ear.

"You have your cell phone with you?"

"When on an adventure, one should always be prepared for any emergency," she replied, before speaking softly into the phone.

"Please don't tell me you called 911," he said, when she pushed the off button.

"Of course not." She replaced the phone in her backpack. "I called the police."

"That's even worse," Marco muttered.

"What?"

"Nothing."

Comprehension dawned in her eyes, and her hand went to her mouth. "Your brother. He's chief of police. I'm so sorry. I forgot."

"Nothing we can do about it now." He forced a heartiness into his voice that he didn't feel.

"Oh, yes, there is," Gretchen said. "You can let me talk you down from here before there's too much of a commotion."

"Before I embarrass myself any further, you mean."

"You have nothing to be embarrassed about. Everyone has fears, Marco. One of yours just happens to be heights."

The sincerity in her voice warmed him. And soothed his nerves.

"What are you afraid of?" he asked, curious.

"The usual." She settled the backpack on her back. "Spiders. Sharks. Although I've never had a personal encounter with one, thank goodness. Snakes."

"Anything else?" he asked.

"You," she replied immediately.

He could tell by the consternation in her eyes that she regretted the impulsive remark. "If it's any consolation, you rattle me, too, Gretchen."

"As much as being up in this tree?"

"Much more than being up in this tree."

"Oh." Her voice turned brisk. "Time's awastin'. We need to get you on solid ground."

He tightened his grip on the branch. "How do you plan on doing that, seeing as I can't move?"

Next thing he knew, she was standing at his side.

"Here's the plan," she said. "Step by step, branch by branch, we're going to climb down. Together. You and me. Okay?"

He looked down, then quickly shook his head. "I can't move, Gretchen."

"Sure you can," she encouraged.

He shook his head again. "Every time I look down, the world spins."

"Then don't look down."

His gaze found hers. "How can I climb down, if I don't look down?"

"Simple. Look at me. Don't look up. Don't look down. Look only at me. I'll tell you where to place your feet and hands. Trust me?"

Marco stared at her wordlessly. He trusted her, but despite that trust, his fear still held him paralyzed.

Understanding and empathy filled Gretchen's eyes. "Do it for me, Marco," she implored. "Because I have faith in you."

She was so lovely. When those big brown eyes of hers pleaded with him like that, it made him want to promise her anything.

"And because," she added, "if those sirens off in the distance are any indication, your brother and what sounds like the entire police and fire department are on their way."

"I'll try," he said.

Her smile was more brilliant than the sun. "That's the spirit."

It seemed to take forever, but when they finally reached the safety of the ground below, Marco felt a surge of triumph. He'd done it. Sweat poured off him like a river, his legs felt as sturdy as jelly, and his heart thundered louder than an entire drum corps in his ears, but he'd actually done it. He'd climbed a tree and lived to tell the tale.

With Gretchen's help, of course.

He turned to thank her for that help and for her belief in him, but the words died unspoken on his lips. His sense of accomplishment faded. Standing not five feet away, watching them, was his older brother. Parked at the curb, lights flashing, sat a police cruiser and a fire truck. The cavalry had arrived.

Drawing himself up to his full height and squaring his shoulders, Marco faced Carlo. Though his brother was too much of a professional to show his amusement outright, there was a definite gleam in the eyes that raked him from head to toe.

"Hello, Gretchen," Carlo greeted. "Nice to see you again."

"Hi, Carlo. Nice to see you, too."

"The station received a call about a man stuck in a tree."

"I made the call," she said.

"That's what I was told." Carlo turned his attention to Marco. "Which leads me to the conclusion that you were the man stuck in the tree. Unless, that is, someone's still up there."

"No one's up there," Marco replied. He spread his arms. "As you can see, I am no longer stuck."

Carlo's gaze passed from Marco to Gretchen and back to Marco again. "Mind telling me what the two of you are up to?"

"We're having an adventure," Gretchen said.

Marco suppressed a groan. There was no doubt in his mind that his brother was jumping to some pretty interesting conclusions. One meeting he might have dismissed, but two? And in such a short period of time?

After digesting her words silently for a minute, Carlo said, "An adventure. I see. And part of this adventure is climbing a tree?"

Gretchen nodded. "Yes."

"You don't climb trees," Carlo told Marco.

"I know that."

"Antonio is the adventurous one in the family."

"I know that, too."

"Then why were you up there, getting stuck?"

"Because it's a damn silly fear, if you ask me," Marco snapped.

"I agree," Carlo said. "You over it yet?"

Marco gritted his teeth. "I'm getting there."

"Any other adventure I should know about, before I leave?" Carlo asked. "Maybe it would be easier if I just had the truck follow you around."

"We'll manage without it," Marco said.

Carlo tipped his head at them. "The taxpayers of this town thank you for sparing them the expense." His lips twitched. "Have a good adventure, you two. Don't do anything I wouldn't do."

With a wave he headed over to the squad car.

"He's added two and two together and gotten five, hasn't he?" Gretchen asked.

"Yes."

"Your whole family is going to hear about this, aren't they?"

Arm raised to shield his eyes from the sun, Marco watched his brother drive away. The fire engine followed.

"Oh, yes, they certainly are," he confirmed.

"And that really bothers you."

He lowered his arm and turned to face her. "No, Gretchen, it doesn't."

She looked surprised. "It doesn't?"

"No. We're having an adventure here. Let everyone else think what they want to think. It won't stop us from having fun."

"Well, well, well," she drawled, shaking her head and leaning back against the tree.

"What?"

"Yesterday you were nearly apoplectic when your family thought we were sleeping together. Today, you don't care what anyone thinks. You, Dr. Garibaldi, are definitely making progress. I'm impressed."

He *was* making progress, wasn't he? And why not? The sun was shining. He was in the company of a lovely young woman who expected nothing but companionship from him. He'd climbed a tree. And for the next few days he didn't have a care in the world. He'd be a fool not to enjoy it.

"Thank you," he said. "What's our next adventure?"

"How does walking barefoot through the grass sound to you?"

Marco laughed. "After that tree? Like a walk in the park."

The sun was warm on her face, and the grass felt deliciously cool and springy between her toes. Shoes dangling from one hand, Gretchen strolled through the park while, out of the corner of one eye, she covertly studied the man at her side.

Like her own, Marco's steps were measured, those of a man unused to going barefoot and carefully trying to anticipate any hazard awaiting to trip the unwary. Gretchen smiled. What a pair of tenderfeet they were.

The morning certainly hadn't lacked for drama. One thing was certain: there was never a dull moment when Marco Garibaldi was around. Gretchen couldn't help wondering what further surprises might be lying in store for her this week.

Whatever they were, none of them would give her the deep sense of satisfaction she'd experienced when she'd helped him down from the tree. She'd forgotten how good it felt to be needed.

There was no denying that up in that tree Marco had definitely needed her. Far more than he had over the weekend, while he was watching Kristen. The feeling was so seductive, she was half-tempted to find out if he had any other fears that she could aid in putting to rest.

Gretchen brought her thoughts up short. She was entering the danger zone here, and she knew it. If she needed to feel needed, there were plenty of worthy organizations in the greater Pittsburgh area that would gladly accept any and all services she cared to volunteer. What she didn't need was to get any closer to this man who had made his intention of keeping his emotional distance from her more than clear.

But she did feel closer to him. How could she not? They had shared an intensely emotional experience. Things were different between them now. He had to know it, too.

"It isn't wise," Marco said.

Gretchen started. Giving herself a mental shake, she focused on the man at her side.

"What isn't?"

"Thinking deep thoughts while on an adventure. It takes all the fun and spontaneity out of things." His gaze sharpened on her. "That's what you were doing, weren't you? Thinking deep thoughts?"

Not anymore, Gretchen decided. From now on, until the end of their adventure, deep thoughts like the kind she'd been thinking were strictly forbidden. Marco was right on one account: they definitely took all the fun out of things. They wouldn't bring her anything but trouble, either, if she chose to act on them.

"Actually," she said, "I was wondering what brought about your miraculous change in attitude."

"You mean my not caring what Carlo or the rest of my family thinks about our spending time together?"

"Exactly. That's not too deep a thought, is it?"

"I guess not."

"So," she repeated, "what brought about the change? What's different between yesterday and today?"

He shrugged. "It's simple, really. I finally got caught up on my sleep."

Gretchen stopped dead in her tracks. When he realized she was no longer at his side, Marco turned to face her.

"Something wrong?" he asked.

She held up the hand not carrying her shoes. "Let me make sure I understand you correctly. You're saying you were so touchy about what I and everyone else thought because you were suffering from sleep deprivation?"

His grin was wry. "Put like that, it does sound pretty lame."

"You said it, not me."

"And you're not going to settle for anything less than the truth."

She studied him for a minute. Did it really matter? The important thing was that he'd changed his attitude. What good would it do to dissect it to death? She'd only brought the matter up in the first place because she hadn't wanted to tell him what she'd been thinking.

"Only if you feel the need to tell me."

He bent down and picked up a dandelion whose head had turned a fluffy white. Twirling the stem in his fingers, he said, "The simple truth is that, for reasons I don't totally understand myself, I've been overreacting when it came to you and me. I think you'll agree it's time I stopped. Overreacting, that is."

Her skepticism hadn't totally evaporated. "So you're not all worried that your brother's burning up the phone lines about our tree-climbing adventure?"

"Let them jump to all the false conclusions they want. I could care less."

"And you're not worried that I might still have designs on you?"

"No. As far as we're concerned, we know exactly where each other stands."

She certainly knew where she stood with him. In front of him, in back of him, but never beside him. Because he wouldn't allow it.

"Besides," he said, "I seem to recall you promising that you wouldn't deprive me of my confirmed-bachelor status. And you always keep your promises, don't you?"

"Yes," she said flatly, "I do."

He held the dandelion out to her. "Make a wish."

She blinked. "What?"

"Haven't you ever wished on a dandelion before?"

She'd wished on stars, on turkey bones and on birthday cake candles, but never on a dandelion. "Not that I recall."

Marco's voice grew reflective. "It's a Garibaldi family tradition. When we were kids, my brothers and I used to call the ones that had turned white blow balls. What you do is make a wish, and then we take turns blowing the seeds off. Whoever blows the last seed off gets his wish."

"Meanwhile, you've released thousands of seeds into the air, to grow even more weeds next year," she said.

"There is that," he agreed, smiling. "Of course, not everyone thinks of dandelions as weeds."

"Ten-to-one they're not homeowners," she said.

"You have a point. So, are you going to make a wish? I'll even let you go first."

"How magnanimous of you," she murmured, but she couldn't help smiling. Closing her eyes, Gretchen wished for the strength not to fall in love with this man.

"Go ahead," Marco urged. "Blow."

She did, and fully two-thirds of the seeds floated into the air and were carried away. There was no way Marco shouldn't be able to blow the remaining seeds off. She looked away. Today simply wasn't her day for wish fulfillment. Not that she believed in the power of a mere plant to make her wish come true.

To her surprise, though, after he'd taken his turn, Marco handed the dandelion back to her. When she looked at it, Gretchen saw one lonely seed still clinging to the bulb.

"Your turn," he said.

"How did you do that?" she asked.

"Do what?"

"Leave just one seed."

"I guess I didn't blow hard enough."

Or maybe, over the years, he'd blown the seeds off enough dandelions to know exactly how to leave one behind. Had he deliberately left it for her? Did it really matter? Gretchen pursed her lips and blew.

"Looks like you got your wish," Marco said as the last seed floated away.

She gazed at him, her heart thumping madly. She hoped so. Oh, how she truly hoped so.

Chapter 10

One minute they were strolling along in companionable silence. The next, Marco was hopping on one foot and howling in pain.

"What's wrong?" Gretchen cried. "Did you stub your toe?"

"I stepped on a bee," he ground out. "The blasted thing stung me."

"Sit down," she ordered.

While he lowered himself to the grass, she shrugged out of the backpack and pulled out a first-aid kit.

"Let me see." She examined the bottom of his foot, where a black stinger was lodged in the pad of his big toe. "You were stung all right."

"Isn't that what I said?"

Because he was in pain, Gretchen ignored the irritated and combative remark. Instead, she opened the first-aid kit and rummaged around inside.

"What are you doing?" he asked when he saw the tweezers in her hand.

"Pulling out the stinger." She cradled his foot in her lap and lowered the tweezers. "Unless, that is, you'd like to court infection by leaving it in."

"Wait!"

Gretchen looked up. "Yes?"

"Are they sterilized?"

Her gaze encompassed their surroundings. "Does this look like the emergency room to you?"

"You're not going to use them on me, are you?"

With a sigh of exaggerated patience, she said, "Marco, I'm not performing major surgery here. I'm removing a bee's stinger. I will not be breaking the skin. Afterward I'll apply an antiseptic. Okay?"

"You sure you know what you're doing?" he persisted.

Her bedside manner had just about reached its limit. Gretchen pointed to her forehead. "See these eyebrows? I think they prove I know my way around a pair of tweezers."

It took all of thirty seconds to remove the stinger, spray on antiseptic and wrap a Band-Aid around his toe.

"All finished," she said.

"Thanks." He pulled his foot out of her lap.

"How's it feel?"

"Not too bad."

She busied herself putting the first-aid kit back together again. "For the record, you're a lousy patient."

He gave a sheepish grin. "Sorry. Doctors are the worst. Didn't you know that?"

"I do now."

"Maybe we should put our shoes back on," he said.

"That would probably be a good idea," she agreed.

After tying her shoelaces, Gretchen wrapped her arms around her knees and stared off into space. When she lowered her head a minute later, her gaze collided with Marco's. For long seconds they stared silently at each other. Then, as if on cue, they both burst out laughing.

Gretchen laughed until her sides ached and tears ran

down her cheeks. Swiping at them with her hand, she asked, "What was that you were saying about a walk in the park?"

A rueful look on his face, he shook his head. "Some adventurers we are."

"Put it this way," she replied. "Lewis and Clark's reputation is in no danger, as long as we're around."

"You can say that again."

"Thank you," she said instead.

He looked surprised. "For what?"

"I haven't laughed like that in a long time."

"Neither have I."

"Sure felt good."

"Sure did." He leaned back on his elbows. "This isn't turning out to be my day, is it?"

"Want to go home?"

He looked disturbingly attractive, stretched out in the grass. So attractive she was having a hard time not staring. Maybe it would be better for her peace of mind, not to mention her heartbeat, if he did abandon further adventuring for the rest of the day. For the rest of the week, for that matter, although she felt a hollowness at the thought.

"No," he said, "let's keep going. After all, what else could possibly happen?"

Gretchen rolled her eyes. He'd had to ask.

"Please, Marco. Don't tempt fate that way."

He laughed again. "You really believe in fate?"

"I wished on a dandelion, didn't I?"

"In that case, you wouldn't happen to have a shot of whisky in that bottomless backpack of yours, would you? To fortify us, before we move on?"

"No, but I do have a thermos of lemonade."

"Freshly squeezed?"

"Is there any other kind?"

"I'd love some lemonade, Gretchen."

She poured the liquid into the thermos cap and extended it to him. "Careful. I might have missed a few seeds."

"What's freshly squeezed lemonade without a few seeds floating around?"

"With the way your luck is running today," she retorted, "those few seeds will force me to do the Heimlich maneuver on you."

He acknowledged the truth of her words with a wry smile. "I'll keep that in mind."

He drank deeply, sighed with pleasure, then handed the cap back to her.

"That was delicious."

"Thank you."

Marco's gaze seemed to burn into hers. "Aren't you thirsty?"

What would he do, Gretchen wondered, if she told him that he was the long, tall drink she thirsted for?

Averting her eyes from his gaze, she lifted the thermos. Since she hadn't brought along paper cups, Gretchen had no option but to refill the thermos cap. As she raised it to her mouth, she wondered if she was drinking from the same spot that Marco had. Her lips tingled and her pulse thrummed as the sour-sweet liquid slid down her throat.

"Thanks for your help," he said, when she finished.

She looked blankly at him, and he added, "Up in the tree. I wouldn't have gotten down if it weren't for you and your belief in me."

She dried the inside of the cap with a napkin and screwed it back on the thermos. "You wouldn't have been up there in the first place, if it weren't for me."

"True," he acknowledged. "But then you didn't hold a gun to my head and force me to climb."

"Why did you?" she asked.

"I guess I didn't want to look bad in front of you."

"So," she said, unable to resist using the phrase countless parents had spoken over the years, "if I had jumped off a cliff, would you have followed?"

He shook his head at her in mock reproach, then

laughed. "You've been dying to say that for years, haven't you?"

"You bet." She grinned. "Of course, whenever I imagined the occasion arising, I always thought I'd be looking at an adolescent."

"Ouch," he said with a grimace.

"You did ask for it," she told him.

"I suppose I did. Want to hear something funny?"

"Sure."

"Despite everything, I'm having a really good time."

"Why's that so funny?"

He raised his face to the sun and closed his eyes. "I've never felt this relaxed with a woman before."

She didn't know what to say. "Oh."

He opened his eyes and glanced at her. "I guess it's because we've taken sex out of the equation. With that out of the way, we don't have to be on our best behavior. We don't have to worry about impressing each other. We can just be ourselves, let our hair down, have fun. I should have tried this years ago."

"Giving up sex?" she asked flippantly.

He gave her a patient look. "Being just friends with a woman."

So much for her thirst for him. Obviously his thirst for her had dried up. It was ironic, really. For the two years he'd been her tenant, Marco had played a pivotal role in many a fantasy. In none of them had he been her best buddy.

If only she could look at him without melting inside. He might have taken sex out of the equation, but her libido hadn't.

"Are you having a good time, Gretchen?" he asked.

Was she? The day wasn't going at all the way she had planned. She had company, for one thing. Unsettling company, to say the least. And when she hadn't been coaxing Marco down from the tree, she'd spent most of her time trying to remain aloof and emotionally uninvolved. She certainly didn't feel relaxed in his presence, the way he did in hers.

But she did feel alive. Breathlessly, tinglingly, vibrantly alive.

"Yes, Marco," she said softly, "I am."

"I'm glad. Ready to move on?"

She placed the thermos in the backpack. "In a minute. First, I need to make some changes to our schedule."

"What kind of changes?"

She pulled a sheet of paper and a pen out of the front pocket. "Several items on the list involve heights. I'm going to cross them off."

Marco's hand shot out, and his fingers circled her wrist. "Don't change a thing, Gretchen. This is your adventure. I'm the gate crasher here. You do everything exactly the way you planned."

"But your fear…"

"I'll cope," he said firmly.

The determination in his eyes brooked no refusal. He dropped her wrist, and Gretchen's hand covered the skin he had so recently touched. She knew she would feel the imprint of his fingers for a long time to come.

"How do you feel about baseball?" she asked.

His face lit up. "You want to go see a game?"

"No. I want to play a game."

"Even better," he said. He got to his feet and dusted the grass off his shorts. "Follow me."

The local ball field was just a few blocks away. They were in luck. When they arrived, a group of boys was just taking the field.

"Can she play?" Marco asked.

The tallest of the boys, who looked to be about twelve, broke away from the pack and approached them. "You want *her* to play ball with *us?*"

"Yep."

"But she's a girl."

Marco eyed Gretchen up and down, and she went hot all over.

"Yes," he drawled appreciatively, "she certainly is. There a problem with that?"

"Why do you want us to let her play?"

"What's your name?" Marco asked.

"Leo."

"Well, Leo, my name is Marco, and hers is Gretchen. I want you to let Gretchen play because she never has before. You guys look like a pretty fair-minded bunch. We were hoping you'd give her a chance."

Leo turned his head and yelled, "She's never played before."

"Hey, lady," a smaller boy with a freckle-spattered face called, "how come you never played baseball?"

"Her parents wouldn't let her," Marco replied.

"I can speak for myself," Gretchen muttered to him out of the corner of her mouth.

"Shh," he muttered back. "I'm negotiating here."

"You're not Jerry Maguire, and I'm not some hot prospect you're trying to place."

"Maybe not, but I know how the game is played. You want to play, don't you?"

He had her there. "Negotiate away," she said, standing aside.

"Her parents wouldn't let her play?" Leo asked.

Marco shook his head, and his face assumed a sorrowful expression. "She had asthma. They thought physical activity would aggravate her condition."

"Overprotective, huh?"

"Sure were. You know how that is, don't you?"

"Boy, do I." Leo's words were heartfelt. "My mom won't let me stay out after dark, unless I'm with an adult."

"So," Marco said. "Can she play?"

"Let me talk with my teammates over there."

The boys formed a huddle. Gretchen shot Marco an amused look while they awaited the verdict.

"I'm sorry," Leo said when the huddle broke up and he rejoined them, "but this is a grudge match. You see, half of us leave for camp tomorrow. School starts up when we get back. This game decides who is the best team. None of my friends here want to take her on. No offense."

Gretchen bit her lip to keep from smiling. She knew she should be offended that each boy automatically assumed she would be the reason if his team lost. But she didn't take offense. She had no experience. If she were in their place, she wouldn't want her on her team, either. Not when the winners took home the bragging rights.

"How about this," Marco offered. "You give her one at bat before you start the game."

"Just one?" Leo asked.

"Just one."

"You want us to go easy on her?"

"Nope." Marco shook his head. "You pitch to her the way you would to anyone else. And when she hits the ball, you field it the way you normally would."

"*If* she hits the ball."

"She'll hit the ball," Marco said confidently, and Gretchen felt a grateful warmth encircle her heart.

"Three strikes and she's out?" Leo asked.

"Three strikes and she's out," Marco confirmed. "But if you walk her, she gets another at bat."

"I don't know," Leo said. He looked over his shoulder at his friends and then back again. "We really did want to get going with our game."

"I'll pay you ten bucks," Gretchen said.

"Places, everyone!" Leo cried. "The lady gets one at bat."

Gretchen leaned close to Marco and whispered, "Bribery will get them every time. You should know that, having all those brothers."

"I was going to offer him twenty," Marco whispered back.

"And you're supposed to be the great negotiator," she teased. "Next time why don't you let me do the talking?"

His laughter held enjoyment and appreciation. "Next time I might just do that."

The boys scattered, and Leo held out his hand expectantly to Gretchen. He stuffed the ten-dollar bill into a pocket. Repeatedly punching his fist into the center of the mitt, he walked to the pitcher's mound.

"Batter up!" the boy acting as umpire called.

"That's you," Marco said.

"What do I do?" Gretchen asked.

"Choose a bat, stand at home plate, and prepare to swing."

"Where's home plate?"

Marco looked pained as he pointed.

Feeling awkward and anything but athletic, Gretchen had half a mind to flee for home. It was obvious they were all expecting her to make a fool of herself.

She squared her shoulders and stuck out her chin. She was on an adventure. Who cared if she made a fool of herself? All that mattered was that she try. After choosing a bat, she moved to stand at home plate.

"Bend your knees," Marco instructed.

Gretchen bent her knees.

"Hands closer together on the bat," he said.

She slid her hands together.

"Higher."

She moved her hands up higher, then looked over her shoulder at him, awaiting further directions. She felt, rather than saw the ball fly by.

"Strike one!" the umpire called as the ball landed squarely in the catcher's mitt.

"Watch the ball!" Marco yelled.

"Now he tells me," she muttered.

When the next pitch came, she took a wild swing that landed her on her backside. Well after the swing she heard the thump of the ball in the catcher's mitt. There was a general tittering from both the infield and the outfield.

"Strike two!"

"Time out!" Marco called.

Next thing Gretchen knew, he was helping her to her feet and had slid his arms around her. The heat of his body enfolded her, and she sucked in a harsh breath. Her knees went weak and bent even further.

"That's it," Marco said approvingly into her ear as his hands closed around hers on the bat. "Now, about your swing."

He drew her arms up above her head, then brought them around her body in a fluid motion.

"Keep it smooth and firm," he said. He swung her arms again. "Just like that. Okay?"

Gretchen couldn't have uttered a word if her life depended on it. Dry-mouthed, she nodded.

Marco stood back, and she felt the loss of his warmth like a physical blow.

"You can do it," he said softly. "I have faith in you. Watch the ball the whole way in. Don't take your eyes off it. And don't swing until you're ready."

Suddenly all tentativeness left her, and she wanted to hit the ball with the fierceness of a prosecuting attorney determined to convict a repeat offender. She wanted to do it for Jill in memory of all that her friend had missed. She wanted to do it for herself. But most of all, she wanted to do it for Marco. To justify his faith in her.

Leo wound up, and Gretchen watched the ball leave his hand. Something about its trajectory didn't look right to her, so she let it go by.

"Ball one," the umpire called.

"That's it," Marco encouraged. "Good eye. Wait for your pitch."

She let two more balls go by, leaving her with a full count. This was it. Now or never.

To Gretchen's amazement, when she swung at the next

pitch, the aluminum bat made solid contact with the ball. She felt a thrill as, open-mouthed, she watched it soar on the air.

"Run!" she heard Marco call.

Gretchen dropped the bat and ran. She was nearing first base when the ball whizzed by. Fortunately, it went over the first baseman's head, and she rounded the base and headed for second.

Things went a little crazy after that. A golden retriever ran onto the field and scooped up the ball before the first baseman could collect it.

"Get your dog off the field, Rocky!" Leo yelled, before he and everyone else on the field gave chase.

She stopped running to watch the spectacle.

"Gretchen!" she heard Marco call.

When she glanced over at him, he was waving his arms wildly. "Keep going, keep going!"

Gretchen ran. Winded, but triumphant, she crossed home plate. The ball was just a hair's breadth behind her, Leo having wrestled it successfully from the golden retriever.

"Safe!" the umpire called.

Without thinking Gretchen threw herself into Marco's arms. "I did it!" she exulted. "I really did it."

"You certainly did," he said, holding her close. "That's what they call an inside-the-park home run."

He felt too wonderful for words. Without warning, Gretchen found herself consumed by a need to run her hands over every muscle and sinew in his hard body, to thrust her fingers through his hair, to nuzzle her cheek against his.

Whistles and catcalls from the field jolted her back to reality. With painful clarity she realized exactly where she was, what she was doing and who she was doing it to. Abruptly, her heart racing faster than her thoughts, she pulled away.

"I'm sorry," she muttered, not meeting his gaze. "I didn't mean to get carried away like that."

"Gretchen," Marco said softly.

She looked up.

His smile held none of the awareness she was feeling. "Don't apologize," he said. "It's perfectly acceptable for one adventurer to share her enthusiasm with another adventurer."

"Even if that enthusiasm takes the form of a hug?"

"What's a hug between friends?"

What indeed. Amazingly, he was taking her action at face value. He wasn't reading anything else into her spontaneous embrace.

"You really are making progress," she said.

"Yes, I am."

Leo ran over to them. "Great hit, Gretchen."

Smiling she turned to face the youth. "Thanks."

Leo bit his lip and toed the ground in front of him. "The guys and I were talking, and...well, we agreed that you could play in the game. If you want to, that is."

Her smile felt as wide as the Grand Canyon. "I'd love to play." She turned to Marco. "Do you mind?"

"Not at all."

"You can play, too," Leo told Marco.

"No, thanks," Marco replied. "I'm kind of tired right now."

Gretchen couldn't resist. "He's had a strenuous morning."

Amusement flickered in Marco's eyes. And, maybe, just a hint of admiration.

"Yes, I have." He nodded toward the bleachers. "I think I'll go sit and rest my weary bones over there. You guys have fun."

While Gretchen followed Leo to the dugout, she couldn't help reflecting yet again on the change in Marco's attitude between yesterday and today. Clearly, if he was plagued by any unwanted emotions toward her, he held them firmly in check. Based on her consuming need to touch him when she'd thrown herself into his arms, she was rapidly losing control.

He might be making progress, but she was definitely regressing. Worse, she was doing exactly what she'd told herself she wouldn't do. She was falling for him. Hard.

She hadn't gotten her wish after all.

His landlady was going to be the death of him.

Aching in every joint and muscle, Marco pulled on his swimming trunks. His movements were slow and torturous, and he winced in discomfort. The task finally completed, he wrapped a towel around his neck, sank onto the edge of his bed, bowed his head and thrust his fingers through his hair.

It was eleven-thirty Sunday night. Seven days after the start of his and Gretchen's adventure. The week had passed in a blur of activity that made his head spin just thinking about it. He'd never felt this weary in his life. Not even as a resident, when he'd often spent thirty-six hours straight on his feet.

Water. Cold water, he told himself. With a groan, he pushed off the bed and dragged his aching body into the bathroom to splash water on his face.

The man reflected back to him in the mirror looked haggard. One thing was certain: he was definitely out of shape. More than being physically exhausted, though, his mental resources were at an all-time low.

Which was not a good thing, since he was meeting his landlady in just a few minutes.

A picture of Gretchen as he'd last seen her, twenty minutes ago, flashed into his mind. While he felt completely wrung out, she, on the other hand, positively glowed with exhilaration. With each passing adventure she grew more luminous, more beautiful. And so enchanting he could barely take his eyes off her.

Maybe he could make an excuse. Plead a headache, nausea, an inflamed appendix, anything to get out of what he had to do next.

It wasn't the physical activity that bothered him. Riding bikes until his legs ached and riding horses until another part of his anatomy ached, he could handle. Ditto the amusement park rides, the white-water rafting, the bungee-jumping and the hot-air balloon ride. In fact, his fear of heights had all but vanished.

What he was having difficulty dealing with was his growing desire for Gretchen. It was enough to drive a man mad. He'd refilled his well all right. With her.

The words he'd uttered last Monday, on the start of their adventure, echoed in his ears. Had he actually told her that he felt relaxed with her because they'd taken sex out of the equation? What a crock.

She was all he could think about: her smile, her laughter, the way the sunlight gleamed in her hair. Her sense of humor, her sense of adventure, her sense of wonder, all were working their way under his skin. She was getting to him in a way no other woman had.

And he was terrified.

If he believed in witchcraft, Marco would be quick to embrace the notion that she'd cast a spell on him. She even dominated his dreams. So much so that he would wake in the middle of the night with an aching erection that sent him straight to the shower. Whoever said that a cold shower was a remedy for unrelieved desire didn't know what the hell he was talking about. Ten minutes under a cold spray did little, other than to send him back to bed, shivering, his erection still throbbing painfully.

If his landlady wasn't the death of him, self-denial would probably do the trick.

What made it all worse was that his current condition was his own fault. He was the one who had insisted on accompanying her on her adventure. If he'd left well enough alone, he wouldn't be in the fix he was in now.

And if Gretchen was combating similar feelings for him,

he couldn't see it. For all he knew, this week had successfully killed any attraction she had felt for him.

Damn her.

"It's the last adventure," he said to the man in the mirror. "You can do it."

But what an adventure. They were going to take an unauthorized swim in the community pool. Which meant he would see Gretchen in a bathing suit.

"You can do it," he repeated, this time with a lot less conviction.

He should be looking forward to this because once the swim was over it meant his life would return to normal. He and Gretchen would only cross paths occasionally, the way it had always been.

But he wasn't looking forward to this. That was the real reason, not sore muscles, that his movements had been so slow while he was putting on his swimming trunks. Because he and Gretchen would only cross paths occasionally, the way it had always been.

His doorbell rang. Gretchen. Time for his swim.

It was a good thing their adventure was ending, Marco told himself. It was the right thing that they wouldn't be spending any more time together. It was the way it had to be. For both of them.

Chapter 11

Gretchen was uncharacteristically subdued. For his part Marco didn't have much to say, either. They walked side by side, arms swinging loosely, their steps slow and deliberate, neither seemingly in a hurry to arrive at their destination.

Their footsteps echoed along the empty streets. The warm night air and the darkness cloaked them like a protective shield. Marco glanced over at Gretchen's shadowed profile and found himself besieged by a series of emotions. Desire. Regret. Loss. Relief. Unaccountable sadness.

At exactly midnight they approached the six-foot-high chain-link fence surrounding the community pool. As if by unspoken consent, they drew to a halt and stared at it in silence. Compared to the tree, the climb would be nothing. Still, Marco found himself searching for ways to put it off.

"Well," he said, trying to sound cheerful, "this is it. Our last adventure."

Still eyeing the fence, Gretchen replied, "Yes, it is."

"Time sure flew by, didn't it?"

"Faster than I ever thought possible."

"Going to work tomorrow?"

"First thing in the morning. You?"

"First thing."

They lapsed into silence again. So much for small talk, Marco thought.

"It's been quite a week, hasn't it?" he said softly.

Gretchen turned to face Marco then, and he caught his breath. In the moonlight her eyes glimmered, dark and mysterious. They exerted a pull over him, a draw, that was stronger than the force of gravity.

"It's been the most wonderful week of my life," she said.

There was no denying the sincerity in her voice. Just as there was no denying the pleasure that flooded through him at her words. Marco's pulse rate soared, and the heat of desire gathered in his chest and radiated outward.

There was no pretense about her. No artifice. No coyness. That's what made her so difficult to resist. What might make it impossible for him to ever forget her.

He was suddenly glad she couldn't see his face clearly. "It was fun, wasn't it?"

She nodded. "I'm going to miss spending time with you."

"I'm going to miss spending time with you, too. Maybe if you decide to go on another adventure, you could give me a call."

"I just might do that."

But he knew she wouldn't. Beginning just a few hours from now, they would both immerse themselves in the routine of their normal, daily lives, and this week would soon become a distant memory. Marco told himself he welcomed the prospect.

He did have one question he wanted to ask, before they went their separate ways. "Did you learn anything this week?"

"So many things, I don't know where to begin."

"Just name a few. Off the top of your head."

She seemed to think a minute. "I learned that I could eat cotton candy until it made me sick. I learned what ERA and RBI stand for in baseball. I learned that I have a lot more stamina and athletic ability than I ever thought. And I learned that horseback riding is a lot tougher than it looks." She paused. "But that's not what you're asking, is it?"

"No, it isn't."

"You're speaking more in the Dorothy after her adventures in Oz sense. The no-place-like-home sense."

"Yes," he said softly.

"Then I guess I'd have to say that I learned the biggest lesson of all. It's not what you do that matters. It's who you do it with. Truth is, I wouldn't have had half as much fun this week if you hadn't been with me."

Marco's heart started galloping faster than a stampeding herd. She shouldn't say things like that. Because they made him feel things he didn't want to feel. Things he couldn't allow himself to feel.

"What about you, Marco?" Gretchen asked. "Did you learn anything this week?"

He was grateful for the change in focus. "As a matter of fact, I did. I learned that I don't laugh nearly enough."

Her mouth curved. "We did laugh a lot, didn't we?"

That was one of the things he'd miss most, he realized. The banter. And the laughter. She was such fun to be with.

"That we did."

"Laughter is good," she said.

"It's the best medicine," he agreed.

"Did you learn anything else?"

"In the no-place-like-home sense, you mean?"

"Yes."

There was a sudden stillness about her, a piercing regard to the gaze she settled on him, as if she was waiting for something. Though he puzzled over it, Marco couldn't quite figure out what she wanted him to say.

"I learned that conquering my fear of heights was a lot easier than I thought it would be and that I waited far too long to do it. I'll probably try to work on some of my other fears, whenever I have some spare time."

Her shoulders slumped. "Sounds like a plan to me."

"Anything wrong?" he asked.

"No. I just thought..hoped..." She bit her lip and looked away. "Never mind. It's not important."

But it was important. To her. He could tell. Just as he could tell that she didn't want to discuss the subject further.

A glance at his watch told him it was getting late. They both had a big day ahead of them tomorrow. They'd put if off long enough. It was time for their swim.

He looked around to make sure no one was observing them. The edge of the park was to their backs. The few houses he could glimpse in the distance were all silent, their windows black. Not one car had passed while they'd been standing there.

Nodding at the fence, he asked, "Ready?"

She drew a breath. "Ready."

Stealthily, they climbed the fence and dropped to the other side. For the space of a few heartbeats they waited for the outcry that would announce their illicit entry to the world, but nothing came.

They were nearest the shallow end of the pool, and the smell of chlorine reached out to greet them. The water shimmered in the moonlight, its surface smooth and unbroken.

After kicking off her sandals, Gretchen walked to the pool's edge and sat down, dangling her legs over the side. Marco watched curiously while she shrugged off her everpresent backpack and pulled out a bottle of what looked like champagne and two plastic glasses.

"Before we go for our swim," she said, "I'd like to

make a toast.'' She held out the bottle. ''Would you do the honors? I tried not to jostle it too much.''

Marco kicked off his own sandals and sat down next to her. The champagne bottle was cold to his touch. After wrestling with the cork for a minute or two, he heard a loud pop, followed by the flow of liquid froth over his hand. He poured champagne into both glasses, then handed one to Gretchen.

She held her glass up, and the liquid and her eyes sparkled in the moonlight. ''To new friends,'' she said, ''and to the end of a wonderful adventure.''

''Hear, hear,'' he replied, his chest feeling tight as he clinked his glass against hers.

Where their hands touched, the warmth of her skin seared him. When the urge to lean over and taste her grew overpowering, he drained the contents of his glass in one long gulp. Surging to his feet, he dropped his towel, pulled off his shirt and took a few unsteady steps into the welcome coolness of the water.

He looked over his shoulder and saw Gretchen undoing the buttons on her cover-up. Mentally he steeled himself for the sight of her in a bikini. Much to his relief, however, when the garment hit the concrete, he saw that she was wearing a simple, chaste, one-piece black bathing suit.

A swimmer's suit, it covered her from the chest down, flattening her breasts and, other than her long, magnificent legs, leaving her almost sexless. In a strange way Marco didn't quite understand, that suit was sexier than any bikini would have been. Because there wasn't any superfluous skin on view, his imagination went into overdrive trying to picture the mysteries hidden from the naked eye.

His hands fisted at his sides. This midnight swim was going to be more than a test of his physical endurance. His mental resolve was also going to be put through the paces.

''We better get going,'' he said quickly. ''Before someone happens along and discovers us.'' And before the physical evidence of the effect she had on him was plain for her to see.

She slipped into the water. "I know it's been a long week, but are you up for one last race?"

"I do have the advantage of superior strength," he told her.

She smiled. "Perhaps. But maybe, just maybe, I might surprise you. You game?"

Where was the man who'd been so tired and achy he could barely move? In Gretchen's presence he felt rejuvenated.

"After you," he said.

She dived cleanly into the water and struck out for the other end of the pool. She was a wonderful swimmer, her kick strong and her stroke fluid, and for a long moment he allowed himself the pleasure of simply watching her. Then before he, like the hare, dawdled too long and lost the race, he dived into the water and swam after her.

He beat her, but just barely. Gasping for breath, he clung to the side of the pool. Beside him Gretchen treaded water and barely seemed winded.

"Surprised you, didn't I?" she said, her voice threaded with amusement.

"Where'd you learn to swim like that?" he asked. "I thought your parents frowned on physical activity where you were concerned."

Resting her elbows on the small ledge that ran around the inside of the pool, she stretched her long legs out in front of her. "The university I attended won't allow you to graduate unless you can pass a swim test. Freshman year, I ended up in a beginner's class. I liked it so much, I took every class they offered."

"Did you join the swim team?"

She shook her head. "No time. My father needed me. But, if I wanted to, I could get a job as a lifeguard."

"A woman of many talents," he murmured.

"I am, aren't I," she agreed, before turning her face up

to the star-studded sky. "I love the night sky, don't you? It's so beautiful and mysterious."

She was the one who was beautiful and mysterious, Marco thought as he rested his elbows on the ledge and turned his gaze heavenward.

"You know what I find amazing?" he said. "Things change so rapidly, down here on earth, but hundreds of years ago our ancestors gazed at these very same stars."

"Know what I find amazing?" she replied. "Only five thousand stars can be seen with the naked eye. But use a small telescope, and you can see hundreds of thousands. And you can magnify that number a million times over when you get into the really sophisticated telescopic devices."

He stared at her, impressed.

"When I was ten years old," she said, "I really got into astronomy. I even studied all the myths surrounding the formation of the stars. Don't laugh, but one of my recurring daydreams was that, one day, like the gods and goddesses of those Greek myths, I would also be glowing up in the heavens."

"You wanted to be a star?" he asked.

"Most young girls dream of being a star in Hollywood. Me, I wanted to be up in the sky. Silly, isn't it?"

He shook his head. "I don't think so."

"It was during the time my dad was unemployed." She sighed. "Since there wasn't much money for material things, I guess I started wishing for things that money couldn't buy."

"And," he added, "being a star in the sky would take you far, far away from the stress caused by your father being out of work."

"Yes," she agreed. "You're probably right."

"See that star over there?" he asked.

"Which one?"

He leaned close enough to see the water glistening on

her eyelashes. "That one," he said, pointing. "The one on the tip of the Little Dipper."

"That's Polaris," she said. "The North Star."

"I know that now. But after my mother died, my brother Carlo gathered us all together, took us outside and pointed up to that star in the night sky. He told us it was our mother. If we were feeling lonely or lost or scared, or just needed to talk, all we had to do was talk to that star, and she'd listen. I was fourteen at the time, too old to really believe it, but it gave me a lot of comfort to think of my mother being up there, watching over me. Over the years I guess I've spoken to that star hundreds of times."

"What a lovely gift your brother gave you," Gretchen said.

"Carlo sacrificed a lot to make sure the rest of us got what we needed. I'll always be grateful to him for that."

She glanced at him. "What do you think your mother would say if she was looking down on us at this very minute?"

What would his mother say? That she was proud of him for the work he had chosen to do. That she was thankful the family had remained so close. That Gretchen was exactly the kind of woman she would have chosen for him.

Marco slammed the door shut on that train of thought.

"She'd say we're breaking the law and have no business being here," he told her.

Gretchen chuckled. "My mother would say the exact same thing."

"That's mothers for you."

"Tell me about your fiancée," she said.

Marco blinked at the sudden change in subject. "Tess? What do you want to know?"

"When did you start dating?"

"We were high school sweethearts."

"So you knew each other for a long time," she said.

"Ever since we were kids."

"When she broke off the engagement, it must have been hard for you."

He hadn't thought much about it at the time, had in fact been too busy with his studies to really dwell on it overmuch.

"When my mother died," he said, "after the funeral, my sister, Kate, who was only ten at the time, cried that she wished she could die, too. Carlo told her she had no choice but to keep on living. Only God knew when it was our turn to go. In the meantime life went on, whether we wanted it to or not."

"So that's what you did when Tess left you?" Gretchen said. "Moved on with your life?"

He nodded. "I had no other choice."

"And you made a decision to remain a bachelor."

He knew what she was getting at, but she couldn't be more wrong. "Yes, but my decision had nothing to do with Tess."

"It didn't?" She sounded skeptical.

He shook his head. "No. Tess was right to break our engagement. I didn't have the time to give our relationship, to give any relationship, the attention it deserved. I still don't. That's why I made myself that promise."

"And it had nothing to do with Tess," she repeated.

He felt a rising irritation. "No, it didn't."

He thought she muttered something like, "If you say so," but refrained from commenting. So far as Marco was concerned, the discussion was over.

"What was your fiancé like?" he asked.

"A lot like me," Gretchen said. "Dedicated to his work. Dependable to a fault. Boring."

"You're wrong," he said in a low voice, his irritation forgotten. "You're not boring at all."

She went suddenly still. "What am I, Marco? What am I really?"

The urgency in her words conveyed itself to him, and he couldn't deny her the truth. "You're a warm, funny, beautiful, desirable woman. A woman who will fulfill every promise she made to Jill, and who, one day very soon, will find herself in the throes of an extremely wild, crazy affair.''

She would never know how much it cost him to say those words, or how it killed him to think of her in another man's arms. Instead of relaxing, the way he thought she would, she seemed to grow even more tense.

''But not with you,'' she said.

Earlier, when he'd been dreading this outing, he'd thought he was the only one doing battle against a desire he couldn't ignore. But he'd been wrong. Gretchen still wanted him as much as he wanted her. She'd just been better at hiding it than he had.

She wasn't hiding it now, though. There was no ambivalence in the heated look that burned straight to his very soul.

And if he took her up on her unspoken invitation, he knew he would be lost. He couldn't change who he was, just as he knew she couldn't change who she was. The end result would be disastrous.

''No,'' he agreed. ''Not if your definition of wild, crazy affair still includes the terms love, commitment and marriage. I believe that's how you defined it for me.''

Her smile was wry. ''You have a good memory.''

''A good memory helps when you need to memorize dozens of symptoms for an even greater number of illnesses.''

She looked down at the water. ''Thank you, Marco. About the warm, funny, beautiful and desirable part, I mean. I really needed that.''

''I was only speaking the truth,'' he said lightly.

''And I can always count on you for that, can't I?''

''I like to think so.''

''In that case…'' Her head suddenly came up. ''Am I totally reading you wrong? Do you want to kiss me? Do you want me at all?''

The air rushed out of his lungs, and his heart thudded painfully. "You know I do," he said roughly. "The same way you know why I won't kiss you."

"Is it so easy for you?" she demanded. "Because, let me tell you, it's not easy for me at all."

"It's not easy for me either, Gretchen." He thrust the fingers of one hand through his hair and felt rivulets of water run down his face. "The hell of it is, I feel closer to you than I've ever felt to another person. I feel as if I truly know you. I know the key events in your life that shaped you. And you know me, in a way no other woman has. Not even Tess."

He gave a harsh laugh. "Do I want to kiss you? Right now, Gretchen, I want to kiss you so badly I ache."

"I want you to kiss me, too."

"I know. That's what makes it worse. But if we don't give in to temptation, no one gets hurt."

They lapsed into silence. Marco had never been more aware of sensation, of the way the water lapped at their bodies, the smell of chlorine on the air, the sporadic sounds of traffic in the distance, the heat of Gretchen's skin, so close and yet so far away.

With a strangled groan, he grasped the edge of the pool and hauled himself out of the water.

Gretchen was climbing out when they heard a shout. Marco looked over his shoulder, and saw a flashlight beam shining through the fence.

"Seems we've been found out," Gretchen said.

"What happens if they catch us here?" he asked.

"I'm not sure," she replied. "They could arrest us for trespassing, or maybe they'll just give us a ticket and send us on our way."

"You forget," he said, "that my brother is the chief of police."

"In that case we'll probably just get a slap on the wrist."

"And by tomorrow morning the whole town will know what we were doing in here."

She turned away. "Can't have that, can we?" she said stiffly.

"Gretchen," he said softly. "Look at me. Please."

When she did, he saw the hurt in her eyes. "I don't give a damn what anyone thinks. But as for sharing this moment with the rest of the town, forget it. Call me selfish, but this is our last adventure. I don't want anything to spoil the memory."

"We'll always have Paris?" she asked.

The reference to *Casablanca* and another relationship with no future left him feeling glum. "No matter what."

Her sudden smile took him by surprise. "Want to make a run for it?"

He forced a smile of his own. "I'm right behind you."

They dashed to the other end of the pool and grabbed their belongings. Ignoring the champagne bottle and glasses, they scaled the fence and disappeared into the safety of the darkened park.

Gretchen had a stitch in her side by the time they reached the safety of her duplex. Along with the stitch, there was an ache in her chest that had nothing to do with physical exertion.

Breathing hard, she dumped her backpack and her sandals onto the porch. A sudden shiver had her shrugging into her cover-up. After fastening each button securely, she sat down on the top step, pressed her back against the post and stretched out her legs. Thankfully, the stitch in her side had eased, although the ache in her chest remained.

Marco dropped his belongings on the ground beside him at the foot of the stairs. Placing his palms against his thighs, he leaned forward and gasped for air. The pool of light shining through her living room window bathed him like a spotlight.

At the sight of his bent head, his hair still wet and spiky

from their swim, Gretchen felt a jolt of lust shoot through her. How was it possible, she wondered, to feel elated, depressed and deliciously wanton all at the same time? She was elated that they had eluded capture, depressed that her time with him was coming to an end and wanton because, well, because he was Marco. And she loved him.

She'd known the truth of her feelings after the first day of their adventure, had hugged the knowledge tightly to her chest as she lay in bed that night, and had even dared to dream each night afterward that he might come to feel the same way for her. The week had been magical, even if she hadn't gotten her wish. With each shared adventure, each shared laugh, each shared confidence, she'd fallen more deeply in love with him.

And not ten minutes ago he'd made it plainer than the nose on his face that nothing had changed. *If we don't give in to temptation, no one gets hurt,* he'd said. Meaning her, Gretchen supposed. Marco might desire her, but he had no intention of surrendering his heart to her. To reveal her love to him now would only cause them both discomfort and embarrassment.

A lump formed in her throat, and she swallowed it back. The key to getting through the next few minutes with a modicum of dignity, she decided, was to keep things light. Free. Easy.

"I feel like Bonnie and Clyde after a successful bank robbery," she said.

His head came up. "Just be thankful it didn't end like their last fateful ride."

She winced. "Quite the optimist, aren't you?"

"Sorry," he said, still breathing hard. "I guess I just can't find all that much to be happy about right at this moment."

She was with him there. "It is depressing that we have to go back to work in a few hours. Plus, according to Doppler radar, it's supposed to rain all week."

''Not to mention,'' he replied, ''that in a few minutes we'll be saying goodbye.''

How was she supposed to keep things light and easy if he refused to cooperate? Gretchen dropped her head and examined a board on the porch floor.

''Yes,'' she managed to choke out.

It wasn't fair. She didn't want to say goodbye. In fact, she'd been dreading this moment all week.

They did talk-shows about women like her. Women who knew that the object of their affection was unattainable and who handed their heart away, anyway. Women who sat on the stage and wailed and cried and bemoaned their sorry fate.

Gretchen supposed it had been too much to hope that, when he'd faced and conquered his fear of heights, Marco would have done the same with his fear of falling in love. Of course, in order to conquer that fear he would have to acknowledge its existence, something he'd also made clear he wasn't ready to do.

It was all Jill's fault, or rather it was the fault of those blasted promises of hers. If Gretchen had never made them, she wouldn't be in the fix she was in now, wanting a man she could never have. Loving a man who would never allow himself to return that love.

Even though all she really wanted to do was weep, Gretchen picked herself up off the porch, drew a deep breath and stuck out her hand. Might as well get it over with.

''Thank you for the adventure, Marco. I had a wonderful time.''

He straightened to his full height. Instead of taking her hand, he said, ''Play for me, Gretchen.''

She blinked. ''What?''

''The piano. I want to hear you play.''

She put up a token protest. ''It's late, Marco, and I'm tired.''

He dashed her protest with a smoldering look. "Please."

"We're only putting off the inevitable."

"I know. But before we say goodbye, I want to hear you play for me. I want to have one last memory of our time together."

For the sake of her peace of mind, and her dignity, she knew she would be better off shaking his hand and wishing him well with his life. Instead, after gathering up her belongings, Gretchen found herself leading Marco up the stairs to her second floor and the piano in the guest bedroom.

Eyes steadfastly averted from the double bed, she spread her towel across the piano bench to protect the wood from her wet bathing suit. After adjusting the bench's position several times, she sat down, licked her dry lips, readied her foot at the pedal and extended her fingers over the keys. Feeling unaccountably shy under his intense regard, she asked, "What would you like me to play?"

He moved to stand directly behind her, making her intensely aware of the fact that, because he'd left his towel, T-shirt and sandals at the foot of her porch steps, his only garment was his bathing suit. The smooth skin of his chest, the hard muscles of his forearms, the flat plane of his stomach, the firmness of his thighs, all were on view were she but to turn her head and look. And touch. Her hands started trembling.

"You choose," he said.

For a minute, as the heat of his skin enveloped her and her insides seemed to melt into a flow of hot, aching need, her mind went blank. Then, as if of their own volition, her fingers picked out the opening bars of Debussy's "Clair de Lune." It seemed appropriate, given their adventure that evening, to play about the wonders of moonlight.

Even though he wasn't touching her, Gretchen couldn't relax. She sat with her back rigid, her fingers feeling clumsy, the notes she played sounding forced, false. A third of the way through, she hit a wrong note. The discordant chord grated on her already stretched nerves. Abruptly she dropped her hands from the keyboard and stared down at her lap.

"I'm sorry," she said, unable to look at him. "I lost my way."

"Don't stop," he implored. "I've never heard anything so beautiful."

This would be his last memory of her. When he thought of her, and of this moment—if he thought of it at all—she wanted him to recall it as something special. Besides, if she couldn't play for him now, what chance did she have, three months from now, before hundreds of strangers, at the piano competition?

Gretchen closed her eyes and drew a deep breath. Banishing everything from her mind but the music, she willed her consciousness to a place where nothing could touch her, and poised her fingers above the keyboard.

This time there was no hesitancy in the notes she played, no clumsiness, no awareness of Marco himself and no discordant chords to jar her concentration. Unknowingly she poured her heart, her soul and every ounce of the yearning she had for him into the haunting tune.

When she finished and the last notes echoed on the air, Gretchen felt drained and more than a little dazed. Behind her Marco was silent. When the silence continued, she slowly pivoted on the piano bench and slanted a look up at him.

The expression on his face drew a startled gasp from her throat. He looked as if someone had sucker punched him in the stomach.

"Marco," she cried, rising to her feet. "Are you in pain?"

He hauled her roughly into his arms and buried his face in her neck. "Yes, Gretchen," he said, his voice thick, "I am. I ache all over. For you. Heaven help me, I don't have the strength to resist you anymore. I'm too weak.''

He ran his hands through her hair, down her arms, across her back, and she felt the burn of his touch low and deep in her belly. Shivers of delight left her weak and trembling as he trailed kisses over the sensitive skin of her neck, and Gretchen clutched at him the way a drowning woman would a life preserver.

''God, you feel so good,'' he said, his mouth moving to nibble at her earlobe, his hot breath teasing her skin.

Something snapped inside her then—the last vestige of restraint. Gretchen tightened her arms around him and plastered her body to his, trying to get as close as possible to him, to climb into his skin.

''Marco,'' she murmured, placing kisses along the column of his throat. ''Marco, Marco, Marco.''

A minute later he gently cupped her face between his hands and tilted her head back. His dark-brown eyes blazed with emotion.

''Tell me to stop, Gretchen, and I will. Tell me to go home, and I'll leave this very minute. But I don't have the strength to do it on my own. I want you too badly.''

Gretchen could only stare at him in wonder. Why was she trying so hard to resist him? She couldn't remember. She couldn't think at all. All she was aware of was a desire that threatened to consume her.

She was so tired of fighting her feelings for him. As the song went, she'd fought for so long that she'd totally forgotten what she'd started fighting for.

''I can't,'' she whispered. ''I want you, too.''

His mouth came down on hers then, and Gretchen tasted heaven. Marco's lips were hard and insistent, his tongue feverishly plumbing the depths of her mouth, his arms encircling her, his hands pressing against the middle of her back with a force that crushed her breasts to his chest. Sinking her fingers into the springiness of his hair,

Gretchen felt the hardness of his arousal pressing against her and instinctively rocked her pelvis, eliciting a groan from deep in his throat.

So this was what wild-and-crazy felt like. Gretchen had thought she'd known desire before. But what she'd experienced in the past had been nothing like being in Marco's arms, a brush fire compared to a raging forest fire, a kitten compared to a wild cat, a cloudburst compared to a hurricane.

When they finally resurfaced for air, they were both breathing hard. Leaning forward, Marco placed his forehead against hers.

"I know I have no right to ask this of you," he said, "but will you give me this one night? I can't offer you the lifelong commitment you need, but I can offer you pleasure. It won't be the wild, crazy affair Jill made you promise to have, but, until the real thing comes along, it could be pretty damn good."

One last time Gretchen strove for rational thought. She could say goodbye now, this very minute, and have her heart break. Or she could have one night in Marco's arms and let her heartbreak wait until morning.

It took her less than a fraction of a second to make up her mind. She was only human, after all. What woman didn't yearn to be held in the arms of the man she adored?

She'd have this one night with him, memories to treasure during the lonely days ahead. If that meant a member of Oprah's staff would be calling to book her for a future show, so be it.

Gretchen backed out of his arms. Taking him by the hand, she led him out of the guest bedroom and into the hallway.

At the doorway to her bedroom she paused, half expecting the physical activity to have brought at least one of them to their senses. But when she looked at Marco, she wanted him more than ever. And the look in his eyes told her that he wanted her, too.

A gentle tug on his hand brought him across the threshold. "Stay right there," she ordered.

Moving surefootedly through the darkness, she made her way to a bedside table and bent to turn on a lamp. A soft glow suffused the room. Looking over her shoulder, she saw Marco where she had left him, leaning against a wall, watching her. Pleasure filled her, and visions of what was to come sent a wave of liquid heat straight to the core of her femininity.

Fastening her gaze on his, she grasped the bedcovers and lowered them to the foot of the bed. Turning to face him, she undid the buttons on her cover-up. When it dropped to the floor, she reached for the straps of her bathing suit.

"Before this gets to the point of no return," Marco said, making her pause, "what about birth control?"

Birth control. In the white-hot haze of desire, she'd forgotten all about it. She couldn't believe it. Of course Marco, the commitmentphobic, would be the one to remember.

"No problem," she said.

Crossing quickly to the dresser, she opened the sweater drawer and rummaged around inside. In triumph, a minute later, she raised the package of condoms above her head.

Marco's lips twitched. "You hid them under your sweaters?"

She shrugged. "I never bought condoms before. I wasn't quite sure where to keep them."

"And someone using your bathroom, someone who might not have any scruples about searching through your cabinets, wouldn't be likely to find them if you put them at the bottom of your sweater drawer."

She had to smile. "That thought might have crossed my mind."

"When did you buy them?"

"The day after I made my promise to Jill." After she'd decided to try to seduce him.

"So you had them the night you agreed to help me out with Kristen."

"Yes."

"But you told me you didn't have any birth control."

"I didn't. Not with me, anyway."

He didn't say anything for a long minute. "I see."

She wondered exactly what he did see. Did he see how much she loved him? If he did, surely he wouldn't be standing just inside her bedroom door, looking so impossibly wonderful she was certain she would awake any minute to find she'd dreamed the whole thing.

"The truth is, Marco, I was afraid that if you knew I had birth control close at hand, you might persuade me to fetch it. And, at the time, I was still feeling ambivalent about sleeping with you."

"But you're not feeling ambivalent now," he said.

She lowered the strap of her bathing suit over one shoulder and sent him a teasing look. "What do you think?"

For someone who looked as though he was leaning negligently against her wall, he sure could move fast. Marco was at her side in an instant.

"I think," he said, his fingers joining hers, "that this is my job."

Gretchen dropped her hands to her sides and watched, not daring to breathe, as he lowered both straps over her shoulders and rolled the fabric of her bathing suit to her waist.

She'd expected to feel shy with him, but when his gaze lowered to her breasts and she heard the soft catch of his breath, what she felt was a sense of pride that her body could affect him so.

"You're beautiful," he said, and for the first time in her life Gretchen believed it.

He pressed his hand, his wonderful healing hand to her chest, and for a moment simply held it there, his thumb gently caressing the hollow of her throat.

"I can feel your heart beating," he said.

"Oh, good," she replied breathlessly. "'Cause for a minute there I was sure it had stopped."

He laughed softly, and his hand lowered to cup her left breast. Instantly Gretchen felt her nipples harden. For a minute his finger made teasing circles around her nipple, then he bent his head and his mouth closed on her tender flesh.

Her head fell back and she moaned. She had no strength to protest when Marco took advantage of her sudden weakness to catch her beneath her knees and scoop her up into his arms. There weren't many men who could lift a woman of her height as easily as if she weighed no more than a bag of feathers. But then, there weren't many men like Marco. In his presence Gretchen actually felt petite.

His eyes glittered with promise in the soft light as he lowered her gently to the bed. With movements so quick and deft she was barely aware of them, he slid her bathing suit down her legs and dropped it to the floor. A second later his bathing trunks lay next to it.

The bed gave as he settled beside her. When he moved to take her into his arms, she took hold of his hands. Climbing to her knees, she maneuvered him onto his back, saying, "It's my turn."

Obligingly Marco laced his hands behind his head. "Ladies first," he said in a voice that wasn't quite steady.

Gretchen placed the flat of her palms against his chest, delighting in the feel of the smooth warm skin beneath her fingers. "I can feel your heart beating, too," she told him, then proceeded to move her hands the length of his torso.

Bending her head, she trailed kisses over the skin her fingers had so recently caressed. His smell was wonderfully musky, and he tasted of chlorine and salt and something so deliciously male it made her head spin.

When she kissed the flatness of his abdomen, she felt his muscles tighten.

"Gretchen." The word was both a plea and a groan.

She looked into his eyes, then at his arousal. Gazing into his eyes again, she curled her hand around him. Marveling that something so hard could also feel so silky and soft, Gretchen slid her hand the length of his shaft. Then, lowering her head, she tasted him.

Marco arched his back. "Gretchen," he moaned again.

She raised her head. "Do you want me to stop?"

His eyes looked dazed. "Please, don't."

When she sensed him reaching his limit, she drew back. "Love me, Marco," she pleaded, uncertain whether it was the physical act or the emotional tie that she was really begging for.

Lying on her back and watching Marco take a condom from the package and sheathe himself, Gretchen felt hot, liquid and languid. When he entered her, she gasped with pleasure. Nothing had ever felt so good, so wonderful or so right.

They moved slowly at first, then with mounting intensity. This was the way it should be between a man and a woman, she thought as she curled her fingers into his shoulder blades and soft cries escaped her throat. If only Marco weren't so afraid of being vulnerable to the power of love. If only she could tell him how much she loved him.

All doubts, all worries, all consciousness was forgotten in a spiral of pleasure so intense it was almost unbearable. After it was over, it took Gretchen a long time to reorient herself. When she did, she was stretched out next to Marco, her head cradled on his chest.

"What time is it?" she asked.

He turned his head to look at the clock. "Two o'clock."

Two o'clock. She had to get up for work in four hours. So did he.

"It's pretty late," she said. "Do you want to go home?"

His arms tightened around her. "I'd like to stay, if you don't mind."

If she didn't mind? He could stay forever, as far as she was concerned. Reaching across him she snapped the light off.

"I don't mind at all."

Within minutes she was fast asleep in the warm haven of his arms.

Chapter 12

"You look radiant," Gary said.

"Thank you." After giving him a distracted smile, Gretchen made a final notation in the file she was reviewing, then closed it and motioned for him to take a seat. "What can I do for you?"

"Nothing. I just stopped by to pass the time. I haven't seen much of you since your return from your week off."

"I guess we've both been busy," she said.

It wasn't a total lie. Yes, she had been swamped with work, but she'd also been avoiding him. She knew he wanted to hear about her adventure. Even if she left Marco out of it, Gary was incredibly perceptive. She couldn't dismiss the possibility—correction...probability— that he would read between the lines.

"Who's the man?" Gary asked.

She blinked at the unexpectedness of the question. "Th-the man?"

"The one who's making you look so radiant."

"What makes you think it's a man?" she hedged. "After all, as you yourself acknowledged, I recently had a week off. I got a lot of fresh air that week.''

"Yes," he replied. "And you were exceedingly radiant the day you returned."

Leaning back in her chair, she spread her arms. "Well, there you have it."

"That was two weeks ago, Gretchen. And your radiance has grown with every passing day."

Her arms dropped to her lap, and she felt her cheeks heat. "It has?"

He nodded. "Indeed it has. And since you've been getting precious little fresh air of late, in my experience only one thing could cause the flush in your cheeks, the sparkle in your eyes and the spring in your step. A man, Gretchen. You're having the wild, crazy affair you promised Jill you would have. Aren't you?"

There was no use for further prevarication. She didn't even have to speak for Gary to read between the lines. Besides, she needed to talk to somebody about the unexpected turn her life had taken.

"Yes."

"Who is he?"

"Marco Garibaldi," she said softly.

"The tenant doctor."

Gretchen nodded.

"I thought you said he wasn't interested."

"I was mistaken."

"Obviously."

Briefly Gretchen explained how Marco came to join her on her adventure, then outlined the events that had culminated in their fateful midnight swim.

"So it was only to be for one night?" Gary said.

"That's what he said."

He peered closely at her. "But it hasn't been just one night. Has it?"

"No."

"It's been all night, every night."

She had to smile. Gary was making them sound like a pair of rabbits. "Not exactly."

"What exactly is it, then?"

With all her heart, she wished she knew. "During the day, we go about our lives as normal."

"And at night?"

"He comes to me."

"And you make love."

Gretchen felt the heat in her cheeks intensify. "Unless one of us is too tired." Which wasn't often.

"What happens then?"

"We just hold each other."

There was a long silence.

"Uh-oh," Gary said.

"What?"

"I hate to be the one to break it to you, but you're not having a wild, crazy affair."

"I'm not?"

"Nope. What you're having is a relationship."

If only that were true. The pleasure she found in Marco's arms was always tinged with bittersweetness. Every time they made love, she waited for the fever pitch of desire to fade. She knew that when it did her affair with him would be over. The prospect made her heart contract with pain.

"I'm not having a relationship, Gary."

"Trust me," he replied, "when a man comes over at night just to hold you in his arms, it's a relationship."

"If it is, it's going nowhere."

"The good doctor determined to hold on to his bachelor status, is he?"

"No matter what the cost."

"And you're in love with him," Gary said softly.

The gentle understanding in his eyes had her blinking back sudden tears. "Desperately."

"Have you told him?"

She felt her lips twist. "Do I look like a fool? He'd run for the hills."

"He could change his mind, you know. Confirmed bachelors get married every day."

The likelihood of that event was on a par with Gary suddenly deciding that he was no longer gay. Gretchen picked up her pen and proceeded to click the ball point in and out of position.

"So I hear."

"What's he have to say about this nonrelationship you two are having?" Gary asked.

Dropping the pen to the blotter, she drew a long breath and exhaled slowly. "That's the thing. Neither of us has said a word. It's as if we're afraid to break the spell."

"Do you think he loves you?"

Gretchen's throat grew thick with emotion. "I don't think Marco wants to love anybody."

"Not wanting to and falling in love, despite not wanting to, are two very different things."

"As are hope and false hope," she retorted.

Gary inclined his head in acknowledgment. "Somebody's going to have to say something sometime."

"I know," she replied. "I know."

The stick turned blue.

Hands shaking like an addict going through withdrawal, Gretchen placed it on the bathroom sink alongside the stick with the plus sign and the stick with the vivid pink line. She sank onto the closed lid of the toilet and gazed unseeingly around the room. There was no denying it any longer. Her period, which was as regular as the sunrise, was seven days late. And three home pregnancy tests all said the same thing. She was going to have Marco's baby.

With a groan she buried her face in her hands. How could this have happened? They'd used protection. Every time.

The words her mother had spoken to her as a teenager

echoed in her ears. *No birth control method is 100 percent effective. Abstinence is the only foolproof method against unwanted pregnancy.*

Over the past twenty days, Gretchen had hardly been abstinent. At least once during that time, one of the condoms Marco had worn had not done its job.

Being a doctor, he was surely aware of the failure rate associated with condom use. Which was probably why, in the past, he had always required that both he and his partner use protection.

But he hadn't required it in her case. His mistake. And hers.

Gretchen lowered her hands to her lap. Straightening her spine, she raised her head and looked at her reflection in the mirror. Her face was pale and strained, but the light of determination shone in her eyes.

Gary had been right. She and Marco were going to have to talk. And it looked as if she was going to be the one to initiate the discussion.

Because she had to tell him that he was going to be a father. It was the right thing—the only thing—to do.

And after she told him, then what? What would Marco say? What would he do? What would she do?

Gretchen had no idea.

"We'll get married, of course," Marco said.

Gretchen's stomach had more knots tied in it than all the lassos at a rodeo. She wished she could see his eyes, tell what he was thinking. But he continued to stand the way he had been since she dropped her bombshell on him, with his back to her, his hands shoved into his pants pockets and his gaze aimed out the window. His tone of voice was as unrevealing as his stance.

She wanted to reach out, to touch his hard cheek, to tell him that everything would be all right. But she couldn't, because she wasn't sure anything would ever be right again.

He couldn't be happy about this; she wasn't happy about this. And *she* hadn't spent her entire adult life avoiding commitment.

"You never wanted to get married," she said.

"What I wanted doesn't matter anymore. There's an innocent child involved. You didn't get pregnant by yourself, Gretchen."

She was grateful for the concession. He was taking equal responsibility for the pregnancy. He wasn't questioning whether the child was his, nor did he accuse her of poking holes into the package of condoms she'd supplied, a package they'd exhausted during their first few nights together.

There were men who wouldn't hesitate to make either of those accusations, and dozens more besides. If Marco had turned out to be one of them, she would have lost all faith in her ability to judge character. She would also have thrown him out of her apartment.

Still, whenever she'd envisioned this conversation, she'd never once thought he would offer marriage.

"Marriage is the only option," he said.

"Since when?" Gretchen replied. "This isn't the Dark Ages, Marco. We have lots of options here."

He whirled to face her, and for the first time she saw emotion on his face. Anger.

"Abortion, you mean?" he accused.

In a motion that was pure reflex, her hands covered her stomach protectively. She could no more abort the child growing inside her than she could take a gun in hand and walk into a fast-food restaurant and start shooting.

"Of course not."

He seemed to relax. "That leaves marriage, then."

"Not necessarily. There are other options."

"Name one."

"Adoption. I could have this child and surrender it to a couple who would give it a good home."

He was shaking his head before she'd finished speaking. "Could you really give it up?"

She didn't have to think. She was carrying the baby of the man she loved. She was probably being selfish, but once she held the child in her arms, once she felt it kicking and moving inside her, she knew she would never be able to let it go.

"No," she said softly.

"Neither could I, Gretchen. A child needs both its parents. I firmly believe that."

"I would allow you liberal visitation," she said. "Or, if you insist, we could work out a shared custody agreement."

"Under the same roof," he said.

His expression was remote, turned inward. Watching him now, Gretchen found it hard to believe that this was the same man who, just last night, had stared at her out of eyes blazing with passion, and who had called her name at the peak of his pleasure in a voice thick with emotion.

"Some people might call your proposal extremely outmoded and old-fashioned," she said.

"Just because an idea has been around for years doesn't make it outmoded. On the contrary, it only proves that it's stood the test of time. Our child needs us living together under the same roof. As husband and wife."

She drew an uneven breath. "Even if we don't love each other?" Oh, how it hurt to say those words out loud.

He turned to look out the window again. "Even then. All that matters to kids is that both of their parents are there. We're good people, Gretchen. We won't scream and throw things at each other. We'll treat each other with kindness and respect. It will be a good environment for our child."

But what about her and Marco? What kind of environment would it be for them?

His mother's death had affected him far more deeply than she had suspected, if he was willing to surrender his prized bachelorhood for his unborn child. It was a gallant gesture, but could she really take him up on it?

This wasn't the way she wanted him. How did women who deliberately set out to get pregnant live with their actions afterward? It had to be a hollow victory at best. And from that time forward a nagging question had to always be in the back of their minds: Would he have married me without the baby?

That was one question that would never nag at the back of Gretchen's mind. Because she knew the answer was a resounding no.

She loved him. He cared for her, at least a little. He desired her. Was it enough?

She couldn't think of herself now. She had to think of what was best for her baby.

Her thoughts flashed back to the weekend she and Marco had baby-sat Kristen together. Despite his doubts about his ability to care for the child, he'd been great with her. He would be a wonderful father. Gretchen couldn't deprive her child of that experience. No matter the personal cost to herself.

"Very well, Marco," she said, her heart aching for a love she knew would never be returned. "I'll marry you."

He turned back to her again. "I have to be honest with you. I believe the odds are stacked pretty high against us. It probably won't be easy. But I promise you that I will do my best to make you a good husband, and our child a good father."

They were being disgustingly adult and depressingly civil about the whole matter, she thought. If only he would show some emotion, throw something, kick and scream, rail at the unfairness of it all. If only she could let him see how scared she was, how vulnerable she was feeling. Anything but this stilted, polite conversation that left her wanting to scream and cry her eyes out at the same time.

"I know you will, Marco. I'll promise to do my best by you, too." She paused. "So, what do we do next?"

"Make all the necessary arrangements."

"Do you want to go to a justice of the peace?"

"No, Gretchen. We'll do it up right and proper. My family will expect that. Your family, if they were here, would expect it, too."

She couldn't deny the truth of that statement. "But that will take time."

"Not too long. While we're waiting, we can house hunt."

"House hunt?"

"You don't expect us to continue living in separate duplexes, do you?"

"No, but…"

"If all goes well, we can close on a house one day and get married the next."

"But a house…" Things were starting to move far faster than she had expected them to. This was all becoming a little too much.

"Is there anyone you want to invite?" he asked.

She gave her head a brief shake to clear her muddled thoughts. "Gary, my boss. A few colleagues from work. Some of the neighbors."

The scene was surreal. They were discussing marriage—*their* marriage—as if the decisions involved had no more import than the choosing of one's outfit for the day, or the selection of which brand of toothpaste to buy.

"Are you going to tell your family about the baby?" she asked.

"No."

"They're going to figure it out, Marco. Especially if we wait a month or two to get married."

He waved a hand in dismissal. "So let them figure it out. This is nobody's business but ours."

"If that's how you want to play it."

"It's how I want to play it." He studied her for a long minute. "Do you want this baby, Gretchen?"

She met his gaze directly. This was one truth she could give him. "Yes, Marco, I do."

He hesitated, as if waiting for her to ask the same question of him. But she couldn't. She was too afraid of the answer he might give.

Emotion flickered in his eyes, but it came and went too quickly for her to identify it. He turned away.

"It's been a long week," he said, thrusting a hand through his hair. "If you don't mind, I think I'll go home and go to bed."

Gretchen sat motionless as he walked out of the room. A few seconds later she heard the soft click of her front door.

Tears spilled out of her eyes and ran down her cheeks. For the first time since their midnight swim, and on the night she needed him the most, they were going to be sleeping alone.

They were married six weeks later, on the first Saturday of October. Sunlight poured through the stained-glass windows of the church, bathing the sanctuary in a gentle warmth. Friends and family claimed the pews at the front of the church. Clad in a white suit and carrying a bouquet of tea roses and baby's breath, Gretchen walked unattended down the aisle to her groom. Her heart melted at how darkly handsome Marco looked, waiting for her on the marble altar, in a plain, black suit.

Between work, buying and readying their new home, the surprise bridal showers thrown by Marco's sister, Kate, and Gretchen's co-workers, and the wedding planning itself, they had had little time alone together. Nor had they made love since Gretchen had told Marco about her pregnancy. In a surprisingly old-fashioned and unexpected gesture, Marco had insisted on waiting until their wedding night before being intimate again. He had said it would make a special night even more special if they denied themselves beforehand.

Though Gretchen had been genuinely touched, she hadn't been able to dismiss a nagging certainty that he was deliberately keeping a distance between them. But if he had been dreading their upcoming nuptials, she hadn't been able to tell. He'd entered into every transaction, every negotiation, every discussion about what needed to be done, seemingly as eager as she was to have things be just right on their wedding day. She supposed he was making the best of their situation.

Miraculously things had fallen into place with little difficulty: they'd been able to secure the church on relatively short notice; the priest, after meeting with them, had consented to perform the ceremony without their attending the prerequisite premarital classes. They'd even managed to secure a photographer, a videographer and a band to play at the reception.

They'd both fallen in love with the first house their real estate agent had shown them, a beautiful Tudor with a large yard that was just perfect for a sandbox and a swing set. Because the owner was willing to provide financing, they didn't have to wait on a bank and were able to close on the deal within the month.

Marco had moved in ahead of her. They'd used his belongings to fill the den, dining room, master bedroom, study and kitchen. Other than a few cherished items, Gretchen's furniture, which had mostly belonged to her parents, would remain at the duplex, her half of which they would rent out furnished. The living room, spare bedrooms and nursery were still empty, the furniture they'd ordered was not scheduled to arrive for several more weeks yet.

There were times, when she pondered everything they'd accomplished, that she almost deluded herself into believing their marriage was going to be a real one. Of course, it would be real in the sense that it would be legal and binding. What made it less than ideal, less real, was that its foundation was weak because it wasn't built on love. She only hoped that the mutual admiration and respect she and Marco had for each other would form a strong enough foundation to hold the marriage together.

They weren't taking a honeymoon. Gretchen had exhausted the last of her vacation on her adventure, and Marco's week off officially ended Sunday evening. Since they both were expected back at work early Monday morning, they had decided to spend their wedding night, together for the first time, in their new home.

Gretchen remembered little of the ceremony itself, which passed in a haze. What she did recall, vividly, was the recitation of her vows, another promise that she was making. While she gazed into Marco's eyes and spoke of loving and honoring him all the days of her life, in good times and in bad and in sickness and in health, words she meant with all her heart, the memory of a previous pledge echoed in her ears. A pledge she had made to him on the weekend they'd watched Kristen. *Neither now, nor anytime in the future, will I try to deprive you of your confirmed-bachelor status. You have my solemn vow.*

It was the first promise she had ever broken.

If Marco's family thought there was anything odd about the rushed nature of their wedding, they hid it well. Even Marco's father, who had traveled up from Florida, seemed to approve of the match.

If only Gretchen could be as certain as everyone else seemed to be that they were doing the right thing.

Roberto and his wife, Louise, had insisted on hosting the wedding reception as their gift to Marco and Gretchen, in honor of which they closed the doors of Café Garibaldi to the public. When she walked into the main dining room, Gretchen caught her breath. Everything was a vision in white, from the table coverings to the streamers of wedding bells that were suspended overhead, the floral centerpieces that adorned each table, the suits of the band members, who were softly playing swing music, and the three-tiered wedding cake that Gretchen instinctively knew Roberto had baked himself.

Just when she thought she might go blind with the blizzard of white, she glanced out the floor-to-ceiling windows overlooking the city and was greeted by the blaze of autumn foliage. It was the perfect backdrop.

"Oh, Roberto," she murmured, turning to her host. "It's beautiful. Thank you."

The pleasure on Roberto's face warmed her heart. "Not nearly as beautiful as my new sister-in-law. Don't you agree, Marco?"

"Nothing could be that beautiful," Marco replied, his eyes virtually burning into her.

The intensity of the look sent a rush of excitement through her. Gretchen knew he was thinking of later tonight, when they would consummate their marriage. She had wondered if his self-imposed celibacy had driven him as crazy as it had her, and now she knew.

Suddenly all doubts fled before the wave of the sensual haze that enveloped her, and she couldn't wait to be alone with him.

Roberto chuckled and wagged an admonishing finger between them. "Uh,-uh,-uh, you two. Not just yet. The festivities have just gotten under way."

Gretchen felt her face flame, but Marco simply laughed.

"I think you both need some time apart to cool down," Roberto said, taking her by the arm and ushering her away. With a last, longing look over her shoulder, she went with him.

Roberto showed her around the room, pointing out the small touches that each of Marco's brothers and his sister had contributed. That everyone had gone to such trouble for them warmed Gretchen's heart.

She glanced across the room and saw Marco talking with Gary. He laughed at something her boss said, and she stared at his throat, at the way the strong muscles moved, and felt a love so fierce it was almost a physical pain.

"I knew this was going to happen the day I saw you up that tree," Carlo said later, after she and Marco had cut the cake and their guests were still gathered around them. "Only true love would have gotten you up there in the first place."

"Well I knew it the day he brought her to Sunday brunch," Franco replied. "When he got all defensive about their relationship, it was obvious he was stuck on her."

"Welcome to the family," Kate said warmly, raising a glass of champagne in a toast. "I promise you there will never be a dull minute."

She had a family again, Gretchen realized, and fought back sudden tears. As she gazed from smiling face to smiling face, she was filled with a happiness she was almost afraid to trust.

Marco didn't carry her across the threshold, for which Gretchen felt mixed emotions. The lack of ceremony served as another reminder of how their marriage was different from everyone else's.

When they entered the front hallway, he surprised her by saying, "Close your eyes."

"Why?"

"I have a surprise for you."

"A surprise?"

"Yes, Gretchen, a surprise." A smile played over his lips. "Now, are you going to close your eyes, or am I going to have to blindfold you?"

Obediently she did as he requested and felt the warmth of his hands settle on her shoulders. "This way," he said, guiding her into the living room. There was a pause as she felt him reach across her, and she heard the overhead light click on.

"Okay, you can look now."

Gretchen opened her eyes and saw a seven-foot grand piano sitting in the middle of the still-empty room. The lid was propped open, and the rich mahogany of the beautiful instrument gleamed like molten chocolate in the light.

She caught her breath and tears sprang to her eyes. In wordless wonder she turned to Marco. "For me?"

Marco, too, seemed strangely moved. "My wedding gift to you," he said softly.

She looked back at the piano. "I've never seen anything so beautiful in my life. Thank you."

When she didn't move, he gave her a gentle push. "Go ahead. Try it out. You know you're dying to."

She sat down on the bench and reverently ran her fingers over the keys. "They're ivory."

"Antonio is an auction junkie. He found this at an auction a few weeks ago. It's a hundred years old, but the last owner had it restored. Antonio assures me it is top quality."

A hundred-year-old Steinway was more than top quality. It was a treasure.

"You shouldn't have, Marco. This is far too generous a gift."

He dismissed her protest with a wave of his hand. "Play for me, Gretchen."

The first note transported her to a faraway place. The tone was rich, soaring on the air like an eagle and filling the room with sound. Never had she played a more responsive and wondrous instrument.

She was so enraptured she had no idea how long she played. It could have been thirty seconds, it could have been an hour. But when she felt Marco's hands settle on her shoulders, and his thumbs began making rhythmic circles on the sensitive skin of her neck, a familiar weakness invaded her body.

Her fingers stumbled over the keys, the music forgotten. His breath was in her hair, the heat of him enveloping her like a fever. Her nerve endings hummed the way the piano strings had while she was playing.

"You're like a drug in my veins," he said thickly, into her ear. "I can't get enough of you."

His teeth closed gently on her earlobe, and she dropped her head back to give him easier access. "I can't get enough of you, either."

He teased her earlobe until the pleasure was almost pain, then moved on to her cheek and temple. When she could no longer endure his touch without doing some touching of her own, Gretchen stood and turned into his arms. The look in his eyes scrambled her thoughts, not that they'd been all that coherent to begin with.

"I've been waiting for this moment for what seems like forever," he told her. "For the past six weeks, it's all I could think about, dream about. You don't know how hard it's been for me to keep my hands off you."

Gretchen divested him of his suit coat and dropped it to the floor. Running her hands down his shirtsleeves, she plastered her body tightly against his, thrilling to the way he trembled at her touch.

"You were the one who insisted we stay away from each other," she teased.

He ran his tongue along the inside of her lower lip, and she made a low sound deep in her throat. "And I think it's time I was rewarded for such a sacrifice. Don't you?"

"The one thing I firmly believe in," she said huskily, "is that we should all receive our just rewards."

Slowly she began rocking her pelvis back and forth against his. With a low moan, Marco lowered her to the floor.

"We're wearing too damn many clothes," he said, tearing at his tie.

"Let me help." She reached for the buttons of his shirt.

In minutes they were both naked. Gretchen felt the softness of the carpet beneath her shoulders and hips as Marco fitted his body to her body and his mouth to her mouth.

They were both voracious in their need to touch, to taste, to meld into each other. Long minutes later, when Marco abandoned her mouth in favor of her breasts, Gretchen threaded her fingers through his hair. He teased her nipples with his tongue, then traced it slowly down the length of her abdomen. Hovering over the core of her femininity, he raised his head and gave her a smoldering look.

Gretchen felt her stomach muscles tighten, and she held her breath in anticipation. When he lowered his head again, she dug her fingers into his skull. The pleasure was so intense, she cried out. Arching her back, she held on for dear life.

She was nearing the peak when Marco moved over her again. In one swift movement he entered her, his strokes hard and rhythmic. She met him stroke for stroke as the pleasure mounted between them.

"You drive me out of my mind," he groaned as they climaxed together.

Beneath the shadow of the grand piano, they consummated their marriage a second time. This time the pace was more leisurely, more tender and, while no less satisfying, infinitely more sweet.

Afterward, Gretchen lay spent in his arms. Ear to his chest, she listened to the strong beat of his heart and felt the first quiet ray of hope she'd felt in weeks. Was it possible after all that, after the passage of time, their marriage might turn into what she'd always dreamed of, a union based on mutual love and respect? He'd cared enough to buy her this beautiful piano. Surely that was a good sign.

For now it was enough.

For now.

Chapter 13

Twenty days later it was no longer enough, and Gretchen was spoiling for a fight.

It was Friday night; she and Marco had both had a long, hard day at work; and, instead of going out to a movie or cuddling up in front of the television together as she had suggested, she was working on a jigsaw puzzle in the den—the same puzzle they'd started all those weeks ago—and Marco was upstairs in the nursery, painting.

She had offered to help, but he'd waved her away. Paint fumes weren't good for a pregnant woman to breathe, he'd said. She'd be much safer in a different part of the house.

He had the following week off, forty-plus hours while she was away at work to paint in, and he'd chosen tonight of all nights to begin this particular project. Couldn't he have at least waited until tomorrow morning? Couldn't he see that all she wanted to do was spend some time with him? She didn't care what they did, so long as they were together.

Sadly, spending time apart while physically under the

same roof was not unusual for them. On the contrary, it was the norm. Of the 480 hours that had elapsed since they'd said I do, Marco had spent 260 hours at the hospital, forty hours commuting to and from the hospital, 120 hours sleeping and approximately thirty-seven hours making love to her.

Gretchen knew all this because in a moment of frustration she had hauled out her calculator and figured it out. And how had he used the twenty-three precious, remaining hours that they could have spent together? He'd squandered them reading the newspaper and endless medical reports, checking stock prices on the Internet, raking leaves, washing cars, puttering around in the garage and, tonight, painting.

To make matters worse, she was nauseous every morning until she managed—very slowly—to down a piece of dry toast. Her waist was thickening, and her clothes were growing tight. She was in that awful in-between stage in her pregnancy, when she wasn't big enough for maternity clothes but her regular clothes only succeeded in making her look fat.

She could cope with the long hours Marco worked, the missed dinners, even looking fat. What she couldn't cope with were the silences whenever they were together. It seemed to Gretchen that from the moment Marco had slid the simple gold band on her ring finger he'd turned into a stranger. He never talked to her anymore, and it seemed that the only time they saw each other was in bed at night, where their lovemaking was as tempestuous as ever. While the thirty-seven hours of lovemaking had been wonderful, they weren't conversation. And it was conversation Gretchen was beginning to crave even more than she did vanilla ice cream and dill pickles.

If the only common ground they had was sex, she often wondered, what would happen when her belly was hugely rounded with his child, when her face, feet and ankles were swollen with retained water, when her walk had turned to a penguin-like waddle, and when she was feeling anything but sexy? Would she lose those hours, too?

Maybe when the baby came, she kept telling herself, things would be different. Maybe then he would open up to her more.

Or maybe she would be even more alone.

She didn't know how to reach him. He seemed to withdraw further from her with every passing day. Night after night she would lie awake while Marco slept beside her, and she would feel an aching, echoing emptiness. If things continued this way, she wasn't sure how much more she could take.

This was not a marriage, she told herself as she fitted another piece into the puzzle, her temper brewing. This was two people living separate lives under the same roof.

She'd worked herself into a fine state by the time she climbed into bed and drew the covers up over her body. Her nerves stretched way past the point of relaxation and any hope of sleep, she lay rigidly on her side with her back to the middle of the bed and waited for Marco to come to her. She knew, without a doubt, that when he did join her he would expect her to make love with him.

Well, tonight his expectations were not going to be met.

Around midnight she heard the door of the nursery open and close. The tread of Marco's shoes echoed heavily on the wood floor of the upstairs hallway. Lately it seemed that his footsteps were sounding heavier and heavier, as if he were carrying the weight of the world on his shoulders, and that weight was increasing exponentially with the passage of time.

He walked quietly past the bed, and a second later the soft glow of the bathroom light snuck its way into the room. Gretchen didn't make a sound while he washed his face and brushed his teeth. A quiet rustling indicated he was removing his clothing and depositing each item on the bathroom floor.

She felt another shaft of irritation. She knew that in the

morning he would gather them up, take them out into the hall and feed them to the clothes chute. Still, was it asking too much to expect him to put his dirty clothes down the clothes chute when he took them off?

After turning off the bathroom light, Marco climbed, naked, into bed with her. As she had predicted, he immediately slid his arms around her and drew her close. A minute later she felt his growing arousal pressing against her.

"No," she said, pulling back. It was the first time she had denied him.

She felt him rise up on one elbow and look down at her in the darkness. "Something wrong?"

"I'm just not in the mood."

"I see," he said slowly.

After a long silence he lay flat on his back. Gretchen waited, but he didn't say anything else.

"Don't you want to know why I'm not in the mood?"

"I'm assuming you're tired," he replied.

She turned on her back then, but made sure their bodies didn't touch. "I'm wide awake, Marco. I came to bed an hour ago. If I was tired, I would have been fast asleep by now."

"Okay." He sounded wary. "Since it's obvious you want me to ask, why aren't you in the mood?"

"Because you just can't ignore me all night and expect me to suddenly desire you."

Sitting up, he reached over and snapped on the bedside light. "Ignore you? I was painting the nursery. How was that ignoring you?"

Gretchen sat up, too. For the first time, the blatant masculinity of his broad chest and the rippling muscles in his arms failed to arouse her. She pointed to her barely rounded stomach.

"And it was imperative that you paint the nursery on this night, seeing as how I'm about to pop any second now." She made her voice as sarcastic as possible.

He looked taken aback by her attack. "The furniture will be here at the end of next week," he said stiffly. "I just wanted everything to be ready. I assumed you did, too."

"You assumed wrong. As of four hours ago you have the next nine days off. You didn't have to paint tonight, but you chose to, anyway. Do you have any idea why? Or do you need me to spell it out to you?"

"I told you why I chose to paint." The wariness had turned to defensiveness. "Obviously, you have a different spin on things."

She was nearing the end of her rope. "You're damn right I do. You're deliberately shutting me out, Marco. You're avoiding me. You're punishing me for depriving you of your precious bachelorhood."

He looked at her as if she'd started speaking in tongues. "Where'd you get that ridiculous notion?"

"From your behavior over the past three weeks, that's where. The only time I have your complete attention is when we make love. Do you know how that makes me feel?"

She didn't wait for his reply before giving him an answer. "Like a prostitute, that's how. Like my services have been bought and paid for, with this house, the ring on my finger and that piano downstairs."

She was stretching things, but not far. She was in a fighting mood, and the words certainly got his attention.

A spark of anger flared in Marco's eyes. "Are you saying my touch makes you feel like a prostitute?"

"No, Marco. I'm saying that I feel like the only time you really want me around you is when you need to satisfy your baser urges. That's what makes me feel like a prostitute. The only time I see you is at night, in this bed."

He was silent for a long minute. "I told you what marriage to me would be like. I'm dedicated to my career, Gretchen. Most of the time we'll have to spend together will be in this very bed."

"But not all of it," she responded. "Like tonight. You told me you worked long hours, Marco, and I accepted that. I don't need a nursemaid, and I don't need someone to entertain me twenty-four hours a day. What I can't accept is that you've stopped talking to me altogether. Even when you're here, you're not here."

"I do talk to you," he maintained.

She nodded. "Yes, when the occasion calls for it. Like when you want to know if the dry cleaners delivered your shirts, or where I'd like you to hang a particular painting. Otherwise, you have little to say to me. You're acting like you're still single. You're not trying, Marco."

He suddenly looked weary. "What do you mean, I'm not trying? We bought a house together, Gretchen. Together we're making it into a home. We're going to have a baby. How much harder can I try?"

"You can give of yourself."

He shook his head. "I don't even know what that means."

All the anger went out of her, and she stared down at the bedspread. One finger traced over its pattern. "That's the problem."

"What do you want from me, Gretchen? Just tell me, and I'll try to give it to you."

She looked up. "I want you to talk to me. For starters, you can tell me about what happened at work today."

This time Marco seemed to be the one who'd reached the end of his tether. "You want to know what happened at work today? Fine. I'll tell you what happened at work today. I saw a homeless man who will probably go blind soon, and maybe even lose a leg, because he's a diabetic and doesn't take good enough care of himself. I treated three gunshot wounds, one of which proved to be fatal. I shocked a thirty-eight-year-old man's heart back into beating. I treated a fourteen-year-old girl who had been gangraped and who will never be able to bear children as a result. Do you want to hear more?"

"No," she said quietly, holding back tears. "I've heard enough."

"Isn't this a lovely conversation we're having? Doesn't it make you feel all warm and cuddly inside?"

He looked away. "Why do you think I never talk about my work? Because I live with it twelve to sixteen hours a day. Because here in this peaceful refuge we're building together, for a few hours each day, I can get away from the sights and smells and sounds of death. I can forget what so-called civilized human beings do to each other in the name of love. I may be dedicated to my job, but I don't want to live with it twenty-four/seven."

His words only served to underscore exactly how little they knew about each other.

"I'm sorry," she said. "I never realized. I won't pry anymore."

Marco bit off a curse and thrust his fingers through his hair. "No, Gretchen," he said. "I'm the one who's sorry. I understand what you're saying. Really, I do. I guess I'm just not used to living with anyone. I'm not used to sharing a bathroom, let alone my thoughts. I'll try to do better."

"I will, too."

He shot her a smile. "How was your day?"

"I went to the obstetrician," she said.

"Is everything okay?" he asked quickly.

His obvious concern soothed her frayed nerves.

"Everything's fine," she reassured him. Excitement filled her voice. "I heard the baby's heartbeat for the first time."

He sat up straight. "You did? How did it sound?"

"Fast. And very strong. The doctor said it was good and strong. It was the most wonderful sound I have ever heard."

He reached over and placed his hand across her belly. Regret filled his eyes. "I wish I could have been there with you."

"I wish you could have, too," she said softly.

He raised his head, and his gaze met hers. "How's the morning sickness? Getting any better?"

She hadn't realized he was aware that she suffered from it. Perhaps he was paying more attention to her than she gave him credit for.

"It's about the same."

He nodded. "Give it a little more time. It should pass."

"I don't have much choice, do I?" she replied with a grin.

An answering grin played about his mouth. "No, I guess you don't."

She sobered. "I miss the laughter, Marco. The fun."

"I miss it, too," he said. "But we're not on an adventure here, Gretchen."

His hand still rested on her belly, and she covered it with both of hers. "That's where you're wrong. We are definitely on an adventure here. It's called life. It's faster than any roller coaster, higher than any Ferris wheel. It's the most thrilling ride of all…if you'll only climb on board."

His thumb started making slow circles on her stomach. Gretchen caught her breath at the shiver of desire that radiated outward from his touch. When she looked into his eyes, they glittered with invitation. He circled his free arm around her shoulders and drew her to him.

"I know another thrilling ride," he whispered seductively while nibbling on her earlobe. "That is, if your mood has changed."

Because she loved him so much, and because she felt closer to him than she had for a long time, Gretchen allowed herself to surrender to Marco's lovemaking. But even while she was trembling at his touch, in the back of her mind she couldn't escape the niggling realization that he had neatly sidestepped the subject.

It had been a long day. After working for twelve hours, which included eating her lunch at her desk, Gretchen had returned home to practice for the piano competition for an additional three hours and, after weeks of effort, to finally place the last piece into the jigsaw puzzle. A glance at her watch told her it was eleven-fifteen.

Yawning and rubbing at the crick in her neck, she sat back to admire her handiwork. She was so tired her eyes were nearly crossing, but she didn't want to go to bed just yet.

During the evening rush hour, a runaway truck had plowed into a crowd of pedestrians in downtown Pittsburgh. Since he hadn't come home yet, and since Bridgeton Memorial Hospital boasted one of the most advanced trauma units in the area, Gretchen knew that Marco had to be one of the physicians feverishly working to save the injured. She knew the toll the experience would take on him, and she wanted to be awake and waiting for him when he got home. Even if it meant she'd be asleep on her feet tomorrow at work.

Her gaze ran over the puzzle again. She supposed that a small part of her, deep inside, had wished it could symbolize her marriage to Marco, that each piece she entered would cement it tighter together. Maybe Marco had felt similarly, because, instead of tearing it apart and returning the pieces to the box, he'd gone to the effort of having the puzzle transported in its semicompleted state during the move.

She felt her lips twist wryly. She really was a cockeyed optimist.

"You finished it," Marco said from the doorway.

"Hi," she said, whirling to face him. He looked exhausted, and the grim set of his mouth told its own tale. Gretchen's heart went out to him. "I didn't hear you come in."

"I didn't want to disturb you, in case you were asleep. Sorry I'm so late."

"Can I get you something to eat? There's roast beef in the refrigerator. I could make you a sandwich."

He shook his head. "I'm not hungry. Why'd you wait up?"

"I saw the news tonight," she replied. "I know about the accident. Was it as bad as they described?"

His face took on a haunted look. "Worse."

"How many victims?"

He tossed his coat onto the leather sofa. "Fifteen total. Seven of them were transported to us, three of them life flighted."

In the twelve days that had passed since their argument, things had gotten better between them. It had helped that Marco had had that week off from work. The more he'd relaxed, the more he'd opened up to her. Several nights Gretchen had even come home from work to discover that he'd prepared dinner.

"How are they doing?" she asked.

"Three are in intensive care, in guarded condition. Two were treated and released. One is in critical condition, but his vital signs are good. He should improve rapidly."

"And the seventh?" Gretchen asked.

His gaze skittered away from hers. "She died," he said hollowly, adding, "She was six months pregnant. We couldn't save the child. I just left her husband."

How hard it must have been for him, Gretchen thought, to tell that young man of his loss and then come home to his pregnant wife. "Oh, Marco, I'm so sorry."

He ran a hand across the back of his neck. "Me, too. If you don't mind, I think I'll go take a hot shower."

She had everything ready when, towel draped around his waist, he opened the bathroom door and let out a cloud of steam. In a glance, Gretchen saw him take in the dim lighting, the bedcovers that she'd rolled to the foot of the bed, the towel spread across the sheets, and the bowls of fragrant oil she'd placed on the table on his side of the bed. Marco looked from her to the bed and back to her again.

"What's all this?"

"I thought I'd give you a massage," she said. "Unless, that is, you'd rather just go to sleep."

"A massage sounds wonderful."

"Great." She patted the bed. "On your stomach, please."

Dropping the towel, Marco quickly complied.

Gretchen started with his shoulders, rubbing in the oil and kneading his tight muscles.

"God, that feels so good," he said with a groan.

"That's the whole point," she replied. "I took a course in therapeutic massage when my dad was sick. It helped him relax, too."

"You can help me relax anytime," he said.

As she worked her way down his back and arms to his legs and feet, she could literally feel the tension melt and drain away from him. By the time she finished with his toes, Marco was hovering on the edge of sleep. Gretchen felt a tug on her heart as she pulled the sheet up over him.

She was in the bathroom washing the oil from her hands when she heard the phone ring. Who could be calling at this time of the night?

Grabbing a hand towel and stifling a curse, she ran for the bedroom, but she was too late. Marco was already sitting up, his legs swung over the side of the bed, the receiver to his ear. He talked softly for a few minutes, then quietly hung up the phone. Shoulders hunched and head bowed, he sat unmoving, as if gathering his strength. Surely that couldn't have been the hospital, demanding that he come back in?

"Who was it?" she asked.

"Brian," he said dully. "Val has asked him for a divorce. She's assured him that there's no chance of a reconciliation."

"Oh, no." Gretchen's heart broke for the couple she'd come to know and like. And for Kristen, whose life would never be the same. "Are you okay?"

The eyes he raised to hers were turbulent with emotion.

"It's not like I haven't known for some time now that they were on shaky ground."

"Still," she said, "this must be really hard for you." Especially after the day he'd just had.

"Harder than I ever thought it would be."

"I understand. Your friend is hurting, and that's painful for you to watch."

He shook his head. "If only that were all."

"What do you mean?"

The turbulence in his eyes increased. "Can't you see? I was certain that if any marriage could survive the wear and tear of a demanding job, Brian and Val's would. But if their marriage, a union based on love, can fail, what chance do the two of us have?"

Throat working, he tore his gaze from hers. "What chance do we have?" he repeated softly.

Gretchen felt the impact of his words like a punch to the stomach. Her heart gave a hard, painful twist. If she looked closely enough, she was certain she'd be able to see the ruins of her world crumbled at her feet.

She didn't say anything. She didn't trust herself to speak, and, after all, what was there left for her to say? Any hope she'd had that Marco would tear down the walls he'd built to protect himself from intimacy had just died.

At least the death had been swift and merciful.

He stood up and began pulling on clothes. "I have to go. Brian needs me. I'll be back later. Don't wait up."

Marco's taillights disappeared from view, and Gretchen let the curtain fall back into place. Eyes burning, she turned to survey the bedroom. Her gaze fell on the empty bed, where the indentation of his head against the pillow was still visible, and with a cry of despair she sank to the floor.

Pulling her knees to her chest, Gretchen wrapped her arms around her legs and, rocking back and forth, let the tears fall. She cried for a long time, then sat motionless

for an even longer period. Finally, dry-eyed and determined, she climbed to her feet.

She had filled one suitcase by the time Marco returned.
Without bothering to acknowledge his arrival, she emptied
the contents of her underwear drawer into a second.

"What are you doing?" He sounded wary.

She drew an unsteady breath and ruthlessly stemmed a
fresh round of tears. She refused to cry in front of him.
Nor would she get emotional about what she had to do.
After everything he had been through today, the last thing
Marco needed was her weeping all over him. And, in the
future, when she looked back on this moment, she would
like to think that she'd kept her dignity.

"Packing," she replied in a surprisingly steady voice.

"Going on a business trip?"

"I'm going home, Marco." Thank goodness she'd put
off finding new tenants for the duplex, and that they'd left
her half furnished. Maybe, in some small corner of her
mind, she'd known that she would be returning.

She snapped the suitcase shut and placed it on the floor
beside its twin. She would collect the rest of her belongings later, preferably when Marco was at the hospital.

"This is home, Gretchen," he said.

"No, Marco, it's not. This was just a temporary way
station."

"Look, I'm sorry I ran out on you like that. But Brian
needed me."

"I'm not angry that you went to be with your friend,"
she said softly. "How could I be angry about that?"

"Then why are you leaving?"

Not why are you leaving me, but why are you leaving.
"I guess you could say I've finally come to my senses.
My only regret is that this didn't happen before I obligated
you to me by marriage."

"It's two o'clock in the morning," he said heavily.
"Can't this wait at least until sunrise?"

Even from the depths of her despair, Gretchen could feel

compassion for him. He'd had a hell of a day, and she wasn't helping matters. But if she didn't leave now, if she climbed into bed beside him and waited until morning, she might not have the strength to do what she knew she had to do. And to wait any longer was just to open herself up to more pain.

"I don't think so, Marco."

He sat on the edge of the bed. "Just a couple of hours ago you were giving me a massage. Now you're leaving. If not because of Brian, then why?"

"Because of what you said."

"What did I say?"

"That if Val and Brian's marriage, a union based on love, couldn't make it, what chance does our marriage, a union not based on love, have?"

It was all so clear to her now, had been from the minute Marco had driven off in his car. No matter how much she hoped and prayed otherwise, he would never let himself love her. While she could wish for a bright future for them in which that love was a possibility, knowing it would never come to pass, that Marco probably spent every waking minute regretting the impulsive act that had led to this hasty marriage, made it all futile. How he must resent her for that. If that resentment continued to grow, would he pass it on to their innocent child?

The sad truth was that, weak and pitiful as it made her, she needed to be needed. And Marco didn't need anything but his work.

"You're right, you know," she said, her heart heavy. "Our marriage doesn't stand a chance. I'm not blaming you, and I'm not blaming me. It's no one's fault. This marriage never should have taken place."

Leaning forward, he placed his elbows on his thighs and folded his hands together. "Have you forgotten why we did this?" he asked in a low voice.

"Of course I haven't forgotten. Our hearts were in the right place. It was our reasoning that was skewed."

"How so?"

"We got so wrapped up in doing what was right, of providing our child with two parents who lived under the same roof, that we forgot to look to the years ahead. The long, empty years ahead.

"I remember how close my parents were. There was never a question in my mind of their devotion to each other. Every time they laughed, every time they embraced, I felt warm and safe inside.

"I want my child to grow up in that same kind of atmosphere. He or she deserves more than what this marriage can give. I deserve more. We all deserve more. That's why I'm leaving. Don't worry. I would never prevent you from seeing your child."

She waited for him to protest, to ask her to stay. If only he would ask her to stay. But he just sat there, so remote and contained she felt a suffocating despair take hold of her.

"You're right," he finally said. "You do deserve more."

That was it, then. Gretchen felt her shoulders slump. Picking up her suitcases, she headed for the door. She'd taken three steps when the anger took over.

The suitcases made a loud thud when she dropped them to the carpet and whirled to face him. Her life was falling apart, and he just sat there, impassive. In the long run, she supposed, her dignity wasn't as important as the things she needed to say.

"Before I go, I have one last thing to tell you. One last truth you need to hear. It's not the job that's preventing you from having a successful relationship, Marco. Just as some doctors make bad marriages, so do people in all professions. But many doctors have good and lasting marriages. You could, too, if you weren't so afraid."

His back went ramrod straight. "Afraid?" he said, his voice dangerously soft.

"Yes, Marco. Afraid. Of love. The fear was born in you

the day your mother died. It intensified when Tess broke your engagement. You're afraid that if you fall in love with any woman, you'll lose that love the way you lost your mother. Medicine is safe. Medicine will never leave you. That's why you've dedicated your life to your work.''

Her hands covered her stomach. ''This is what life is all about,'' she said fiercely. ''Not some career, no matter how much good it does.''

She drew a deep breath and forged ahead before he could respond. ''There's a hole in your heart. I can hear the wind whistling through it. That's the real reason I'm leaving. I'm afraid that if I don't, I'll wind up with a hole in mine.''

Spent, Gretchen turned on her heel, picked up her suitcases and walked out the door.

Chapter 14

Marco stared at the silent piano. Outside, a storm raged, rain pounding and wind howling. Inside, all was so quiet and still he thought that if he concentrated hard enough he'd be able to hear his heart beating.

Amazing how a heart could feel as if it had cracked in two, yet still go on beating. It was totally illogical.

Gretchen had been gone for two days, and he felt as if all the life had been sucked out of the house. It wasn't a home to him anymore. No longer would the swell of piano music fill the air, nor would the sound of her laughter echo off the walls. It was just a place for him to hang his hat and coat while he wasn't working.

When the sight of the piano became too much to bear, Marco turned his back on it. There was no respite to be found, however. Everything he saw bore Gretchen's touch. The pillows on the sofa. The paintings on the wall. The matching terrariums on either end of the mantelpiece.

His shoulders sagged. He'd known this would happen

from the very beginning. He'd known she would leave. He just hadn't expected her to go so soon.

Nor had he expected the force of the pain that knifed through him whenever he thought of her. Each time, it felt as if someone had punched a fist through his chest, grabbed hold of his heart and squeezed hard.

His mistake had been in allowing himself to hope. And to care. Thank goodness he had his work. Without it he didn't know how he would be able to go on.

The only thing that kept him from drowning his sorrows in a bottle of whisky this very minute was his job. But in two weeks, on the first night of his week off, he planned on getting stinking drunk.

When the doorbell rang, Marco had half a mind to ignore it. But what if it was Gretchen? Maybe she'd forgotten her key.

"You look like hell," Carlo said when he opened the door.

"And you look like a drowned rat," he growled back.

Carlo raised his eyebrows. "Testy, are we? Hard day at work?"

If only that were the reason for his foul mood. "Hard week."

"As you can see," Carlo said, looking pointedly around him, "it's raining out here. Can I come in?"

Marco didn't feel up to company. But Carlo wasn't one to be easily dismissed without a lengthy explanation. Besides, he had to let his family know sometime that his marriage was over. Now seemed as good a time as any. Without a word he stood back and motioned his brother inside.

"What brings you out on this ugly evening?" he asked.

Carlo held up a videotape. "This. It's from your wedding. I thought you and Gretchen would like to see it. It has some priceless footage of Antonio dancing with a lampshade on his head. Although where he got that lampshade in the first place, I'll never know."

Carlo looked around him, seemingly aware for the first time of just how quiet the house was. "Where's Gretchen?"

Marco supposed there was no use mincing words. "Gone."

Carlo's brow furrowed. "Gone where? Shopping? It's a lousy night to be out shopping."

"She's gone home, Carlo."

"This is home."

If only she had felt the same way he and his brother did. "Not to her. Our marriage is over. She left me."

"When?"

"Two days ago."

"What happened?" Carlo asked. "What did you do?"

"What did *I* do?" Anger seized him. He counted off on his fingers. "I bought her this house. I gave her a wedding I thought she'd never forget. I worked my fingers to the bone day in and day out to prepare for our future. That's what I did."

He turned away, and his voice lowered. "It wasn't enough. She left me, anyway."

"Come with me," Carlo ordered.

"Where?"

"The den. I want you to see something."

They took a seat in front of the television set, and Carlo put the tape into the VCR and fast-forwarded. When he reached the spot he wanted, he pushed the play button.

"Tell me what you see," he said.

Gretchen's lovely face filled the screen. It was hard for Marco to speak past the lump that had formed in his throat.

"Gretchen saying her vows," he said in a low voice.

"Look closer," Carlo said. "At the expression in her eyes. If that's not a woman in love, I don't know what is."

Marco wanted to believe. Oh, how he wanted to believe. The same way he'd wanted to beg her to stay on the night she left him.

"It's just a trick of the light, Carlo."

His brother looked as though he wanted to strangle him. "Why are you being so damned obstinate?"

"Because you don't know the truth. You're just seeing what you want to see."

"And what is the truth?"

"She's pregnant," Marco said flatly.

"In that case, even more reason for the two of you to stay together."

Marco shook his head. "You don't understand. The only reason she married me was because of her pregnancy. All I was to her was an affair. She's still looking for Mr. Right. She doesn't love me."

"She told you that?"

"Not in so many words. But the implication was clear. We wanted each other. We had each other. It was only supposed to be a temporary thing."

Carlo was silent for a long moment before asking, "Have you told her you love her?"

"No."

"But you do love her."

When had he fallen in love with her? When she'd propositioned him? When he'd watched her cradling Kristen in her arms? When she'd coaxed him from that tree? Or while they were floating in the deep end of the pool, and she'd gazed at him with those big brown eyes of hers and seduced him body and soul?

The answer was yes to all of them. He'd fallen a little bit more in love with her with each moment they had spent together. A fact he had finally acknowledged when she'd floated down the aisle to him, looking so achingly beautiful he hadn't been able to believe his luck. She was going to be his.

Almost immediately he'd been seized by fear. He'd been terrified that it was all a dream. He'd been terrified that he would lose her.

And now he had lost her. Which was why he'd fought so hard against falling in love with her in the first place.

"Yes, Carlo. I love her."

"Why haven't you told her?"

"Because, when she told me she was pregnant, all she could talk about was adoption and visitation and shared custody. Telling her I loved her hardly seemed appropriate. Especially when I had to practically twist her arm to get her to agree to marry me."

"Did it ever occur to you that if you had told her you loved her, you might not have had to twist her arm so hard?"

"And did it ever occur to you," Marco shot back, "that if I had said those words, she would have believed I was only saying them to get her to marry me?"

"What about your wedding night?" Carlo asked. "Couldn't you have said something then?"

Marco was silent.

"You were afraid, weren't you?"

Instead of answering, Marco said, "Every relationship I've ever had, the woman has been the one to break it off. They leave, Carlo. They always leave."

"Maybe," Carlo replied, giving him a sad smile, "it's time you figured out why they always leave."

"Sounds to me like you have your own theory."

"I might."

"Care to share it with me?"

Carlo shook his head. "Sorry, brother. I know we all meddle in each other's business a lot, but this is one thing you're going to have to work out on your own. Because, until you do, they'll just keep leaving."

"The bloom is definitely off the rose."

Gretchen raised her head from the file she'd buried it in to say, "Hi, Gary," before burying it again.

The upholstered leather chair in front of her desk made

a crunching sound when he sat down. "Do you know what time it is?"

She looked at her watch. "Nine o'clock."

"That's p.m., not a.m."

"I'm aware of that."

"Why are you still here?" he asked.

She nodded toward the pile of files on her desk. "I'm swamped. Which you must be, also, because you're still here."

"*I* don't have a brand-new husband waiting for me at home."

She turned a page and strove to keep her voice neutral. "Neither do I."

"Marco working late?"

"I have no idea." She raised her head and met her friend's gaze. "I've left him, Gary. I moved back into the duplex. My marriage is over."

"When did this happen?"

"A week ago."

"That would explain why you've been walking around like a lost soul."

She just looked at him.

"I don't understand," Gary said. "When we spoke in August, you were in love with him. You married him the first weekend in October. Only five weeks have passed since then. What happened?"

"What happened is that, in between my talk with you in August and my marriage to Marco in October, I got pregnant."

There was a long silence. "So what you're saying is…"

"Marco did the noble thing and offered to make an honest woman of me. The only reason he married me is because I'm pregnant."

"I could have sworn…"

"What?" she asked.

"You should have seen your faces during the wedding ceremony. I could have sworn the emotion was real."

"For show only." At least on Marco's part. "Marco's great at putting a good face on things."

"Why did you leave him?"

"He—" She drew a deep breath when her voice cracked. "He doesn't love me."

"From what you told me, he didn't love you when he married you. Nothing's changed. So why leave now?"

Even though it was the truth, the words still hurt. "Let me rephrase. He'll never love me." She bit her lip. "I thought I could live with that. I discovered I can't."

"You sure give up awfully quick."

Gretchen sat back in her chair and blinked at him. Where was the sympathy, the pat on the back, the shoulder for crying on?

"What are you saying?"

Gary shrugged. "Only that your marriage must not have meant that much to you in the first place if you could walk away from it so easily."

The pain cut her swiftly, its aim more accurate than a master marksman's. She felt tears spring to her eyes.

"How can you say that to me?"

"What things in your life do you feel passionate about?" he asked. "What would you fight for with your last breath? And don't tell me it's this job. You're wonderful at it, Gretchen, but you don't live for it."

"I...I don't understand," she said.

"That's the problem. Let me explain. I fought passionately to build this business. I fought passionately to earn respect as a gay businessman in a straight world. What have you fought passionately for?"

Gretchen could only stare at him in silence.

Gary stood. "Word of advice from a friend? Go home, Gretchen. You won't be doing yourself, or your unborn child, any favors if you let yourself get run-down. And while you're home, do some thinking. Decide what things you feel most passionately about. If they're missing from your life, start fighting for them." He swept an arm out indicating the files on her desk. "Otherwise, this is your future."

A woman carrying a clipboard ushered Gretchen down a long corridor lined with practice rooms. As they passed each room, she heard snatches of different sonatas from behind the closed doors. Her fellow contestants were practicing their selected pieces one final time.

Gretchen drew a deep breath and tried to slow the staccato beating of her heart. This was it. Her big chance. After today she would know whether or not she should pursue the childhood dream that she'd thought she'd left far behind her.

The competition was divided into two parts. The first part was the audition phase. Twenty contestants would each perform a sonata of their own choosing. From those twenty contestants, six finalists would be selected. The six finalists would then perform a composition for piano and orchestra, the performance to be held one week after the auditions. The top three placers, who would be ranked by a jury of five, would receive monetary prizes, along with a medal and the chance to enroll in a larger, more prestigious competition.

Gretchen was realistic about her chances. It was highly unlikely that she would advance past the audition stage. She would be pitting her skills against performers who had spent many more hours at the keyboard than she had in recent years, and whose repertoires were far larger than her own.

The woman with the clipboard stopped in front of a room with the number twelve painted on the door. It corresponded to the number Gretchen had drawn when she registered, and signified the order in which she would play.

"Good luck," the woman said with a smile.

Gretchen's answering smile felt forced. "Thank you."

Inside, the small room was bare of any ornamentation save the console piano that looked as if it had seen better days. The cinder-block walls were painted pale yellow, the floor was covered by gray tile that at one time might have been white, and the lone window was in need of a good washing.

Thankfully, though battered, the piano was mostly in tune. Gretchen played scales for ten minutes, warming up her fingers. Then, too nervous to sit still any longer, she rose to her feet and began pacing.

She knew she should close her eyes and visualize herself on the stage, and that when that picture grew clear in her mind she should start playing. But she couldn't. She tried to console herself with the knowledge that if she wasn't prepared by now, she never would be.

She'd done enough practicing over the past months, especially the last ten days since she'd left Marco. Without a tenant next door, she'd been able to practice whenever the spirit moved her, early in the morning before work, late into the night when her demons wouldn't let her sleep.

Since she had walked away from her marriage, Gretchen had tried to keep her mind a careful blank. She'd succeeded by filling every available minute with work and music. In all likelihood, after this afternoon she wouldn't have the music to keep her mind off her troubles. What would she do then?

The words Gary had spoken to her echoed in her brain. *What things in your life do you feel passionate about? What would you fight for with your last breath? Start fighting for them. Otherwise, this is your future.*

What *did* she feel passionate about? she asked herself. Definitely her music. The child growing in her womb. And, despite it all, Marco.

She'd fought for her music by entering this competition and by practicing as hard as she could. She knew instinctively that if called upon she would fight like a tigress for her baby. But she hadn't fought for Marco, the man she loved. On the contrary, she had reverted to old habits and had cut and run. Why?

Because she didn't have his love. He certainly hadn't tried to stop her when she walked away.

"Why should he have?" she said out loud. When it came down to it, she hadn't expected their marriage to last, either. She certainly hadn't overwhelmed Marco with declarations of love.

Now that she thought about it, he hadn't said their marriage had no chance. What he had done, in those first vulnerable moments after hearing about Brian and Val, and while his emotions were still raw and on the surface, was to ask what kind of chance it did have.

Instead of reassuring him and telling him that it had a wonderful chance because she loved him, she had turned her back on him and walked out the door. Why should she have expected him to put himself on the line, to beg her to stay, when she hadn't been willing to put herself on the same line?

There was a knock on the practice room door, and the woman with the clipboard peeked in to tell her that it was time. Gretchen drew a deep breath, straightened the folds of her white silk blouse and ran her hands down the fabric of her ankle-length black skirt.

As she followed the woman down the corridor and into the wings off the stage, she made one more promise, this time to herself. It was the most important promise of her life. She would fight for the man she loved. No holds barred. Life was just too short not to do otherwise. And she wouldn't give up the battle until *he* told her that the cause was hopeless. But the telling would have to come from Marco himself, not her insecurities.

Wasn't that the real reason Jill had asked her to make those promises? So she would, for once in her life, stand up for herself and fight for what she wanted. Passionately.

When she sat down at the piano, Gretchen made the mistake of looking out at the crowd. At the sight of all those faces looking expectantly at her, the magnitude of what she was about to do froze her in her seat. Her mind went blank. Like Marco at the top of that tree, she couldn't move, couldn't think, couldn't blink, even when people began murmuring and shifting restlessly in their seats.

A movement caught the corner of her eye. She was able to turn her head far enough to see Marco stand up from the middle of the audience. Relief rushed through her, accompanied by a sense of elation. He had come.

"You can do it, Gretchen," he called. "Play for me, sweetheart. Play just for me."

She did. Gretchen poured her heart and soul, all the love she had for Marco, into her music. When she finished, she knew she had played better than she had in her life. But she didn't even hear the applause. Nor did she worry that she had played well enough to final. She only had eyes for the man making his way to the front of the auditorium.

She met him in the wings. Marco looked big and strong and impossibly wonderful, and it was all she could do not to throw herself into his arms.

"Why are you here?" she asked breathlessly. "Shouldn't you be at work?"

"I had to see you. I couldn't let you do this alone."

She drew a deep breath and mentally steeled herself for what she had to do. "I'm glad you're here. I need to talk to you."

He held up a hand. "Me first, please. I have a few things to say, and I'd like you to hear me out."

He looked so serious, Gretchen's heart lurched. Had he chosen this time and this place to serve divorce papers on her?

She squared her shoulders and stuck out her chin. Where was her backbone? She'd met the first obstacle, and already she was ready to give up? Not a chance. She'd made a promise, and she intended to keep it. If he was here to end their marriage, he was in for the fight of his life.

"Not here," she said, taking him by the arm and leading him off the stage and out into the corridor lined with practice rooms. This time the sound of music could be heard behind only a few of the closed doors. They passed the woman with the clipboard, who was leading the next contestant, and Gretchen gave the nervous man an encouraging smile.

Marco preceded her into room number twelve and moved to stand in front of the window. She placed her back to the door, her hand on the knob. Blocking him from escaping before she'd had her say?

"What did you want to tell me, Marco?"

He turned to face her. "I've been a fool, Gretchen. A coward and a fool."

His words took her by such surprise she could only stare at him dumbly.

"Remember asking me if I'd ever let myself go with a woman, if I'd ever lost myself so completely in her that I didn't know where she ended or where I began?"

Still bemused, she nodded.

"I lose myself that way every time I look at you, Gretchen. Every time I touch you."

"Then why did you let me go?" she burst out.

"Because I was afraid. Being with you felt so right that I spent every waking moment terrified I would lose you."

"The way you lost your mother and Tess," she murmured.

"Yes. But I understand now that I drove Tess away. The way I drove away every woman I've been involved with. The way I drove you away. My fear of loving was all tied up with my feelings of loss. But I'm here to tell you today that I am no longer afraid. And I'm not letting you go."

Though her heart threatened to take wings and soar, there were still a few things they needed to set straight between them. "What are you saying, Marco?"

He took a step toward her. "I'm saying that when you told me you were pregnant, I was thrilled. Because it allowed me to do what deep in my heart I really wanted to do, even though I wasn't ready to admit it to myself. It allowed me to marry you. I'm saying that losing you, the way I lost my mother, would be indescribable. But losing you and knowing that you are somewhere out in the world, alive and vital and not in my arms, is a thousand times worse."

He took another step. "I'm saying that I love you, Gretchen. I want our marriage to continue, and not just because of the baby you're carrying, although I want our child more than words can say."

She started trembling. "What about your work?"

"It will always be a priority. But you, Gretchen, and our children, will be number one in my heart. You always make me see what's right and good about the world. I'm a lesser man when you're not by my side. I love you, Gretchen, and I'll continue telling you so until you beg me to stop. I'm putting you on notice right here and now that I'm fighting for you and our child. I'm not walking away until I get your complete surrender."

She couldn't hold back any longer. Flying across the room, she threw herself into his arms. "I love you, too, Marco, and I'll never leave you again," she managed to say before his lips claimed hers in a fiercely possessive kiss.

Two hours later they stood in the wings while the six finalists were announced. Gretchen's name was not among them.

"There are other competitions," Marco said. "We'll enter you in one the minute we get home."

Heart full, Gretchen shook her head. "No."

"Why not?"

"It's not necessary. The point of entering this competition was for me to figure out what I want to do with my music. I've figured it out."

"You have?"

She smiled. "I want to be a piano teacher."

"What about your job at Curtis, Walker, Davis and Associates?"

"I'm quitting. I want to be home with our children, Marco. And I want to work at a job that I'll love as much as I do you. Giving piano lessons will fill both wants. Plus, we'll have one entire week a month together. That's more than most couples have."

"How is Gary going to take this?" he asked.

"He'll pitch a fit, and then he'll wish me luck."

Marco laid a hand tenderly on the side of her face. "I will always love you, Gretchen. That is my promise to you. My promise to keep."

She took his hand and laced her fingers through his. "Come on. Let's get out of here. Let's go start our wild, crazy affair with life."

* * * * *

Silhouette

I N T I M A T E   M O M E N T S™

presents a riveting new continuity series:

FIRSTBORN SONS

Bound by the legacy of their fathers, these Firstborn Sons are about to discover the stuff true heroes—and true love—are made of!

The adventure continues in November 2001 with:

BORN IN SECRET by **Kylie Brant**

When Walker James was assigned to infiltrate a terrorist compound and discover the location of a deadly virus, the suave international spy was less than thrilled to be teamed up with Jasmine LeBarr. He'd tangled with the clever secret agent once before, and her covert maneuvers had done a hatchet job on his macho pride. Come hell or high water, he was not about to cave in to their sizzling desire ever again!
Or so he thought....

July: **BORN A HERO**
by **Paula Detmer Riggs** (IM #1088)
August: **BORN OF PASSION**
by **Carla Cassidy** (IM #1094)
September: **BORN TO PROTECT**
by **Virginia Kantra** (IM #1100)
October: **BORN BRAVE**
by **Ruth Wind** (IM #1106)
November: **BORN IN SECRET**
by **Kylie Brant** (IM #1112)
December: **BORN ROYAL**
by **Alexandra Sellers**
(IM #1118)

*Available only from
Silhouette Intimate Moments
at your favorite retail outlet.*

Silhouette®
Where love comes alive™

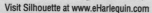

Visit Silhouette at www.eHarlequin.com

SIMFIRST5

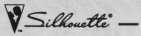

CALL THE ONES YOU LOVE OVER THE HOLIDAYS!

Save $25 off future book purchases when you buy any four Harlequin® or Silhouette® books in October, November and December 2001,

PLUS

receive a phone card good for 15 minutes of long-distance calls to anyone you want in North America!

WHAT AN INCREDIBLE DEAL!

Just fill out this form and attach 4 proofs of purchase (cash register receipts) from October, November and December 2001 books, and Harlequin Books will send you a coupon booklet worth a total savings of $25 off future purchases of Harlequin® and Silhouette® books, AND a 15-minute phone card to call the ones you love, anywhere in North America.

Please send this form, along with your cash register receipts
as proofs of purchase, to:
In the USA: Harlequin Books, P.O. Box 9057, Buffalo, NY 14269-9057
In Canada: Harlequin Books, P.O. Box 622, Fort Erie, Ontario L2A 5X3
Cash register receipts must be dated no later than December 31, 2001.
Limit of 1 coupon booklet and phone card per household.
Please allow 4-6 weeks for delivery.

I accept your offer! Please send me my coupon booklet and a 15-minute phone card:

Name: _____

Address: _____ City: _____

State/Prov.: _____ Zip/Postal Code: _____

Account Number (if available): _____

---

097 KJB DAGL
PHQ4012